I0788124

Controlled Chaos

A LOVE & LYRICS NOVEL

USA TODAY BESTSELLING AUTHOR

NIKKI ASH

She believed she could, so she did.

Author's Note

Like real life, the characters are far from perfect, make morally gray decisions, and deal with subjects that may be sensitive for some readers. If you are looking for a safe romance, this series is not for you. Trigger warnings (which contain spoilers) can be found on my website: Love & Lyrics Trigger Warnings

Playlist

"That Should Be Me" – Justin Bieber
"Eenie Meenie"– Sean Kingston & Justin Bieber
"Perfect" – Ed Sheeran
"Break Up with Him" – Old Dominion
"Trumpets" – Jason Derulo
"Here Without You" – 3 Doors Down
"Love Like This" – Natasha Bedingfield (feat. Sean Kingston)
"One Call Away" – Charlie Puth

It should be me, kissing you, touching you, inside you
But instead, it's him, getting you, every fuckin' piece of you
Those pieces should be mine
- Camden Blackwood, Raging Chaos

One

Camden

The Present: High School Pre-Graduation Party

"SO YOU'RE REALLY GOING TO LET IT HAPPEN, HUH?" DECLAN ASKS, TAKING A SIP OF HIS beer. "You're going to let her go off to college with that asshole without telling her how you feel?"

I flip the hood of my jacket up and tug on the strings, tightening it to cover my head. "She's in love," I say dryly, then take a swig of my beer, chugging it down in the hopes of getting drunk enough to believe the words I'm spewing.

"I missed my chance, and I'm not about to be *that* guy." Draining the last of my beer, I drop the empty bottle onto the table and stand so I can grab another one.

"I'd bet my ass if she knew how you felt, she wouldn't be with him," Declan points out as we push through the crowded room of our classmates celebrating our impending graduation in various ways—some legal, some not so much—to the kitchen.

"She knows how I feel." I scoff, grabbing a Solo cup and a bottle of vodka so I can mix myself a stronger drink. Beer isn't going to cut it tonight. Not if I want to forget.

Declan barks out an obnoxious laugh. "Sure, she knows you care about her… as a *friend*, but you've never actually told her you're in love with her."

"And when the hell was I supposed to do that?" I huff, forgetting the cup and guzzling straight from the bottle. I welcome the burn as the liquid slides down my throat and into my belly, warming my insides.

"I don't know, but if you don't tell her soon, it really will be too late."

"What if she turns me down?" I ask, sounding like a damn pussy.

"I can't imagine it," Declan says, taking a sip of his drink. "For the past three years, every time that girl looks at you, it's as if you both are the only two people in the room."

I love my best friend, but the guy is such a fucking hopeless romantic, which is ironic since his parents are the least loving people I've ever met in my life. "Then why is she with him?"

"Maybe because she doesn't know you're an option."

Like a moth to a flame, my eyes find her as she makes her way through the living room alone. I'm shocked her boyfriend isn't with her. The guy never leaves her side, especially if he knows I'll be there. She's dressed in a sexy as hell red minidress that shows off all of her curves, with her chestnut hair down in long waves. Our gazes lock, and like it always does when I see her, my heart thumps against my rib cage. It's been like this every time I've seen her since we met.

Two

Camden

The Past: Sophomore Year

"DAMN, CAM, THIS SONG IS DEEP AS FUCK," BRAXTON SAYS. USING THE NECK OF HIS GUITAR to prop himself up, he's reading over the lyrics I just gave each guy a copy of. We just finished practicing our usual set list, and I figured I'd show them the song I finished writing last night.

"Thanks, man. I was thinking we could try it out, and if it works, we can play it Friday night at Ricky's party." Every few weeks, one of the kids at our school throws a kegger—whoever's parents are out of town that weekend—and we use them as a way to practice in front of a crowd. Obviously, they don't pay, but our classmates are assholes and have no problem telling us if something we play sucks.

"I'm down," Gage says, walking over to the drums and having a seat.

"Let's do it," Declan agrees, picking up his bass guitar and getting into position.

We spend the next couple of hours in the studio, messing with the instrumentals and getting them to mesh with my words. We stop and start again damn near a hundred times until we get the sound we're looking for—only stopping when my dad makes an appearance.

"New song?" he asks, knowing all of our songs.

"Yeah, what do you think?" I ask, holding my breath. Most kids my age don't give a shit what their parents think, but most kids' parents aren't Easton Blackwood, president of Blackwood Records. With locations in New York and California and over five hundred artists and bands signed, it's one of the most prominent record labels in the country. And I'm hoping after I graduate, my band will be one of them.

"It sounds good," Dad says with a smile that tells me he genuinely means it. He spends a little while giving us pointers like he always does, and we try them out, but then since it's getting late, the guys take off.

I'm about to start on my science homework when I remember I left my books in my mom's car. I run out, grab my stuff, and am heading back inside when a girl sitting on the steps of the house next door catches my eye. The place has been empty for several months but recently sold.

As I step toward her, getting a closer look, I notice her shoulders are shaking, and it sounds like she's crying. "Hey, are you okay?"

Her head springs up, and her tearstained eyes meet mine. "Umm, yeah." She swipes at her tears and sniffles.

"Doesn't sound like it." I jump over the fence separating our houses and have a seat next to her on the steps. "You move in here?" I nod toward the house behind us, which is identical to mine. The four-story townhouses on this street each have their own garage, driveway, and small yard in the back.

"Yeah," she says, her voice coming out hoarse. "Today. I start school tomorrow."

"At Brooklyn High?"

"Yep. Sophomore."

"Same. Where are you from?"

"Michigan. Dad got a job offer he couldn't turn down. Had to leave my friends, my boyfriend… It's going to suck to start at a new school tomorrow without knowing anyone."

I can't really relate since I've lived in this home most of my life and have gone to school with the same people from day one, but I can imagine how bad it would suck to start over in high school.

"You know me," I say, extending my hand. She glances up at me and smiles. "I'm Camden Blackwood."

"I'm Layla Higgins." Her hand connects with mine, and I notice how small it is. Even sitting down, I can tell she's a tiny thing.

"What's with the camera?" I ask, noticing it's sitting in her lap.

"I love documenting everything. Pictures, videos. It's kind of my thing." She shrugs. "As an 'I'm sorry for moving you away from the only life you've ever known' gift, my dad got me a new editing program, so I came out here to take some pictures."

"And then you ended up sitting here crying?"

She snorts out a half-laugh, half-cry. "Yeah." Her brown eyes lock with my green. "I've only been gone for a day, and I already miss my home." She sighs, and a fresh set of tears well up in her eyes. "I don't really feel like documenting anything right now."

"What do you feel like doing?"

"Honestly, I just feel like wallowing," she says with a watery laugh.

"Wallowing?" I repeat. I know the word, but you usually don't hear teenagers saying it.

"It's what my mom says I do when I'm upset." She looks out at the road in front of us. "I just want to sit here and wallow."

"Here." I pull one earbud out and hand it to her. "I have the perfect wallowing music."

I scroll through my selection of songs on my phone until I find one that she might be able to connect with and click play.

We sit together, listening to "Here Without You" by 3 Doors Down, while Layla cries. I'm not sure what to do, so I do the only thing I can think of and put my arm around her, pulling her closer to me so I can try to comfort this sad girl who's now my next-door neighbor. I'm shocked when she not only comes willingly but lays her head on my shoulder.

When the song ends, I find another one—"Home" by Machine Gun Kelly—and after that, in hope of lightening the mood, I click on "I Can See Clearly Now" by Johnny Nash. When the lyrics start, I feel Layla's shoulders shake with laughter. She glances up at me and grants me a full ear-to-ear smile. And holy shit, she is pretty. She's got two dimples, one on each cheek, and when she isn't crying, her brown eyes brighten up to the color of caramel. Lyrics flood my head, and I have to shake them out to focus on what she's saying.

"You have quite the playlist," she points out, her smile remaining.

"I love music." I shrug. "All of it."

"Even country?"

"Country, pop, rap, rock… If the lyrics say something worth hearing, I'll listen."

"Camden," a voice calls out. I look over and find my mom standing on the doorstep. "Everything okay?"

"Yeah." I stand, and Layla joins me. When I look at her, my earlier suspicions are confirmed. I'm five-ten, and she only comes up to the top of my chest, putting her a good half a foot shorter than me. "This is Layla, our new neighbor."

Mom meets us halfway. "Nice to meet you. I'm Sophia Blackwood."

"It's nice to meet you," Layla says softly.

"Will you be attending Brooklyn High?" Mom asks.

"Yeah, my mom got me registered, so I can start tomorrow."

"You'll love it," Mom says before turning her attention to me. "It's late, and you have school in the morning as well. Come in soon, please." She looks back at Layla. "It was nice to meet you. I'll have to stop by tomorrow to introduce myself to… your parents?"

"Yeah, my mom and dad."

"Good luck on your first day tomorrow. If you need anything, I'm sure Camden can help you." With a smile and a wink, Mom excuses herself.

"Here, put your number in," I say, handing her my phone. She raises a single brow. "So if you're lost or anything tomorrow, you can text me," I add. "Don't worry, I heard the part about you having a boyfriend."

Her face falls at the mention of the guy she had to leave behind. She inputs her number, and once she hands me back my phone, I pull it up and hit call. Her phone rings in her pocket, and I click end. "Now you have my number, in case you need anything."

"CAN WE PLEASE STOP BY STARBUCKS ON THE WAY TO SCHOOL?" BAILEY GROANS AS WE walk to the car. Oscar, our driver, opens the door, and I'm about to get in when I see Layla stepping outside with a frown marring her features. She's dressed in the girls' version of our school uniform—a blue, yellow, and white plaid skirt, a white button-down shirt with a matching plaid tie, and black flats—with her backpack situated on her shoulders and her camera around her neck.

When she sees me watching her, a small smile appears.

"Who's that?" my younger sister asks.

"Our new neighbor." I wave Layla over. "You on your way to school?"

"Yeah. I have my GPS pulled up…"

"Get in," I tell her. "It'll take a good thirty minutes to walk and even longer on the train since it's the morning rush."

She eyes the vehicle, Oscar, then my sister.

"This is Oscar, our driver." Oscar tips his hat—yes, he actually has a hat like the drivers you see in movies and speaks in a British accent. He's been our driver for years and is awesome about not telling on us for the shit he sees us do.

"And this is my little sister, Bailey. She's a freshman."

"His much *cooler* sister," Bailey adds with a side-eye.

After Layla introduces herself, we pile in, and Oscar stops by Starbucks so we can run in and grab coffee and breakfast on our way to school. Layla asks if she can roll down the window during our drive, and she snaps pictures of everything in sight.

When she says she's never even so much as visited the city before moving here, I offer to show her around this weekend.

"That would be amazing," she gushes in excitement. "This place is like a photographer's playground."

When we arrive, Bailey takes off toward her friends, and Layla stands in place with a coffee in her hand, checking everything out. It must be daunting coming from a small town to the city. Brooklyn isn't huge compared to Manhattan, but our high school is three stories and houses almost three thousand students. Even though my dad is a famous musician, and my family is hella rich, we've gone to a public school our entire lives. My parents want us to stay humble, and that's fine by me. Had I been forced to attend private school, I never would've met my boys.

"You're not going to take any pictures?" I ask, nodding toward the camera still around her neck.

She glances down as if just remembering it's still there and pulls it over her head, pushing it into her backpack. When I give her a questioning look, she simply shrugs and says, "Don't want to be the weird new girl with a camera around her neck."

I nudge her hip lightly. "There's nothing weird about you, Shutterbug."

She smiles at the nickname. It's not original by any means, but it fits her.

"You ready?" I ask, taking her hand in mine.

She glances down at our joined hands, swallows thickly, and briefly closes her eyes. "Not even close." But then, she opens her lids and, with renewed strength, nods once and saunters forward.

While she's speaking to the lady in the front office to get her schedule, Braxton texts me in our group chat asking where I am, and I tell him I'll see him at lunch.

We find out Layla has three classes with me, including first period, so after she finishes in the office, I walk her to class. When we get inside, the bell is just ringing, and everyone is piling in. I always sit in the back with Declan, who also has English first period.

When he walks in, he notices Layla right away, giving me a raised brow, clearly appreciating what he sees. Feeling an odd sense of protectiveness over Layla, I shake my head, making it clear she's off-limits. Sure, she has a boyfriend, but he isn't here—and let's be honest, at fifteen and living hundreds of miles apart, they aren't going to last. Her simply having a boyfriend won't stop the guys from swooping in like vultures and trying to pick apart the fresh meat.

As I'm introducing Layla to Declan, Kaylee and Tori walk in. They're cool chicks, so I nod for them to come over and introduce them to Layla. The girls hit it off right away and spend the next few minutes getting to know each other while we wait for the teacher to start class.

"WHAT'S WITH YOU AND THE NEW GIRL?" BRAXTON ASKS LATER AT LUNCH. WORD HAS already gotten out around school that there's a new girl, and since I walked her to our first three classes, she's obviously been linked to me.

I'm scribbling words into my notebook, hoping eventually some of them will get turned into lyrics, so I don't look up when I say, "Nothing. She's my new next-door neighbor."

"She's hot as hell," Gage says, sitting next to me and dropping his tray of shitty food on the table.

"Fuck yeah, she is," Declan agrees, sitting next to Braxton and across from me. "But not as hot as your sister."

I look up and glare at him. "Don't talk about my sister." I point my finger at him. Fucking dick has been obsessed with my older sister, Kendall, since he met her. She's seven years older than us and doesn't even know he exists. "And she's off-limits."

"No shit. She's dating that actor…"

"Not her… though she's definitely off-limits as well, even if she wasn't dating that dumbass. I'm talking about Layla. She's off-limits."

Braxton's brows hit his forehead. "You laying claim on her?"

"She has a boyfriend back in Michigan. But even if she didn't, it's not happening." There's no way I'm letting my asshole friends anywhere near her. They would use her up and spit her out just like they do the rest of the girls at this school.

Declan scoffs. "It's sounding a whole lot like her boyfriend is sitting at this table."

"We're friends," I say dryly, going back to working on some lyrics.

"Whatcha got there?" a feminine voice asks a few minutes later.

Looking up, I find Layla sitting next to me, her raspberry-vanilla scent invading my nostrils, and her eyes on my notebook.

"That's his journal," Braxton says, answering for me. "It's where he writes all his secrets."

"Aw, that's cute," Layla coos. "I have one too. I keep it under my bed…" She scrunches her face up in an adorable way, making her twin dimples pop out. "But I probably shouldn't have said that out loud, huh?"

"Good to know," Braxton says, "in case I'm ever in your room." He shoots her a wink, and I kick him in the shin, making him groan in pain.

"This isn't a journal like that. It's where I jot down my ideas for songs."

"You write songs?" Her voice perks up, and she moves closer to sneak a peek.

I close my book. Nobody's allowed to see what I write—hence Braxton talking shit. "I do," I tell her. "We're in a band." I nod to the other guys.

"Really? You didn't tell me that last night." She playfully jabs my side. "You any good?"

"Damn good," Kaylee says. "They'll be playing Friday night at the party Ricky's throwing. You should totally come."

"I'm there." Layla's eyes meet mine. "I can't wait to see you guys play."

After school, since Layla and I don't have our last class together, I text her, telling her to meet me in the student pickup so she can ride home with the guys and me. Bailey texts that she's going home with a friend.

When we get home, Layla says she'll see us tomorrow and then heads over to her house. Before she gets to her door, I call out her name. "We'll be practicing all afternoon if you want to come over and hang out."

A huge grin spreads across her face. "Let me just say hi to my mom, and then I'll come over."

The afternoon is spent practicing while Layla videos and takes pictures. I'm not sure what she's doing, but she's so into the music and us, I don't question it. At some point, Dad comes home, and I introduce him to Layla.

"Did you make that today?" he asks her from behind her laptop. I'm on the other side so I can't see what he's talking about.

"Yeah, I'm just messing around. My dad bought me this new program."

"Can you play it back for me from the beginning?" he asks.

Curious, the guys and I walk around behind her to check it out. It's a rough cut of us practicing, homing in on each of us from different angles—still shots, video clips—showcasing each of our best attributes. I've seen my sister and dad play, have watched their live performances and music videos, but this is the first time I've seen myself and the guys as an outsider. We've been playing for years, but at this moment as I watch ourselves from Layla's perspective, I feel like we're actually a fucking band.

"This is really good," Dad says, making Layla blush with his compliment. "You considering videography as a career?"

She nods. "I'm not sure what I want to do with it, but yeah."

"From that video, it's clear you have a keen eye for detail. The way you captured their passion and love for the music. You could make a very good living working in the music industry. If you ever want to intern at Blackwood, just say the word."

Her eyes light up, and I can't help the way my insides tighten.

"Really?" she says. "That would be amazing."

Three

Camden

Junior Year

Layla: SOS My house.

"SHIT, I GOTTA GO." WITHOUT WAITING FOR ANY OF THE GUYS TO SAY ANYTHING, I HAUL ASS upstairs and head straight for the front door. Layla only texts me SOS when it's an emergency—it's our thing. When one of us needs the other to bail us out, or when we're having a bad day and need to talk, we text SOS. Layla was supposed to be in Michigan, staying with her aunt so she could visit her friends and boyfriend for two weeks before school starts back up. She's been looking forward to this all summer. She's only been gone for a few days, so for her to be back already means something went wrong.

Without knocking, since I know her dad's at work and her mom treats me like I'm her own son, I swing the door open and go in search of Layla.

"She's in her room," her mom says with a sad smile from the kitchen where she's stirring something on the stove.

"Thanks."

I sprint up the stairs to the fourth floor, where her room is, and with a small knock, walk right in, stopping in my place for a moment when I see her lying in her bed, curled up like a shrimp, with tears streaming down her cheeks.

"Ah, hell, Shutterbug, what happened?"

Lifting her into my arms, I sit against the headboard and hold her tight while she sobs against my chest. I have a feeling I know what, or I should say *who*, has caused her to cry: Taylor, her dumbass boyfriend. And while I hate to see her cry, if he's the cause of her tears, that probably means one thing—they broke up—and selfishly, that makes me happy because Layla deserves better than that guy.

When she's finally calmed down enough to talk, she sniffles a few times and glances up at me with her red-rimmed eyes that have me wanting to kill the fucker who would dare to break her heart.

"He's been cheating on me for the past several months," she chokes out, "with Mariah." A fresh sob wracks her body, and she nestles her face back into my chest. I lean over and kiss the top of her head, inhaling the raspberry scent of her hair and the vanilla from her lotion. "I showed up as a surprise, and instead, I was the one surprised."

Over winter and spring break, she offered to visit Taylor, but he gave her excuses that he was too busy with school and sports and work and wouldn't be able to spend quality time with her. I wanted to call bullshit, tell her to dump that asshole and find someone who would make her the center of his world, but I kept my mouth shut, knowing she needed to get through this her way. I knew he would eventually fuck up, and once he did, I'd be here for her. When summer came around, he mentioned he had football camp in the beginning, so she called his mom to ask when it was over to plan a visit and surprise him.

I had a bad feeling something like this was going to happen. I could see the signs that he'd been pulling back, not calling and texting her like he used to when she first moved here, but for Layla's sake, I was hoping I was wrong. Because, with the way she wears her heart on her sleeve, I knew she'd be devastated the day he broke her heart. I've learned over the past year from getting to know Layla that when she gives you her heart, she's all in. She's loyal to a fault and probably the most forgiving person I've ever met. She's also the best person I know.

"I'm such an idiot."

"You are *not* an idiot," I tell her, tipping her chin up to look at me. "He doesn't deserve you." Nobody does… but if she would ever give me a chance, I'd do everything in my power to be worthy of her love.

"It hurts," she croaks, fresh tears filling her lids.

"I know, but you'll get through this." I kiss her forehead and hold her tighter while she continues to cry in my arms. When her eyes eventually shut, I spend the next couple of hours watching her, wondering how long it will take for her to get over this guy. I know that sounds bad, but the truth is, at some point in the past year, I fell in love with Layla. I've waited for the day I can finally tell her and hopefully make her mine.

Eventually, her eyes flutter open, and she stretches her limbs, glancing up at me with a soft smile. "Sorry, I guess I fell asleep."

"It's all good."

As if she suddenly remembers something, her eyes light up slightly. "I have something for you." She reaches across the bed and grabs a small box off the nightstand. "When I first flew into Michigan, my aunt took me to this cute little shop she opened up a few months ago. She makes all types of jewelry and house stuff. Anyway, when I was looking around, I saw this necklace." She opens the box and pulls it out. "My aunt said it's a friendship necklace." She opens the clasp and puts it around my neck. "I know you're a guy, but lots of guys wear jewelry, and it's manly."

I glance down at it and smile. I've never been one to wear jewelry, but as far as jewelry goes, it's not half bad. The beads are all black, with pieces of metal between them.

"Thanks."

Layla sniffles softly and encircles her arms around me. "Thank you for being my friend. I don't know what I would do without you in my life."

"Well, it's a good thing you'll never have to find out." And once she gets past her dumbass ex-boyfriend hurting her, hopefully, we can work on our friendship becoming something more.

"I'M READY!" LAYLA SAYS, JOGGING DOWN THE STAIRS TO THE STUDIO A COUPLE OF DAYS later. After I held her all night, we spent the next day watching chick flicks while eating a shitload of junk food that her mom swore would heal her broken heart. That night, I reluctantly left to go home since my mom was giving me crap about being gone for so long, but sometime in the middle of the night, Layla texted me she needed me, and I ended up back at her house, in her bed, holding her for the rest of the night. Yesterday, Kaylee and Tori came over and dragged her out for a girls' day, where they got their nails and hair done. Once she was home, she snuck over after her parents fell asleep and slept in my arms, leaving some time before I woke up.

"What are you ready for?" I ask, flipping my hood onto my head and tugging on the strings as I take in her appearance. Unlike the past couple of days, when she's been dressing in sweats and oversized hoodies, today, she's wearing a tiny jean skirt, a light-pink tank top that shows off her belly ring, and flip-flops. She's wearing more makeup than usual, and her usually wavy hair is straight.

"Life," she says with a wide grin, making those damn dimples pop out. My heart pounds against my chest at how beautiful and happy she looks. "I'm ready to finally live my life."

I set my notebook on the table and walk toward her, wondering how long I have to wait to tell her how I feel. Then she speaks her next words, halting me in place.

"More specifically, the single life." Her hands land on her hips, and she nods once quickly for emphasis. "I've spent the past two years locked down by a boy who didn't deserve me. I spent too many hours giving him my time when I should've been focusing on me. So this year is all about me. And to start it off, guess what I'm doing?"

Her eyes light up in excitement while my heart deflates.

When I don't answer quick enough, Braxton does for me. "What're you doing?"

"I'm trying out for cheerleading!"

Kaylee and Tori cheer—since they're both on the squad and have been begging Layla to join—at the same time the guys snort out a laugh.

"This is going to be so much fun!" Kaylee squeals, running over to Layla and hugging her. "Guys are overrated. I say we make this year about girl power!"

"I'm in!" Tori agrees.

So much for telling her how I feel.

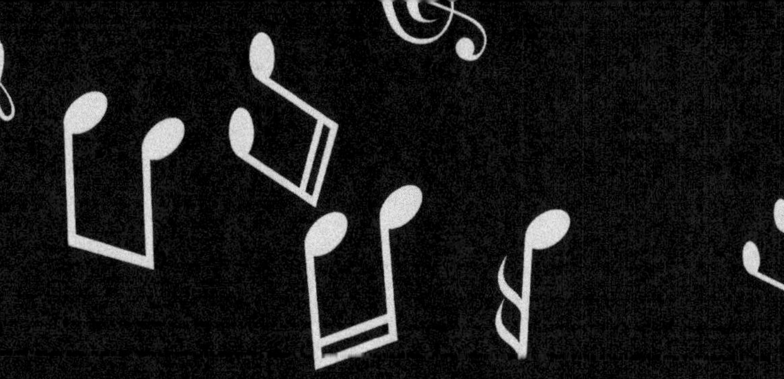

Four

Camden

Senior Year

"CAMDEN, I SERIOUSLY CAN'T THANK YOU ENOUGH." MY SISTER, KENDALL, WRAPS HER ARMS around me and kisses my cheek. "I know you would've rather been hanging with your friends all summer." She isn't wrong. I was definitely looking forward to hanging out with my friends and relaxing all summer, but when Kendall broke up with her boyfriend—who's opening up for her while on tour—and begged me to join her, I couldn't say no to my sister. She's several years older than me, but we've always been close.

"It's all good. I had fun on the road with you, and I learned a shit ton about touring."

She grins. "Never know… I could be visiting you while you're on tour in a few years."

"Oh, it's happening," I tell her, stepping off Blackwood Records's private jet. "Mark my words, within a year of us graduating, we'll be touring."

Her shoulders shake with laughter. "How is it that we grew up listening to nothing but pop and country, and you ended up being a metalhead?"

"Hey!" I feign offense. "I am *not* a metalhead. Would you call Aerosmith a metalhead? How about Matchbox Twenty or OneRepublic? No, you wouldn't, and I'm not either." Not that there's anything wrong with someone being one. I grew up listening to Led Zeppelin and Black Sabbath. They're just a couple of the reasons I fell in love with rock instead of the pop shit my dad and sister sing.

But when Braxton and I sat down in the sixth grade and decided to start a band, I knew I wanted my lyrics to be less heavy and a bit more soulful. Braxton agreed. And when we met Declan—who is a hopeless romantic—and a year later, Gage—who didn't give a fuck what we sang as long as he could beat the shit out of the drums— they were both on board with the vibe we wanted to create.

"Whatever." Kendall rolls her eyes playfully. "It all sounds the same to me."

"And so does your bubblegum pop crap."

She laughs as we get into the Town Car taking us home. Technically, Kendall lives in California, but after a tour, she always spends time at home so our parents can spoil the shit out of her before she goes back to LA to record her next album. She could easily record her album in New York, but she swears the California beach speaks to her, and she has no desire to live anywhere else.

Dad has already said if he signs us after graduation—yeah, *if*, because he refuses to agree to anything until after the four of us have our diplomas—we'll have to move to LA, at least for a while since that's where Earl James is located—one of the best producers in our genre.

When we get to the house, our mom fawns over us, crying about how much she's missed us, while Dad asks us how the tour went, even though he knows everything that goes on with Blackwood.

"Breakfast is ready," Maria says, popping her head in and shooting a wink my way, silently telling me she's made my favorite. Maria is officially our nanny/housekeeper, but unofficially, she's our nanna—at least that's what we've been calling her since I was born. She was hired to help when Mom was pregnant with me and eventually moved in.

While our parents have always been there, they're still busy with Blackwood since Dad is the president, and Mom is Blackwood's attorney and VP. When Dad's parents retired several years ago, they stepped down. Dad retired from making music and instead focuses on running the family business. The first musician he signed was none other than Kendall.

"Cream cheese French toast," Mom says, sitting at the table. "You haven't made these since—"

"Since my birthday," I say, stabbing a piece with my fork. "Because they're my favorite. Thanks, Nanna."

She smiles brightly, sitting at the table with her own plate of food. She's in her late seventies now, and Mom insisted years ago that she stop doing anything around the house and relax. She's hired someone else to do the cleaning and cooking, but Maria swears she gets bored if she's not taking care of our family. I'm not going to argue since she always makes my favorites and cleans my dirty clothes even though we do our own laundry. And before you get on me, I've never asked her to do it. She's like the laundry fairy. My clothes go from the hamper to my drawers, and I've never even seen her do it, but I know it's her. Nanna's been spoiling me since I was born, and everyone knows I'm her favorite.

"Anything for you, my boy," Nanna says with a wink that has everyone at the table, besides me, groaning. "It's been quiet around here all summer without you and those boys making a ruckus downstairs." Her eyes meet mine, and they're a bit glassy. "Sure gonna miss you when you're in LA."

"Oh, Maria!" Mom wraps her arms around her. "No crying. Besides, we still have a year before they leave." She glances at my sister, then back at Maria. "And they always come back."

"But if you're worried about missing me, you're more than welcome to tag along. You can live with me, enjoy the beach and the sun, and make me French toast every morning."

Dad kicks me under the table, Mom glares, and my youngest sister, Phoebe, who's eleven, scoffs. "She's not going anywhere. She still has to take care of me. Right, Nanna?"

Nanna laughs. "I'm not going anywhere, dear. If your brother wants my famous French toast, he'll have to come back here."

"You couldn't keep me away," I tell her as I stuff a bite of delicious food into my mouth.

After breakfast is over, I head up to my room to shower. While I'm waiting for the water to heat, I scroll through my social media, checking out Layla's photos. She hasn't posted a lot this summer, but the few pictures from her time at the beach have all been saved to my phone. And one in particular, where she's lying on a towel and laughing at the camera, has become my background. We've texted almost every day, up until a couple of weeks ago, when the tour went overseas. Between the time difference and my phone rarely having reliable service, we've only spoken a few times.

Before I get into the shower, I pull up her name and shoot her a quick text: **I'm home. Where are you? I need to talk to you.**

This past year, I've given her the space she wanted and remained her friend while she stuck to her ridiculous no-boy pact. At first, I didn't believe she would last all year. I figured she was just heartbroken and needed time, but she stuck to that shit like glue. She joined the cheer squad like she wanted to, and she, Tori, and Kaylee spent the year boyfriend-less. Luckily, staying away from guys doesn't include me, so nothing between us has changed. She still spent plenty of afternoons and weekends hanging out in the studio and going to the parties we performed at. Layla also started a YouTube channel, documenting our shows and practices, and it's blown up like crazy.

I'm excited as hell to be back. I've written several songs while on tour with my sister, and I can't wait to get back to practicing and performing and hanging out with my girl. This year is going to be my year. I can feel it. Braxton mentioned he and Kaylee started dating this summer, and so did Gage and Tori. I was shocked as shit my friends actually got girlfriends, but I'm happy for them. I'm also happy because that means the no-boyfriend pact is over, and I can finally tell Layla how I feel.

Since Layla hasn't texted back yet, I take a quick shower, then get dressed, ready to go find her ass. I shoot a text to the group chat with the guys, letting them know I'm home and asking where they are, figuring since they're dating Layla's best friends, they're probably all together.

Within seconds Braxton texts me back: **At Serendipities. It's hot AF today, and the girls wanted ice cream. <insert rolling eyes emoji>**

I chuckle at my pussy-whipped friend.

Me: Layla with you guys?

Braxton: Yeah

Me: See if everyone wants to come over and chill in the studio.

Before he can respond, Layla responds to my text: **Hey you! Welcome home. Brax said we're going to your house. See you soon! <insert kissing emoji>**

About thirty minutes later, everyone piles into my studio. Declan is the first to enter, and he's alone, followed by Braxton, who has his arm around Kaylee, Gage, who's holding hands with Tori, and Layla, who's… What in the actual fuck? She's holding hands with some asshole I've never seen before.

I'm about to ask what the hell is going on when Layla locks eyes with me, her twin dimples I've missed the hell out of popping out. "Camden!" she squeals, running into my arms. "I've missed you so much!"

Her arms wrap around my neck, and I inhale her signature raspberry-vanilla scent. Fuck, I've missed this girl. My gaze goes over her shoulder to the guy she was holding hands with, and he's glaring daggers my way. I tell myself this can't be right. There's no way I left for two months, and she found a boyfriend, but when we separate, and she walks over to stand next to him, my heart sinks, knowing that's exactly what happened.

"Camden, I want you to meet David Kessler… my boyfriend."

My eyes dart from him over to my friends, who are all standing silent, waiting to see how I'm going to handle this. They know I'm in love with Layla and have been waiting for her to be ready. And based on the way they're avoiding looking my way, they've known about Layla and this guy for however long this has been going on and didn't fucking tell me.

"David," Layla continues. "This is the guy I've been telling you about. Camden, my best friend."

And just like that, I've been friend-zoned.

Just. Fucking. Great.

Five

Camden

PRESENT DAY

High School Pre-Graduation Party

"YOU KNOW WHAT? YOU'RE RIGHT," I SAY, MY GAZE LOCKED ON LAYLA AS SHE ATTEMPTS TO make her way over here only to get stopped by several people. "I'm going to tell her how I feel."

While Layla and I have remained close, it hasn't been easy. David is a possessive asshole—not that I can blame him since Layla is the entire package, and he's worried she'll leave him for someone else. But if Layla and I were together, I wouldn't treat her the way he does—trying to keep her from her friends and hog all her time. I wouldn't fear she'd leave me because I'd treat her so good she wouldn't want to be with anyone else.

We still ride to school together every day, but once we're there, David makes it a point to drag her away, wanting alone time with her. She still hangs out in the studio, but it doesn't take long before he's texting her, wanting to hang out. She still goes to parties, but he's always all over her, not giving her any space. Kaylee once said he only acts like that around me, that when I'm not around, he's normal and doesn't get all possessive, which tells me he's scared of losing her to me.

The funny thing is, up until now, I'd never go after another man's woman, so he had nothing to be worried about. But now, despite knowing it's wrong, I need to finally be honest with her. I'm not going to ask her to break up with David, but I need for her to at least know how I feel before she takes off to college with him—because once she said where she wanted to go, suddenly, he wanted to go there as well. The fact is, I've been holding on to these feelings for three years, and I need to get them out, so at least she knows.

I steal one of the shots Declan poured for himself and throw it back, needing a bit of liquid courage. "Fuck it. At this point, what do I have to lose?"

"That's what I'm talking about." Declan clasps his hand on my shoulder.

As I'm pushing off the counter, ready to lay it all out to her, a couple of our fellow students speaking next to me stops me in my place.

"…that picture… Braxton is going to kill him."

"Kill who?"

The two girls look up, their eyes going wide. "Umm…"

"Who the fuck is Braxton going to kill?" I snatch the phone from the girl's hand so I can see what she's looking at. The last thing we need is Braxton getting into any fights the night before we all walk across that damn stage and get our diplomas. Sure, technically, we're graduates, but who knows what the school would do if he got arrested for fighting, and Braxton is notorious for his no-shits-given attitude.

When I see the photo on the screen of his girlfriend half-naked in bed with another guy, I fling the phone back at the girl. "Where is this?"

"I don't know." She shrugs. "Probably here since I saw Kaylee earlier." She turns back to her friend. "I always knew she was a skank. Always trying to act like she's so perfect. Guess the homecoming queen has been dethroned."

"What happened?" Declan asks.

"We need to find Brax. Now."

I sprint out of the kitchen, already dialing Braxton's number, but before it goes through, Gage's name appears on my screen.

"Hey, man, have you seen Brax?" There's silence over the line. "Gage, you there? This is important. Gage…"

"She… She's gone."

I halt on the sidewalk, a shiver racing up my spine. Gage's girlfriend, Tori, has been going through some shit lately, but there's no way he could mean…

"Gage, what the hell are you talking about? Where is she?"

"Tori's dead. I'm at the hospital. She's gone, man." A choked sob comes through the phone, sending goose bumps up my arms.

"Stay right there," I tell him. "I'm on my way. Don't fucking move!"

The line goes dead, and I glance over at Declan. "Something happened to Tori. I need to go to Gage. I need you to find Braxton. There's a picture going around of Kaylee and another guy. Find Braxton and don't let him kill anyone."

Declan nods, and we take off in opposite directions. I call my parents on the way and ask them to meet me at the hospital.

We arrive at the same time, finding Gage sitting in a chair at the hospital, his head in his hands, his entire body shaking uncontrollably.

"Gage." His face pops up, his bloodshot eyes meeting mine. "What happened?"

He shakes his head, and I drop onto the ground next to him. "She texted she wouldn't be able to make it to the party. I knew she'd been down lately, and I didn't want her to miss our last night." A sob escapes his lips. "I showed up at her house..." He swallows thickly. "I was too late... Fuck!" He roars. "I was too fucking late. She's gone." Tears slide down his face, and I pull him into my arms, holding him tight. "She's gone," he repeats over and over again while we sit here, me holding him while he cries into my chest.

At some point, he gets himself together and stands. "Where are you going?"

"I don't know," he says, looking around. "I... I don't fucking know. Her parents wouldn't even let me see her. I just wanted to see her."

"You're coming home with us," my mom insists. "We'll deal with this together as a family."

I give her a sad smile, thankful as hell to have the parents I have. A few months ago, Gage aged out of the system, and the people giving him a place to live said he needed to go. Without hesitation, Mom told him he'd be staying with us.

My phone buzzes in my pocket, and remembering everything that's going on, I pull it out so I can get everyone caught up to speed.

Declan: Not good. Kaylee cheated on Brax, and I can't find him.

I check to make sure Declan didn't text me in the group chat and then reply: **Gage found Tori dead. Find Brax and get to my house ASAP. He needs us.**

Declan: Fuck...There's something you need to know. It's bad timing, but I don't want you finding out from someone else.

Me: Worse than Kaylee cheating and Tori dying?

A link comes through, and I click on it, waiting for it to open so I can see what the next blow tonight will be.

When it loads, I find a picture of Layla and David with smiling faces, but that's not what has my attention. Because also in the picture is her hand, with a diamond ring on her left finger. The caption reads: **He asked, and I said yes!**

And just like that, my entire world is blown apart.

Six

Layla

FIVE YEARS LATER

"MOM, CHECK OUT THIS MOVE," FELIX SAYS, SHAKING HIS BUTT TO JUSTIN BIEBER'S "BABY."
He turns in a circle, mimicking what Justin is doing on the television.
Justin drops into some cool dance move I couldn't replicate to save
my life, but somehow, my four-year-old does it perfectly, making it
look like he's part of the concert, only in our living room.

"Good job," I tell him. "After this song, I need you to stop and
clean up before—"

My sentence is cut off by the opening and slamming of the front
door. Felix's eyes go wide, and he runs to turn off the TV, but he's
not fast enough. Before he can cut it off, David steps into the living
room with a scowl on his face.

"What did I say about letting our son spend his time dancing?"
he barks. "Dancing is for girls. If he's bored, enroll him in a damn
sport."

I mentally roll my eyes at his sexist remark, not bothering to
comment on it. We've had this argument too many times lately.

With my passion for videography, Felix has grown up watching various music videos, and along the way, he found his love of dance—and for his age, he's actually really freaking good. When I mentioned him taking dance lessons, David nearly flipped his shit and refused to allow it. Since then, I've made it a point not to have Felix dance when David is around. That way, he can't make Felix feel bad about it.

"Well, aren't you in a lovely mood," I say dryly, then glance over at Felix. "Why don't you go clean your room? I'll let you know when dinner is ready."

Felix nods and runs out of the room, thankful for the out.

"I take it you didn't get the promotion you were hoping for?" I say to David once we're alone. David lives and breathes his job. If he didn't get this promotion he's been working hard for, he's going to be a pain in the ass to live with. Our marriage is already rocky as it is. I'm not sure we'll be able to weather an unplanned storm.

I sigh, wondering how we got here. Things between us weren't always this bad. At least I don't think they were. It's hard, now, to remember a time when we actually got along, but I'm sure we did. Otherwise, we wouldn't have gotten engaged and left for Boston together. But somewhere along the way, between college and my accidental pregnancy and life, things between us shifted—and not for the better. I keep hoping the rift between us can be fixed, but at some point, I'm going to have to face the facts—that rift is split open so wide, there's no repairing it.

David glares at me. "Actually, I did get the promotion. Thanks for your vote of confidence… but it comes with a stipulation I wasn't aware of: relocation."

"Relocation? Like we have to move?" We've been living in Boston since we moved here for college. I had hoped to move back to New York after college, but when David graduated, he got the job of his dreams, which meant staying—regardless of what I wanted.

"Yeah," he says with a bite in his tone. "Actually, this should make you happy. We're moving back to New York."

"Really?" I gasp because he's right. This does make me happy. I should be totally peeved that he's made the decision without me, but since it means moving back to the place I consider home, I'm not going to bother arguing. Especially since it will mean being closer to my mom.

Last year, we lost my dad, and since then, she's been having a hard time. I know getting to see Felix more often will help. And since David is practically married to his job, it will mean getting to spend lots of quality time with my mom as well.

"Yeah," he says, his nostrils flaring. "We're moving back. But I'm telling you right now, if you think that means you'll be spending all your time with those loser metalheads, you're wrong. I don't want my son around them."

"They're not metalheads," I argue. "And in case you forgot, they don't even live in New York." I'll never understand why David has such an issue with the guys. They've never done anything wrong to him. But if they come on the radio or get mentioned, he damn near loses his shit, like them simply being alive and existing personally offends him.

"His parents do." *His* meaning Camden, who I haven't talked to in several years. But that doesn't stop David from making crazy accusations anyway. "All I'm saying is when we move back there, you need to remember who you're married to."

"I'm well aware of who I'm married to. So when do we move?"

"Soon. With the promotion comes a relocation bonus. I found a place not too far from my parents and signed a six-month lease." Of course, he only mentions his parents because he and my mom don't exactly get along. When she was visiting us after Felix was born, he was rude to me in front of her, and she made a comment about it. Ever since then, he acts like she's trying to break up our marriage when, the truth is, he's doing a fine job of it himself. I already have one foot out the door. And now we're moving home. He might've found a place near his parents, but my mom lives near them.

"When it's up, I'll figure out what I want to do," he continues. "They're opening up a new office and want me to oversee it. I'm hoping once it's up and running, they'll move us somewhere else."

"I don't want to keep moving," I tell him. "Felix is about to start school. I want stability for him. You know how much I hated moving when I was younger. Moving to New York means being close to our families. I want to stay there."

"Well, you don't really have a say," he snaps. "My job pays the bills, so I decide where we live, and New York is not where I want to live."

And here we go again…

"And I'd gladly work, but you keep giving me shit about it."

"Because you belong at home taking care of our son. How about being a little more appreciative that you're able to be home? My mom's been home since I was born, and she appreciates it. Stop acting spoiled."

"I am appreciative of it," I grind out. "I love being home with him, but once he starts school, I'd like to get a job. That doesn't make me spoiled. I want to follow my passions and contribute just like you're doing."

"Your passions?" He scoffs. "Taking pictures is a hobby, not a job. Focus on our son, and I'll focus on taking care of us." He loosens his tie. "I need to get everything in order. We're leaving next Friday."

"FELIX! COME AND EAT, PLEASE," I YELL OVER THE SOUND OF JUSTIN BIEBER. I CAN'T SEE HIM since he's upstairs, but I can imagine him dancing his little butt off to the new music video that just came out. When he doesn't respond, I add, "I made chocolate chip pancakes."

"Coming!" he yells. The music comes to a halt, and then the distinct sound of his feet padding against the wood floor is heard. He flies down the stairs and plops into his chair, diving right into his breakfast.

"Are you excited about school?" I ask, my stomach in knots at the thought of my little boy starting preschool.

"I'm a little scared," he admits. "Ms. Derby seems nice, but I don't know anyone, and I miss my friends."

"I get that, but the good thing is we're close to Grandma and Nona and Papa. And you'll make new friends, I promise." School started a couple of days ago, but it's still early enough that he won't feel too much like the new kid.

I hate that Felix will miss the friends he's made in Boston, but the truth is, I won't miss the place at all. Everyone and everything I love is in New York, and had I not gotten pregnant our freshman year, I doubt I would've stayed in Boston as long as I did. Actually, I know I wouldn't have.

Felix nods slowly, not completely convinced, and continues to eat his food. A few minutes later, he's done, and after cleaning him up, we're off to his new school, which is only a few blocks from where we live. It's September in New York, and still nice out, in the low seventies. Unfortunately, that won't last long, and snow will soon be blanketing the ground.

After snapping several photos of Felix next to his desk and then introducing himself to a couple of kids and being reassured by Mrs. Derby that he'll have a great day and she'll see me later when I pick him up, I head back home to get my chores done. David likes a neat house and tends to bitch and moan when things are amiss, so I straighten up, run the vacuum, wash the dishes from breakfast, and throw a load of laundry into the washer.

When I glance at the time and see it's only been an hour, I send a text to my mom to see what she's up to.

Mom: Walking into yoga. Dinner tonight?

Me: Have fun! And sure. I'll come over after Felix gets out of school.

Then I text Kaylee to see if she's free for coffee.

Kaylee: I wish. Classes all day. Boo.

Kaylee had a rough go of it after her breakup with Braxton. Despite my best efforts to help her get through her first year of college, she failed out and moved back home. She took the rest of the year off and started over again the following year. She buckled down the second time around and will graduate in December. She already has a job lined up that she's excited about.

Bored, I pull up my social media and scroll through everyone's Monday morning posts, a mixture of inspirational and hating Monday memes.

I stop on one post in particular and hover my finger over it, deciding whether to like and comment. It's from Raging Chaos's official page. The picture was taken at a recent award show—Gage, Declan, and Braxton are standing around the man in the middle, who's holding the award in his hand with a huge grin spread across his face: Camden Blackwood. My best friend. Well, my ex-best friend. We haven't spoken in years, not since *that* night when everything changed. When Tori took her life, Kaylee cheated on Braxton, and David asked me to marry him.

Braxton and Kaylee broke up.

We buried Tori.

And then the guys left for LA, never looking back.

None of us even bothered to walk across the stage—our diplomas were mailed to us.

I tried to call Camden, but he said they needed time. Needed some space. So I did what he asked. A few months later, while I was in my dorm room listening to music while studying, their first song hit the radio. "Raging Chaos." It was the name of the song and their band—their introduction to the world.

A couple of months into college, David and I were going through a rough patch—being in college was different than being in high school. I was close to calling off the engagement and ending things between us, but then fate intervened, and despite being on birth control, I found out I was pregnant. David insisted on us getting married before Felix was born, so, in December, we were married. It was a small wedding, just close family and friends. I sent the guys and Camden an invite to our wedding, but they RSVP'd they couldn't make it. The day of the wedding, a gift arrived from Camden congratulating us—it was the newest camera out at the time with a note that read: *So you can capture all the memories.*

In June, I gave birth to Felix, and once again, a box was waiting for me when I got home. It was a baby book to print the pictures I took and create a scrapbook. There was a note inside as well that read: *You're going to make a wonderful mom.*

My heart hurt that he could easily throw our friendship away, reducing it to gifts for the occasions, but I didn't know what to do or how to fix it, so I followed his pages and watched him and the other guys climb up the ladder of fame. I always knew they'd be successful. Between Camden's soothing voice and the raw talent of Gage, Declan, and Braxton backing him up, it was a given. But what I don't think anyone expected was how quickly they would blow up.

Every song has topped the charts for weeks, every album has

won awards, and every tour has sold out. I'm so proud of them. And I miss Camden so damn much.

I click on the picture and comment congratulations even though I'm sure they probably have people handling their social media for them, and none of the guys will even see it.

Closing the app, I pull up Google. Without thinking about it, I find myself searching for videography jobs. With Felix in school and David busy at work, there's no way I'm just going to sit around here doing nothing. I got my videography degree for a reason, and it's time I actually put it to use.

As I'm searching for possible job leads, my phone rings. It's Bailey.

"Hey, long time no hear," I say when I answer.

"Hey, you. I just saw your mom at yoga, and she said you're back! When were you planning to let us know?"

"Umm… soon…"

"That doesn't sound convincing."

The truth is, since Camden stopped talking to me, I kind of shied away from the rest of his family. I always comment and like their posts, but I haven't seen any of them since I moved to Boston, and since David despises New York, my mom always visited us.

"We just got back a few days ago and are still settling in. We actually rented a place not too far from my mom."

"That's awesome. I know how much your mom misses you. Every time Mom and I have lunch with her, she's always talking nonstop about you and Felix."

My heart swells at her words. Even though I was gone, I'm glad she has Sophia. Since we moved in eight years ago, they clicked and have been the best of friends ever since.

"Thank you for keeping her company. I've missed her like crazy."
I've missed everyone like crazy.

"We should totally catch up. Hey! Friday night, I have to attend a charity concert. It's for a good cause, and I have an extra ticket. You should come."

"I don't know." It's been so long since I've been out. David always works late on Friday nights, and I hate to ask my mom to watch Felix when we've just moved back.

"Come on, please. It's been forever since we hung out," she begs.

"Let me see if my mom minds watching Felix, and I'll let you know."

Seven

Layla

"A charity concert in the park."

"Who will be there?"

"Bailey, for sure, and I'm assuming her friends."

"Will *they* be there?"

"Who?" I ask incredulously, confused as to why the hell my husband all of a sudden cares where I'm going and who I'm going with. For the past five years, he's never asked me a single question. He's always been too busy with school and work and doing his own thing.

"Don't play stupid with me, Layla. Raging Chaos." His face twists together like just the name of the band is enough to make him sick.

"You know, you used to be friends with them," I point out. When we first met at the beach, he hit it off with Declan, Gage, and Braxton. We spent two weeks, all of us hanging out. It wasn't until Camden got home that David decided he was above hanging out with a bunch of rockers.

"I put up with them to hang out with you," he corrects. "And once we were together, I didn't have to do that."

What the hell? Not liking his attitude, I throw it back at him. "Well, Camden used to be my best friend, and now that we're home, I wouldn't doubt that we'll see more of them, so you better play nice. You know our families are close."

"I don't give a shit how close your families are. You're married to me, and he isn't welcome anywhere near *my* family."

"Whatever. I'm going tonight. Does you coming home early mean you're keeping Felix?"

"I have a meeting I need to get to. I thought your mom was taking him."

"She is," I snap. "I need to get ready. Keep an eye on Felix, please." After stomping upstairs, I put on an olive-green maxi dress with a halter top and pair it with a cute dark-wash denim jacket. After I finish curling my hair into beach waves, since it's too humid to straighten it, and throw on a pair of strappy sandals, I head back downstairs.

David is in the living room typing away on his computer, and when he sees me enter the room, he does a double take before setting his computer aside and walking toward me.

"You look beautiful," he says, placing his hands on my hips. "We should go out tonight, just the two of us." His tone is gentle, sweet, and very unlike him. It reminds me of when we were in high school, and for a second, my heart softens at it.

"I thought you had to work."

"I can reschedule the meeting. We can drop Felix off at your mom's and go to dinner. What do you say?" He places a tender kiss on the corner of my mouth. "Cancel with Bailey and go out with me."

His last statement has me rearing back. "Or you can go with us?"

His eyes turn into thin slits. "I'm not going to that shit." And there he is… The *real* David Kessler.

"It's for a good cause," I repeat what Bailey had said. "We can get dinner and go to the concert. It will be nice——"

"I have work to do," he says, stepping back. "I grew up years ago. You should try it."

His harsh words hit me like a slap to the face even though they shouldn't surprise me anymore. "Music isn't just for teenagers. You might think of it as a hobby, but many people view it as a career. One I plan to pursue."

He glares like he always does when the subject of me working gets brought up. "If you're bored, you can always reconsider getting pregnant…"

Ugh, not this again. "I already told you that I'm not ready to have another baby." The truth is, I always imagined my kids being close in age, but there's no way I'm bringing another child into our already rocky marriage.

"Fine," he barks. "Then you should do something productive like volunteer at Felix's school. My mom did that when I was little."

"You're such an asshole," I hiss, completely fed up with his shit. "You've known what I've wanted to do for years, and you used to be supportive. What happened?"

"I assumed you would grow out of it."

"Grow out of it? It's my passion, my livelihood. My dream is to make music videos, film documentaries, and photograph musicians. That's never going to change."

During the years I was friends with Camden, I would record them, edit the footage, and post it on YouTube. It was then I realized I wanted to do that on a larger scale one day. The summer before our junior and senior year, Easton, Camden's dad, even let me hang around the studio and learn from one of their videographers. He told me after I finished school, I would always be welcome if I wanted to intern with them. Maybe I should talk to Easton. It would piss off David, but at this point, I don't even care.

"I need to get going," David says, snapping me from my thoughts.

"Of course you do." I roll my eyes.

He ignores my annoyance, gathering his stuff and heading to the front door. Before he walks out, he turns back to me, eyeing me one last time. "Do you think that dress is appropriate for a mom to wear?"

My jaw drops—literally drops. "You just said I looked beautiful."

"And you do. When you're at home or with your husband. I'm just not sure about the kind of message it will send if you're wearing it to a concert, surrounded by drunken men."

"It's a *charity event*, and I don't care if I show up naked. Nothing I wear should send any message to any man, drunk or not. Have a great night at work," I sneer, turning my back on him, done with this asinine conversation.

"ARE YOU *SURE* YOU DON'T MIND WATCHING HIM?" I ASK AS MY MOM PUSHES ME OUT THE door, even though she told me several times she has absolutely no problem with watching her grandson. In fact, she insisted on keeping him for the night to make up for all the time they've missed out on while we were living apart and told me not to pick him up until at least after breakfast tomorrow.

"Layla Isabella, if you ask me that one more time…"

"Okay, okay." I throw my hands up, waving the white flag. "I'm going."

"Have fun, Mommy!" Felix yells from the living room, not even bothering to come over and properly say goodbye since he's too busy checking out all the toys my mom bought for him once she found out she'd be watching him tonight.

"Bye, love you."

I close the door behind me and walk down the steps and over to the Blackwoods, where Bailey told me to meet her. When her mom found out we were going out tonight, she insisted I stop by to see her before we went out.

"Oh my God, Layla!" Sophia wraps me up in a motherly hug. "Seeing pictures of you online is not the same thing. I swear, when you left here, you were still a little girl, but now"—she backs up and drags her gaze up and down, taking me in—"you're a beautiful woman." She hugs me again. "We missed you so much."

"Okay, Mom, we get it," Bailey says, sauntering into the room, dressed in a pair of dark-wash skinny jeans and a black wraparound halter top, complete with tall lace-up stiletto boots. "Now give her some breathing room before you scare her away."

Sophia rolls her eyes lovingly at her daughter and kisses her cheek. "Have a good time tonight and give my boys some lovin' from me. Tell them I expect to see them before they take off back to the other side of the country."

Her words have me freezing in my place. "The guys are going to be there?"

Bailey and Sophia both eye me curiously, and I make it a point to school my features, not wanting them to know just how much I've missed Camden. Hell, how much I've missed them all.

"They're playing at the event," Bailey says, a cautious smile on her face. "I assumed you knew. I'm technically working tonight. I'm sorry. I should've mentioned that. If you don't want to go—"

"What? No! It's all good." I cringe when I hear the false cheer in my voice. "It's just been forever since I've seen them play live," I add, trying to play it off.

Sophia and Bailey both frown, but thankfully, neither one comments on how awkward I sound, like I'm talking about a band and not my once best friend.

"You sure?" Bailey asks.

"Yeah, I can't wait to see them play in person." I should've known the event wasn't just for pleasure. Bailey works for Blackwood, so it only makes sense.

The ride to the concert is long in the city traffic, but Bailey and I use the time to catch up. I learn she's dating someone new—her name is Cynthia, and she works in marketing at Blackwood. She's the first woman Bailey's dated who she can see a future with, so they're taking it slow. Bailey graduated last year and is using her marketing degree to run Blackwood's media department, and when she asks me if I'm still planning to do something in videography, I tell her I've been researching possible internships and jobs.

"You know my dad would be offended if you don't intern with us."

"I wasn't really sure if that was still on the table." I shrug, not wanting Easton to think I've disappeared and then expect him to take me in.

"Layla," she says, placing her hand on my thigh. "I know you and Camden don't…" She flinches, not finishing the sentence, but we both know what she was saying: *we don't talk anymore.* "But that doesn't change the fact that you're like family."

"I appreciate that. I think, for now, I'll keep looking. I don't want to stir the pot."

I can tell she wants to argue, but instead, she says, "Okay, but if you change your mind…"

"I know. Thank you."

When we get to the venue, we're taken backstage. With Bailey's hand in mine, we walk through the throng of people running around and getting ready for the show to start. It's complete madness and makes me smile. I always dreamed of working with musicians, and although I've only been to a handful of concerts, those I've been to, I was lucky enough to be with Camden and get to experience it all from behind the scenes. Every show he took me to solidified what I wanted to do for a living. Being back here amid the chaos reminds me of my dreams. And if David thinks he's going to stop me from achieving them, he's got another thing coming.

"I just need to check in with Cade real quick," she says. "Actually, you'll love to meet him." She grins back at me. "He's our videographer. I'm doing a promotional YouTube series leading up to the next tour for Raging Chaos, and he's getting footage for it."

She searches for him in several areas he should be in, and when she can't find him, she stops and calls him. After the second attempt, he answers. "Hey, Cade, where are you?"

I can't hear what's being said but based on the frown now marring her features, it can't be good. "Is everything okay?" Her frown deepens. "I understand… No, it's okay. You need to focus on her. If you need anything, please let me know."

"What happened?" I ask when she hangs up.

"Cade's girlfriend has been put on bed rest. She's only eighteen weeks pregnant. He's been so distraught that he forgot to call me. He's in LA with her right now."

"Is she okay?"

"Yeah, but he's worried about leaving her. I really wanted to get some footage of the show tonight, but there'll be other shows."

"I could do it," I blurt out. "If you have the camera equipment and lighting, I could record the footage. It's not that hard." Her eyes go wide, and I immediately backtrack. "I mean, I haven't done anything like that in a while, but while I was in college, I videoed a few shows and made some music videos. No, actually, I can't do it. I don't know what I was thinking. Just ignore me. I'm an idiot. I have no idea what I'm even talking about." When a smile spreads across Bailey's face, I stop my rambling. "What?"

"Nothing, I was just listening to you have an entire conversation with yourself. Do you do that often?"

I snort out a laugh. "It's one of the side effects of being a stay-at-home mom."

She laughs. "Sounds like you need some adult interaction."

"David works a lot," I mumble, immediately regretting it when Bailey looks at me curiously. "I mean, he's working his way up the corporate ladder, and with the promotions, he has to be at the office a lot, so it's usually just Felix and me." I sigh, willing myself to shut up.

"So you can do it?" she asks, changing gears.

"Do what?" I ask dumbly.

She rolls her eyes. "Record the show. It would just be during the guys' set, which is only two songs."

"I don't know."

"You would be doing me a huge favor, and let's be real…" She steps closer and leans in like she's about to tell me a secret. "We both know you want to. I bet you're itching to get behind a camera again."

She's right. I totally do, and I totally am. My fingers are literally tingling at the thought of getting my hands on the professional equipment. It's been too long since I've gotten to do anything like this and never at an event this big.

"Yeah, I do," I admit.

She grins. "Then let's do it."

Eight

Layla

equipment is and I get situated, we go to the VIP seats and watch several performances. Some of my favorite bands are playing, and I get lost in the music. It's been way too long since I've been able to let loose and enjoy myself. We dance and laugh and sing and even have a couple of drinks. I'm so wrapped up in the show that I'm momentarily confused when Bailey says it's time to head backstage. Until I remember I'm recording Raging Chaos. Then my heart goes into overdrive because what the hell was I thinking? I haven't seen these guys in person in five years.

Thankfully, since they're on stage and I'm recording from the side, they won't even know I'm there. My plan is to get in and get out.

As I'm setting up, the crowd goes crazy, and a second later, Camden's voice echoes across the speakers. My gaze lands on him, and my heart leaps in my chest. Time has been good to him. He's older looking, more mature. His brown hair is messy, and his skin is sun-kissed from the California sun, making him look more like a surfer than a rock star. I briefly wonder if he lives near the water. If he goes to the beach on his days off.

Camden thanks everyone for being here, and once the crowd has calmed a bit, he explains that them being here is helping a cause close to their heart. My chest tightens at his words as he speaks about it, though he doesn't specifically say Tori's name. It's been years since I've allowed myself to think about her. What happened was so tragic, and it was hard to deal with as a teenager. The night she died, everything changed for all of us. We were young and heartbroken, and we just didn't know how to handle adult shit. Hell, five years later, I might be older, but I still don't think I would be able to handle the seriousness of what went down.

Gage starts the song by counting off on his drums, and I press record, focusing on him. His face is stoic, but I know him well enough to know he was affected by Camden's speech and is hiding his emotions. He looks darker and edgier than he did the last time I saw him five years ago. He's never been carefree, not with everything he's been through in his life, but before, he still had a lightness to him. Now, it's as if it's been snuffed out.

Declan joins in with the bass a few seconds later, smirking playfully at the crowd. Like Camden and Gage, he's now less boy and more man. Braxton adds his guitar, his eyes meeting Declan's for a moment before he gives the crowd his attention. He smirks as well, but it's more devilish. While the band has been good at keeping themselves away from any negative publicity, Braxton's been caught quite a few times in compromising positions with various women, alongside Gage. The media chalks it up to them being manwhores, but since I'm personally familiar with their history, I know it's more about burying their broken hearts than the need to sleep around.

Declan and Braxton move closer, and I zoom in on their

instruments and then on their faces as they bob their heads in time with the music. And then Camden belts out the beginning lyrics of the song "Hate to Love You" from their last album. Their sound is fluid. They've been playing together for so many years, they could probably do it in their sleep. One song blends into two and then three.

Camden's shirt comes off at some point, and sweat glistens on his skin. He chucks it to the side, making fans freak out over who's going to snag it. I've seen plenty of pictures of him shirtless, but none of them compare to seeing him in person. He's all man, rippled and hard everywhere, yet still so damn beautiful.

When the lyrics come to an end, Camden grins while Braxton riles the crowd up with his solo just before the lights flicker off, officially ending the song.

Everyone cheers when the lights come back on, and Camden is sitting on a stool with a mic in his hand. He holds his hand up, and like magic, the place goes silent.

"I thought tonight, here with you, would be the perfect time to play something new. It's a bit slower. What do you think?" The fans scream and shriek, and Camden chuckles under his breath. "All right, since you asked so nicely." More screams.

Gage starts in on the drums, and then the other guys join in. I'm videoing just fine, focusing on what I'm doing… and then Camden opens his mouth. His raspy voice is filled with raw emotion, and I find myself locked on him, forgetting what I'm supposed to be doing. From the moment the first words leave his mouth, I can tell that this song is different from his norm.

Lately, I've been sitting in the dark
Drinking whiskey
Wondering how the hell I let her get ahold of my heart

It wasn't hers to take
It sure as fuck wasn't hers to break

I quickly realize he's singing about a woman who has broken his heart, and I wonder who it could be. As far as I know, he's never been in a serious relationship. Sure, he's been seen out with various women but never more than a few times. Maybe he kept it quiet, under wraps, not wanting his business to be out there.

Looking back, I have to wonder if I was ever even in the game
Guess it doesn't fuckin' matter
'Cause the outcome was always meant to be the same

Sharp, jagged pieces all over the floor
That's all that was left when she walked out the door

Camera in her hands
All I wanted was to see the world through her lens
Would it be beautiful, magical, or would it all be a blur?
Would I ever know what she's thinking?
Or would I always wonder why I was never enough for her?

Sharp, jagged pieces all over the floor
That's all that was left when she walked out the door

At his words, my body stills, chills racing up my spine. My eyes stay locked on Camden as he sings about a woman with a camera. He couldn't be talking about me. There's no way. Mentally, I shake my head for even coming up with such an outlandish notion. It has to be a coincidence. It wouldn't even make any sense because we've never dated, so how could I have possibly broken his heart. No, I'm clearly overthinking things. I chalk my crazy thinking up to the shit David was giving me earlier about Camden, mixed with the couple of drinks Bailey convinced me to get… until he sings the next few lines.

> *Nobody warned me how hard it would be*
> *To watch that gorgeous woman walk away from me*
> *Thousands of miles apart*
> *Should've been easier than this to piece back together my heart*

I suck in a sharp breath, tears filling my lids. This can't be a coincidence. I'm the girl with the camera. I left for Boston and didn't return until now. He moved thousands of miles away. Too many pieces fit together, but none of them make any sense.

> *Like the perfect lens has been shattered*
> *I'm trying to see past her, but she's all that mattered*
> *Life has turned into one blurry mess*
> *I need to refocus, finally put her to rest*

> *Sharp, jagged pieces of my broken heart all over the floor*
> *That's all that was left when she walked out the door*

The crowd cheers when the song ends, clearly loving it. The guys make their way off the stage, but I can't move. My feet are stuck, and my head is numb. My heart is racing beneath my rib cage, causing my body to vibrate. Thoughts of all the times David was pissed about Camden, accusing him of wanting to get in my pants, saying we can't be friends because guys and girls can't just be friends hit me hard. I chalked it up to him being jealous over nothing. But was he right? Was I blind? Did Camden want more with me, and I had no idea?

And then, just before they disappear, Camden stops and glances my way. His eyes land on mine, and I swear, my heart stops. Like literally stops. His eyes widen slightly, his nostrils flaring. I wait with bated breath to see what he'll do. Will he come over? Walk away?

My questions are answered when he steps toward me, not stopping until we're mere inches apart. He's still shirtless, dripping with sweat. It's hard to breathe, and my head is spinning. I open my mouth—to say what, I'm not sure—but before any words can come out, Camden leans in. I think he's going to say something, but his lips softly land on my cheek. Unconsciously, I inhale, and the scent of him damn near knocks me on my ass. He still smells like the same cologne—warm with a spicy undertone. It's the same cologne he's been wearing for years. It's not until his scent hits me that I realize how much I've missed that smell… missed *him*. It's like sitting by the fire on a cold night. I could wrap myself up in his scent and feel content.

He pulls back slightly, and his green eyes bore into mine for a long moment before he finally speaks. "You look good, Shutterbug. Really damn good." Then without another word, he turns his back on me and disappears, leaving me wondering what the hell just happened.

"Layla," a feminine voice says, clearing some of the fog in my head. "Are you okay?"

I look at Bailey, who's biting her lip in worry. "Was that…?" I drag in a breath, then release it harshly. "Was that song… about…?" I can't even finish my question, a lump of emotion clogging my voice. I already know the answer, but I need someone else to say it, to confirm it.

"About you?" she finishes. "Yeah."

"Did you know?"

She shakes her head. "I mean, I knew he wrote it. I'm back and forth between here and LA, and I hear the songs they're recording. But I didn't know he was going to sing it tonight. I swear."

"I don't understand," I breathe. "He said I broke his heart, but it doesn't make any sense. He's the one who left without so much as a goodbye. He's the one who said he needed space."

Bailey eyes me for a moment before she sighs. "Why don't we get out of here and go get a drink?"

We end up at Mitchell's, a hole-in-the-wall dive bar that Bailey frequents when she's in town, and Kaylee, who apparently was watching the performance online, meets us there since she lives in the city and attends NYU.

"It's been too damn long." Kaylee wraps her arms around me for a hug. "I can't believe the warden actually let you out."

"K," I groan, not wanting to hear, *again*, how much she can't stand my husband. Once upon a time, they got along. Until we moved to Boston and shit hit the fan. He wanted to focus on school while Kaylee wanted to drown her sorrows in the bottom of a bottle, and I was stuck in the middle. It led to a lot of fights and me staying home with David and studying instead of partying. She'd constantly tell me he was too controlling and would ruin my college experience. It didn't matter, though, because shortly after the start of our freshman year, I got pregnant, and after that, my life revolved around Felix, school, and David.

After three double shots of Johnny, and an hour of playing catch-up, I bring up the elephant in the room. "So that song… Care to explain it?"

Both women laugh. "I'm pretty sure it was self-explanatory," Bailey says. "That was my brother's poetic attempt to get over you."

"When the hell was he ever into me?" I ask, throwing my hands up in frustration.

"He's been in love with you since you moved here," Kaylee says.

"What?" I gasp in shock. "No…"

"Yes," they both say in unison.

"You're the only one who didn't notice," Kaylee says. "We all saw it, but since you never reciprocated, everyone assumed you didn't feel the same way. And then you got together with David."

"I… I didn't know." I rack my brain, trying to think of any indication Camden would've given that he had feelings for me, but I can't think of anything. "We were just friends."

"Yeah, because you were either dating someone or on a man-break," Kaylee points out. "The guy was head over heels in love with you, and you totally friend-zoned his ass."

"What? No, he wasn't!" This doesn't make any sense. "He never said anything!"

"Because he's not the kind of guy to fuck with a girl while she's in a relationship," Bailey points out.

"Didn't you ever wonder why David hated Camden so much?" Kaylee adds.

"I thought he was just acting crazy." The bartender serves us another round of shots, and I down mine, then ask for another.

"Slow down," Kaylee warns. "When's the last time you drank?"

"Don't worry about me. I can handle it."

Nine

Layla

I OPEN MY EYES, AND THE BRIGHT LIGHTS PEERING THROUGH THE SLATS OF THE BLINDS HAVE me quickly shutting my lids. The room feels like it's spinning, and my head is pounding to the beat of an off-tune drum.

"I think… I drank too much," I groan to myself.

"No shit," Kaylee says, making me jump up and screech.

I push up onto my elbows and glance around, noting that I'm lying in bed with Kaylee, and it's not my bed. "Where am I?"

"My place." She quirks a brow. "Don't you remember?"

I drop back down and grab a pillow to cover my face, willing the throbbing in my head to go away while I try to recall last night. I remember the charity concert, Camden singing the love, *er*, heartbreak song about me, getting drunk at the bar, going to a tattoo shop…

"Oh, shit!" I pop back up, and the room swirls around me. It takes a second for everything to become clear, and once it does, I jump out of bed and run into the en suite bathroom, tugging the sleeve of my shirt down as I go to expose my collarbone.

"I got a tattoo?" I gasp. "Oh, my God! I got a freaking tattoo."

"Were you really that drunk?" Kaylee asks, sitting on the toilet to go pee.

"No… Yes… Ugh, I don't know. I remember getting it. I just can't believe I did that." I stare at the black, gray, and white shaded camera with the cracked lens. There's one word written in script across the front of it: Shattered. The name of the song Camden sang last night. Shards of glass dance up the front of my shoulder and across the top. It's beautiful and sad and…

"What the hell was I thinking?" I murmur, pulling my shirt back up to cover the ink and wondering how the fuck I'm going to hide this from David. He's going to flip his shit when he sees this. Just the idea of me talking to Camden sends him damn near over the edge. When he finds out I got a tattoo… a freaking tattoo with the title of his song on it, he's going to kill me.

Kaylee flushes the toilet and washes her hands, then follows me out of the bathroom. "Only you can answer that, but if I were to guess…" She locks eyes with me. "I think hearing that song stirred something deep inside you."

"Like what?"

"Like feelings for the lead singer of Raging Chaos."

"I'm married," I argue, refusing to acknowledge that what she's saying might be true. Not that it matters because the fact is, *I am married,* and while Camden and I used to be best friends, we're not even acquaintances anymore. "I love my husband."

But as I say those words, a sadness creeps into my chest. Because while it's true, I do love David—he's the father of my son, and I've given him every part of me for the past six years—if I'm honest with myself, I don't think I've been *in love* with him for quite some time. I keep holding out hope that he's going to change, that we're going to to fix the broken in our marriage so we don't have to tear our family apart, but the truth is, I'm not sure if that's possible.

"That doesn't mean you can't have feelings for another man." I'm not sure if she's right or wrong, but I've been cheated on, and it sucks. Having feelings for another man while I'm married might not actually be cheating, but it still doesn't sit right with me.

"I don't want to talk about this anymore," I say, needing to shut down the conversation and get dressed so I can pick up Felix from my mom's. It's already well after breakfast.

When I text her I'm on my way, she replies that she's taken him to the children's museum and to meet her at the house for dinner.

I pull up the thread of texts with David, scrolling through them. He apologized for his attitude and asked what time I'd be home, and apparently, in my drunken state, I told him never. *Yikes.* He proceeded to tell me he's sorry and that he loves me, and I told him I'd be spending the night at Kaylee's. Of course the mention of her pissed him off, and the conversation ended with him telling me not to let her slut rub off on me.

As soon as I get home, I shower, careful with the new tattoo, and then get dressed, putting on a bit more makeup than usual to cover my hangover. David isn't home, which means he's probably working all weekend again. I make sure the shirt I'm wearing fully covers my ink and then head to his office to surprise him for lunch, stopping at his favorite Italian restaurant to get us food. *Yeah, I know. You can smell the guilt I'm bathed in from a mile away.*

When I arrive, the office is locked, and I have to text him that I'm here, so he can let me up. When he comes down, the lack of emotion on his face has my stomach churning. *Something is wrong.*

"I brought a peace offering," I tell him, holding up the bag of food. "Rossi's, your favorite."

David nods, and I swallow thickly as I walk past him and over to the elevator. He's silent the entire ride up to his office floor and doesn't say a word once we're in his office. The silence has my head spinning in worry. Is it possible he heard the song? Does he know it's about me?

The moment we're in his office, he slams the door, making me jump, and is on me, pushing me against the desk. Out of shock, I drop the bag of food and drinks onto the floor as his mouth descends on mine in a punishing kiss. At first, I think he's turned on and wants me, but when he bites my lip hard, making me yelp out in pain, goose bumps prickle my flesh. He's pissed, and I highly doubt it's over our half-assed argument last night. We've had a million of those over the years.

"Ow!" I hiss. "That hurts."

"That hurts?" he barks. "You know what fucking hurts? Learning that my wife was out last night with another man!"

"What the hell are you talking about?" I ask in confusion. "I wasn't with anyone but Bailey and Kaylee last night."

"You're going to lie and say you didn't go to that concert to see Camden fucking Blackwood?" He grips my chin to force me to look at him. "Is that why you didn't want me to go?"

"Are you insane?" I scoff, tugging my face out of his grip. "I asked you to join us. *You* had to work." I might've seen him last night, but I sure as hell didn't go there with the intent to.

"So while I'm busting my ass to provide a cushy life for you and our family, you go out with *him*?" He steps back slightly and runs his fingers through his hair.

"You knew there was a chance he would be playing there. You bitched about it before I left."

"Yeah, but I didn't know you would be all fucking over him!" he booms.

"What? I don't—"

Before I can finish my sentence, he pulls his phone out and

turns it around, and taking up his entire screen is a picture of me… and Camden. It was taken when he approached me after his performance. Somebody must've been recording them walking off stage, and when he stopped to talk to me, they got a picture.

"I… I can explain," I say, staring at the image of Camden leaning so close into me, it looks like he's about to kiss me on the lips instead of on the cheek where he actually kissed me. "It's not what it looks like."

"I knew this move was a bad idea." David glares, throwing his phone onto his desk. "I'm talking to Paul on Monday. They haven't filled my old position yet. I'm telling him I want it back. Moving here was a mistake. I knew this shit would happen."

His eyes are manic, and they scare the shit out of me. I get it. Camden apparently had feelings for me years ago, but the fact is, I never knew that, and I never once cheated on David. I've given him all of me. Even though he hasn't done the same.

"You're acting ridiculous," I tell him, sliding out from between him and the desk. "You might not like Camden, but you have no reason to act like this toward me. Unlike you, I've always been faithful."

"Really? You're going to throw that shit in my face again?" David barks, stalking toward me. "It was one fuckup, and I've apologized a million damn times."

"And I forgave you. I'm just pointing out there's no reason for you to act crazy with jealousy when I haven't done anything wrong. I haven't even seen him in five years. Aside from sending us a wedding and baby gift, he hasn't once tried to speak to me. He saw me standing on the side of the stage and quickly said hello. That's it."

"Why the fuck were you on the side of the stage anyway?"

"Because Raging Chaos's videographer had an emergency, and

Bailey asked me to record their performance."

David's eyes bore into mine. "Don't even fucking think about it."

"Think about what?"

"Getting a job at that fucking record label."

"Blackwood is a huge label. I doubt they'd even hire someone like me… someone with zero experience." I step toward him, putting my hands on his biceps, hoping to calm him down. We can't keep doing this. Going rounds every damn day. It's exhausting, and it's eventually going to affect Felix.

"Please stop acting like this. I didn't know he was performing last night, and when Bailey asked me to fill in, I couldn't say no. You know how much I love videography. It was nothing more than me doing a favor for an old friend. You have nothing to worry about. Camden isn't even part of the equation. I'm married to you."

"Damn right you are, and since I'm the one who pays the bills, I make the decisions, and we're moving back to Boston."

"No, we're not," I say defiantly. "I didn't like it there. It never felt like home. Here, we're close to our families."

"And Camden."

"Would you stop with him already? He lives in California. I'm done with this stupid conversation," I say, walking toward the door.

"Where are you going?"

"To my mom's. I told her I'd have dinner with her when I picked up Felix. You obviously need time to cool off and figure your shit out. I'll see you at home." I glance at the bag of food on the floor we never ate. "Enjoy your food."

Before David can argue, I'm out the door and speed-walking to the elevator. I should probably feel bad that I blew off his accusations, but the truth is, I have nothing to feel guilty about. Well… except for the fact that I got a tattoo in response to a song that Camden sang about me with the title etched across the top. But in my defense, I was drunk, and it's not like I got his name tattooed on me. It's of a camera, something that has meaning for me.

Jesus, if David is pissed about me simply going to a concert where Camden was performing and talking to him for a quick second, I can't imagine how he's going to react when that song hits the radio, and he hears it. Hopefully, he won't listen to it since he hates everything about Raging Chaos. Because if he does, I have no idea how the hell I'm going to explain this tattoo. And there's no way I'm moving back to Boston. He can scratch that crazy idea right out of his head.

By the time I get to my mom's, I'm so worked up over everything, I'm not paying attention when I walk inside... and come face-to-face with Camden Blackwood.

"What are you doing here?"

"Well, hello to you too, Shutterbug." He smirks.

Hearing my nickname on his lips sends liquid heat through my veins. I haven't heard it in five years, and now he's said it twice in twelve hours. It shouldn't affect me like this. *He* shouldn't affect me like this... but it does. *He* does. Fuck, this isn't good.

"Why are you here?"

"Umm... because I live here?" he says with a chuckle.

"No, you live in LA, and I thought you were on tour." *Please don't say you've moved back. My marriage will never survive it.*

"Keeping tabs on me? That's sweet. We are on tour, but in case you forgot, we performed here last night. And since we have a few days before our next show, I'm staying with my parents to get some family time in."

I sigh in relief. Okay, that's okay. It's temporary. Soon, he'll be on his way out of here, and then everything can go back to normal.

We're both silent for a second, and then it hits me...

"Why are you here?"

Camden's brows furrow. "Didn't we just go over this? I'm spending time with—"

"I mean, here, in my house."

He glances around and then laughs. "I'm pretty sure it's your mom's house, and I'm here for dinner. My entire family is."

Oh, shit. This cannot be happening.

Before I can respond, Felix comes barreling down the hall. "Mommy, you're back!" he squeals, throwing himself into my arms. I lift him up, prying my gaze off Camden to give my son my full attention. "I went to the museum with Grandma, and she got me an ice cream. And we made cool art, and I made you something, but it's a secret."

"A secret, huh? What kind of secret?"

Felix's eyes go wide, realizing he let something he wasn't supposed to tell me slip. "I can't tell you! It's a secret."

"Maybe… I'll… tickle it out of you." I tickle his sides playfully, and he squirms.

"No, Mommy! It's a secret."

"Fine." I sigh and stop tickling him. "Were you good for Grandma?"

"Duh." He rolls his eyes, and Camden laughs, reminding me that he's still here.

Our eyes lock, and the softness in his eyes reminds me that he wrote a song about me.

"Mommy, put me down," Felix whines, wiggling his body to get down. "Nanna is letting me mix the potatoes."

"Nanna's here?" I ask, putting him down. I haven't seen her since I moved. Because I spent so much time at Camden's house in high school, she became like a grandma to me, doting on me as much as she did Camden.

Without answering me, Felix runs out of the room and back

into the kitchen.

"Nanna's here?" I ask Camden, since he's still standing in the foyer with me.

"Yeah. She and my mom came over earlier to help your mom cook."

"Well, then you know the food is going to be delicious." I rub my belly. "I can't remember the last time I had a home-cooked meal. I can't cook for shit."

Camden laughs. "That doesn't surprise me in the least. I can still recall putting out quite a few fires when you would try back in the day."

"Oh, hush." I shove him playfully, but before I can move my hand, he grabs it and tugs me toward him, so we're close… too close.

"It's been a long time, Layles." With the hand he's not holding mine with, he tucks a wayward strand of hair behind my ear, causing me to shiver when his flesh brushes against mine.

He notices, and a knowing smirk quirks up on one side of his mouth. "How are you?"

"I'm good," I say, internally cringing at how breathless those two words come out.

"I heard you're back for good. Is that true?"

"Yeah, *we're* back for good." I emphasize the *we're* to remind him—and me—that I'm married.

Camden nods. "That's good. *You* were definitely missed."

I know I'm playing with fire when I say my next words, but I blame it on that damn song because I can't stop thinking about the words and what they mean. Everything about Camden's and my relationship now feels like a lie. I'm overanalyzing every word, every touch, wondering if what everyone said is true. If he really had feelings for me. The song said he had to put me to rest. Does that mean he's over me? Or is he trying to get over me? Could he still have feelings for me?

"Who missed me?"

His eyes dance with what looks like mirth, and when he leans in like he's about to tell me a secret, I hold my breath, waiting for what he's going to say.

"Your mom, of course." He steps back slightly, keeping my hand in his, and looks into my eyes. "I didn't know you'd be at the concert last night. What did you think?"

"About what?" I swallow thickly, completely overwhelmed by this conversation. I imagined seeing Camden again one day, but I never thought our reunion would go like this. Like he didn't just up and leave, and we didn't spend five years apart without saying a single word to each other. Like he didn't become a huge rock star, and I didn't go to college, get pregnant, and then get married.

"The band," he says, knocking me from my chaotic thoughts. "Our performance. Bailey said you videoed it for Cade. Did you enjoy it?"

"You guys were amazing," I say truthfully. "Better than you were in high school."

Camden nods. "And what about the last song?" He squeezes the hand he's holding against his chest, and my heartbeat picks up speed. "What'd you think about it?"

Holy shit. Did he seriously just straight out ask me about that song?

"I think…" I inhale deeply, the scent of him making me feel slightly dizzy, then release a harsh breath, unsure what to say. Thankfully, before I can finish my thought, my mom calls my name, breaking the moment.

"I think I better go see what my mom wants." I pull my hand away from his and turn my back on him, trying to get away quickly without making it look like I'm running.

I'm almost to the kitchen when Camden's strong hand lands on my shoulder, halting me in place. His front presses against my back, and his lips brush against the shell of my ear. I stand here, frozen in my spot, waiting to see what he's going to do, when he leans in and murmurs, "For the record, your mom isn't the only one who missed you, Shutterbug. I've missed you too."

And with those words, he steps around me and saunters into the kitchen, looking unaffected by our interaction as he asks the women if dinner's ready. While I wonder if maybe David was right and moving here was a bad idea. Because the butterflies in my belly that are swarming around… they're not for my husband.

And that's a problem—a big problem.

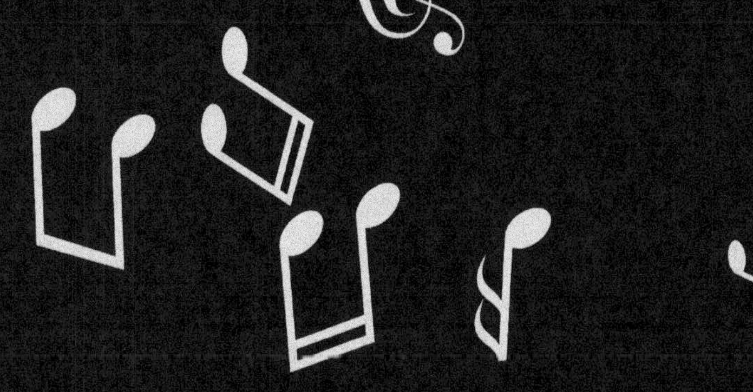

Ten

Layla

"I DON'T WANNA GO HOME," Felix whines, rubbing his fists against his eyes in exhaustion. "I wanna play with Camden."

"You've played enough," I tell him, lifting him into my arms while Camden takes the controller from him.

"But Mom…" he says in a voice that tells me he's about to have a meltdown. He's spent the past few hours playing *Sonic the Hedgehog* with Camden after he found an old Sega Genesis my dad had in the cabinet from many years ago because he loved the classic games— and after asking what it was, Camden set it up so they could play. It's late now, and David texted asking when we would be home. Not wanting to fight anymore, I told him soon.

"Hey, bud," Camden says. "How about you head home with your mom, and if it's okay with her, the next time you come to see your grandma, I'll come over and play with you?"

Felix sighs, not liking it, but then he gives in and nods. "Fine."

I don't bother to mention by then Camden should be back on tour and far away from here. If it means getting Felix to leave without a fight, I'll go along with it and hope he doesn't remember this conversation later.

We make our rounds, saying goodbye to everyone, and then Camden shocks me when he walks us out, holding the door for me while I carry Felix to my car. We don't live far, but I drove, knowing we would be here until after dark.

He opens the passenger door for me, and I slip Felix into his booster seat. He says bye to Camden, his eyes already fluttering closed, and I shut the door, leaving Camden and me alone.

He steps toward me, and I take a step back, not wanting to fall under his trance again.

"Look," I say, putting my hand out so he can't come any closer. "I don't know what happened in there earlier, during our conversation, but..." I swallow down the lump of emotion in my throat, knowing what I say next will most likely send us back to square one—and not the square in high school when we first met, but the one where he left and didn't speak to me for years. "I'm married."

"I know," he says, his mouth curving into a slight frown, which is so unlike the cocky guy I've been in the presence of all night.

"It's inappropriate to flirt with a married woman."

His gaze meets mine. "Who said anything about flirting? I'm just catching up with my best friend." He shrugs innocently.

"Your best friend?" I scoff. "No. You lost that title five years ago when you moved to the West Coast without so much as a goodbye. We *were* best friends. Now..." I look at the older version of the boy I used to know, realizing I know nothing about him anymore. "Now, we're strangers."

His mouth pops open, but before he can say anything, I open my door and slide into my car. "Have a good rest of your tour," I say, closing my door and ending the conversation.

When Felix and I get home, since he's passed out, I take him up to his room and tuck him into bed, not bothering to change him into his pajamas. If he wakes up, he'll be up for hours.

Afterward, I go in search of David, hoping we can talk. I find him in his office, sitting at his desk and drinking whiskey.

"Hey," I say, making my presence known. "Felix is in bed."

The second his dark eyes lock with mine, I know something is wrong. "Come in here and close the door."

I hesitate for a moment, but not wanting to wake Felix with whatever argument we're about to have, I do as he says.

When I turn around, he's standing close to me. He backs me up against his desk until my back hits the hard edge of the wood. "Have you seen social media?"

I shake my head.

"Everyone is linking you to that fucking song. The one where Blackwood admits to being fucking obsessed with you for years. They're wondering who the woman is that Blackwood poured his broken heart out to. I was in a meeting today, and Vanessa asked how you knew Camden Blackwood because that photo is every-fucking-where!" he barks.

Vanessa is his assistant from Boston who moved here to New York. She's always been civil with me, but I could sense a bit of hostility beneath her placating smile, like maybe she has a crush on my husband or doesn't like me for whatever reason. Of course she would be the one to throw me under the bus.

"David, I—"

"Not a fucking word," he booms, reaching down and unbuttoning my shorts. "Do you know how fucked up it is to find out from my assistant that another man wrote and sang a fucking love song about my wife?" He pushes my shorts down, confusing me.

"I didn't know—"

"I said, not a word!" He forcefully cups my jaw, making me jump.

"We haven't even been back for a week, and you're already making a fool out of yourself and me. The song, the photo of you all over him. And don't get me started on the fact that you spent the night with him."

My eyes go wide, and he chuckles humorlessly. "Yeah, your mom loves to post her entire life on social media since you showed her how to use it. Tonight, she posted about her daughter and grandson being home. And in the background, I saw you two." He squeezes my face harder, and the pain in my mouth from his tight grip has me pulling my head back.

"David, I understand it all looks bad, but if you'd let me explain."

"This is mine." He grabs my breast and squeezes. "*You* are mine." His hands fist the two sides of my shirt, and before I can stop him, he yanks it apart. Buttons fly everywhere, leaving me in only my bra and underwear.

I'm so focused on the fact that he just ripped my shirt, I'm not thinking about what he's just exposed. Until his wild eyes land on my collarbone.

"Are you fucking serious right now? This is what you were doing last night after you were all over that fucking loser?"

"It… It doesn't mean anything," I lie because I've never seen David this mad before, and at this moment, I have no idea what he's capable of.

"Don't fucking lie to me!" He whips his hand around, landing on my cheek. The feel of his palm connecting with my face stings like hell, and instinctually, I reach up to rub the area.

It takes me a second to comprehend what just happened, but once I do, I push against his chest as hard as I can. "Get the hell away from me!" I demand, refusing to let him put his hands on me in a violent manner.

David doesn't listen, though, grabbing my wrists and twisting my arms behind my back. My back hits the edge of the desk again, this time harder, and I flinch at the bite of pain.

"What the fuck were you thinking, getting branded with the title of that fucking declaration of his obsession with you?" He shocks me when he pulls his head back and then spits in my face. "Less than a week here and you're turning into a slut!" Who the hell is this man? Because this is not the guy I married. I shake my head, trying to get the spittle out of my eyes.

"You need to get that shit removed immediately." He locks both my wrists with one hand and grips my face with his other, squeezing my cheeks and chin painfully.

"Fuck you!" I hiss. "I'm not removing shit." I shouldn't provoke him, but I've had enough.

"Yes, the fuck you are," he says lowly. "We both know you've been in love with him for years, and I will *not* fuck my wife while she's marred by another man's words. Understand?"

Without waiting for an answer, he releases my wrists. I assume he's going to let me go, but then he fists my mane and yanks me to my knees.

My knees hit the tiled floor, and I cry out in pain. "David, stop!" I beg as he tugs on my hair, causing my scalp to burn painfully.

He pulls harder, forcing my chin up. "I'm not sticking my dick in you until you're rid of that shit, but since you want to act like a little slut, you can suck my dick like one." He unzips his fly and pulls his soft dick out. "Wrap your perfect dick-sucking lips around me, so you can remember who the fuck your husband is."

"I'm not touching you!" I yell. "Let go of me!"

He grabs his dick and strokes it a few times and then pulls my face toward it. I try to shake my head and keep my mouth closed, but he stuffs it into my mouth. I'm in shock, filled with disgust. I never imagined the man I've spent the past six years with could be this cruel. I knew he had a temper, but I didn't think he was capable of this. My body trembles in fear, and I know there's a chance I'm going to regret my next move, but I refuse to be a victim, to sit here while he forces himself on me.

When his dick is all the way in my mouth, I open wide and then bite down on it so hard I taste blood.

"You fucking bitch!" he shouts, yanking on my hair until he brings me to the ground. He slaps me across the face, then straddles my torso. "You want to act like a whore, then I guess I'll have to treat you like one."

He lets go of my hair and flips me onto my stomach, trapping my wrists in his hand and pulling my arms painfully behind my back. At the same time, he rips my underwear to the side. I fight to break free, yelling and cursing at him to stop, but he ignores me as he roughly enters me from behind, tearing me apart. We've never had sex this way, and it burns so badly, tears sting my eyes. The hand not holding my wrists together fists my hair, pulling on it so hard it feels as if my hair is being ripped from my scalp.

The entire time my husband rapes me, I never once give up trying to stop him, but he's stronger, and I can't get away. The more I fight, the harder he pulls my hair, the tighter he locks my wrists together, the deeper he thrusts into me. Finally, when he's found his release, he pushes off me and gets up, leaving me lying on the ground, in pain, shaking and crying and wishing he were dead.

"Get the fuck out of my office," he says, his voice filled with anger and disgust like he isn't the one who just forced himself on his wife. "And don't come anywhere near me until that tattoo is off your body."

I scramble up, grabbing my clothes and putting them on. I want to yell and tell him to go fuck himself, make it clear if I have it my way, he'll never see me again after what he's just done, but I keep my mouth shut, not wanting to give him a reason to hurt me any further. My goal: to get as far away from him as possible. And then, once I do, I can figure out what the hell just happened, so I can ensure it never happens again.

"HE RAPED YOU?" KAYLEE SCREECHES. "ARE YOU FUCKING SERIOUS RIGHT NOW?"

After David stalked out of his office, declaring he'd be at the office working the rest of the night and then left, I showered, trying to rid myself of what he'd done to me. And then I called Kaylee to come over, needing my best friend.

"He… he did it… in my butt," I admit shakily, recalling the bleeding he caused. "It hurt so bad." Fresh tears fill my eyes, and Kaylee pulls me into her arms, hugging me tightly.

"He's dead," she says softly. "I'm going to kill him."

"You can't do that, then you'll be sent to jail, and I need you with me."

She nods in understanding. "What are you going to do?"

"I'm going to file for divorce."

Her eyes go wide, obviously shocked.

"You don't think I should?"

"No, I do," she says. "I absolutely think you should. I also think you should file a restraining order against him. I'm just shocked. I thought you'd say you were going to talk to him, and I would have to convince you to leave him."

"He put his hands on me, spat at me, he *raped* me." The pain, the visual, burns in my brain, like the worst reel on repeat. "I get he's upset over Camden and my drunken tattoo, but that doesn't give him the right to do what he did. There's no coming back from that. *Ever.* I thought about filing a restraining order, but I don't want it to get ugly, and trying to prove my husband raped me will get messy. While I was waiting for you to come over, I was reading about it online and found so many women who tried to prove their husbands were raping them and couldn't. But I am filing for divorce as soon as possible."

"Good. My stepdad will know someone. I'll call him first thing in the morning, and we'll get the ball rolling. But if he so much as lays a finger on you again, you need to file a restraining order so you know you're safe." She takes my hand in hers and squeezes it. "I'm proud of you."

"For what?"

"A lot of women would've made excuses, tried to fix it, or blamed themselves. For years, that's what my mom did with my dad after his accident. He became addicted to drugs and would drink to numb the pain. She felt bad for him and kept hoping he would get better. It took her nearly getting beat to death before she finally left him. I'm proud of you for knowing what he did was wrong and unacceptable and not giving him the chance to do it again." She wraps her arms around me. "We'll get through this. He'll never fucking touch you again."

The next morning, I drop Felix off at my mom's, and Kaylee and I go to the divorce attorney her stepdad recommended. It's Sunday, but he apparently owes her stepdad a favor so he meets with us. After spending the night thinking about what David did to me, I decide to mention the rape, asking his opinion on what I should do.

He tells me what I feared—proving my husband raped me will get messy, and since there are no marks on me from where he slapped me, it would be my word versus his. He tells me he can take it on, but he can't be sure we'll win. It would be a battle that I would most likely lose because our judicial system is far from perfect. Knowing

David will get away with it pisses me off and makes me feel sick to my stomach, but I can't drag my son through a messy court battle. Maybe that makes me weak or a horrible person, but I just can't do it.

After agreeing the best course of action is to simply file for divorce, we go over all the details, and when we're done, he says he'll have the papers filed first thing in the morning, and David will be served by the end of the day. When I explain I'm not sure how I'll be able to pay for this since I'm currently jobless, Kaylee insists she'll cover it, and I can pay her back. I want to argue, but I also want this over with as soon as possible, so I agree and thank her.

Not wanting to be home when David gets the papers, I head over to my mom's so I can tell her everything that's happened. She cries when I give her a less descriptive version and offers to have Felix and me move in with her.

David never calls or texts all day Sunday, so I know he never came home, but we spend the night at my mom's anyway. I don't want to take the chance of being there when he does go home. Monday morning, instead of dropping Felix off at school, I keep him home, unsure of how David will react when he gets the papers. I never thought he was capable of violence, but I was clearly wrong, and I'm not going to risk something happening to my son or me. He'll need time to cool down, and it's best if we stay away until he can do that.

I know when David gets served because my phone starts blowing up with phone calls and texts from him. The texts start off with him upset, asking to talk, but then quickly morph into anger.

"He's going to come here," I tell my mom when I read the text from him that says he was just at the house and we're not there.

Mom nods. "Why don't we have Felix go over to the Blackwood's to play so he's not here?"

"I hate involving them."

"They're like family, Layla. And it's to protect your son."

I agree, and after Mom calls Sophia, I take Felix over there with the Sega Genesis he's become obsessed with. Thankfully, it's only Nanna, Sophia, and Easton at home, so I don't have to see Camden. I thank them for watching Felix and ask that if by some chance David shows up, to please not open the door. Easton promises he'll keep my son safe.

After kissing Felix and telling him I love him and I'll be back soon, I head back over to my mom's. I'm almost to her house when David pulls up. I try to rush inside, but he's faster and catches me before I can make it.

"Were you just at the Blackwood's?" he hisses, pushing me against the front door. "Were you over there fucking him? Is that why you're divorcing me? Because you're fucking that loser?"

"I'm not fucking anyone," I hiss, the vision of him forcing himself on me hitting me hard. It feels like every time I close my eyes, I can see him, feel him, hurting me. "I'm divorcing you because you turned into someone I don't know. You hit and raped me."

"I didn't mean to," he says, his tone softening into the man I used to know. "I was just so upset. The guy's had a hard-on for you for years, and then we move back here, and not even a week later, you're in pictures with him and getting tattoos of his songs on your body."

"It doesn't matter if I got a tattoo of his name on my body. You don't have the right to ever put your hands on me violently. You raped me, David. You hurt me."

"You're my wife! I had sex with my wife. I didn't rape you."

"I begged you to stop. You hurt me. You made me bleed."

"You're overreacting," he scoffs. "Please, Layla." He raises his hand, and I flinch, afraid of what he's going to do. "Don't be afraid of me. I messed up. I was upset, but I love you. You know I love you, right?"

"I know that you hurt me, and I can't let that ever happen again. I want a divorce, and I'm going to live with my mom until everything is final."

He looks at me in pain, reminding me of the man I married, and my heart cracks. We created a life together, a family, and in one day, it all got blown to bits. "I told you moving here was a bad idea," he mutters, scrubbing his hand over his face.

"You can't blame the move or anyone or anything for what happened. *You* did this."

He nods solemnly. "I don't want you to uproot Felix. You can stay in the house. It's your home. I work a lot anyway. I can stay in the office until it all gets sorted."

I release a sigh, grateful that he's calmed down and is acting maturely. "Thank you."

"Maybe you just need some time," he says. "We can go to therapy."

"I don't think so. After what happened, I can't be with you." I don't apologize because I'm not sorry. I didn't do anything wrong, nothing that would ever make it okay for my husband to hurt me the way he did.

He nods and leans in, kissing my cheek. "I'm not giving up yet, but I'll go with the flow for now. I know I fucked up, and you need some time. But I love you, and I'm not giving up on us."

With those final words, he walks back to his vehicle and drives away, leaving me wondering how my life got so messed up so quickly.

Eleven

Camden

TWO MONTHS LATER

"OH, MY GOD, YES! JUST LIKE THAT. FUCK ME HARDER!" AN ALL TOO FAMILIAR VOICE SCREAMS out as Declan and I walk into the penthouse suite we're sharing with Gage and Braxton. Sometimes, we get our own rooms, but at this hotel, in order for security to stay tight, they had to book the only penthouse available, which meant the four of us sharing.

"Yes, yes. Harder!" she yells, moaning loudly.

"Oh, shit," Declan says with a laugh. "I'd recognize that voice anywhere."

Of course he would because we spent the past several months listening to it every damn day. Sure enough, when we step into the living room, we find Everly, our publicist, sandwiched between Braxton and Gage, getting fucked in both her holes. Gage looks like he's barely involved, aside from his dick being part of the equation, and Braxton is angry-fucking her ass with his eyes closed as he pulls on her long brown hair.

"Seriously?" I bark. Both guys glance over at me at the same time, and Everly squeals in embarrassment. "Again?" This isn't the first damn time one of these assholes has fucked a member of our team. And it always ends the same way—her becoming attached and getting her heart broken or us having to fire her because she turns crazy.

"It's the last day of the tour," Braxton says, continuing to fuck her. "She wasn't even all that good at her job. It's not like we're going to hire her back."

Everly gasps in outrage, and I groan, knowing what's coming next.

Pushing Braxton back, she climbs off Gage, who's so high that he doesn't even bother moving. Gage simply lets his head drop back, and his eyes close, leaving his condom-covered dick out in the open for everyone to see.

"Fuck you, Braxton!" she hisses. "I'm good at my job."

"Of course you are," he purrs. "You're awesome at your job. I was just kidding. Now get back on my dick so I can finish, please."

Everly glares, gathering up her clothes and putting them back on in haste. "You can finish your damn self," she says, grabbing her heels and stomping out the door.

"Great," Braxton says dryly. "This"—he points at his now soft dick—"is all your fault. Which one of you is going to suck me off so I don't get blue balls?"

Declan snorts out a laugh, and I roll my eyes. "Thank fuck this tour is over. I need a few months without walking in on you fucking your way across the globe." I shove Gage awake. "And you need to lay off the drugs."

Gage grunts in response, pulling the condom off and dropping it onto the floor as he gets up and stumbles toward his room. "Will do, *Dad*."

"I'm worried about him," Declan says once we can hear his

snoring from the other room.

"Yeah, I am too," I agree. "But we'll be back home in a few days, and we'll keep an eye on him. I spoke to my dad, and aside from a few shows we've already committed to, we're going to take the next six months off to write and record our next album."

"Sounds good," Braxton says, grabbing his pants and pulling them on. "I'm going to take a shower."

"Want a drink?" Declan asks, raising a bottle of Jack.

"Sure."

We take our drinks out onto the balcony, and I pull out my phone to text our tour manager to let her know what happened and to find out what time we're flying out tomorrow. But when my screen lights up, I find several missed calls from damn near everyone in my family.

My stomach drops. Something is wrong.

Since my mom was the last one to call, I hit her name and wait as the phone rings. "Camden, we've been trying to reach you," she says, her voice filled with emotion.

"My phone was on silent, sorry. Everything okay?"

There's a moment of silence on the other end before she says, "No, it's not. Maria is in the hospital, and the doctors aren't sure how long she'll be able to hold on for."

I shoot up in my seat, knocking my drink to the ground. The glass shatters everywhere, but I ignore it, too focused on what my mom just said. "What are you talking about?" I just saw her a couple of months ago when we were in town for the charity concert. She was fine. She even made me my favorite French toast.

"She's been tired a lot lately. I asked her if she was okay, but she blew me off. Today, she had a dizzy spell while she was in her room and hit her head," she chokes out. "She was rushed to the hospital, and the doctors said she has stage four cancer. She never told us.

Didn't want to worry us because it was too late."

"Fuck!" My heart squeezes in pain. "There has to be something we can do. A doctor we can call."

"We've spoken to the oncologist, and there's nothing that can be done. They gave her roughly six months to live. It's been three, but her body is shutting down. They said it can be days or weeks, but she doesn't have long. Right now, she's coherent, and she's asking for you."

"I'm on my way. I'll get a flight out as soon as I can. Tell Nanna I'm coming."

"OH, THERE'S MY BOY," NANNA MURMURS WHEN I WALK INTO THE ROOM SEVERAL HOURS later. She's lying in a hospital bed in a private room, looking so small and fragile. Like simply touching her will break her.

"Nanna," I breathe, tears welling in my eyes.

"Come give me a hug, sweetheart."

I do as she says, hugging her gently and kissing her cheek before I drag a chair over and sit next to her. My parents and Bailey excuse themselves to give us some time alone, but I don't pay them any attention, focusing on the woman in front of me. "Why didn't you tell anyone?" I ask her. "We could've called someone."

"No, you couldn't have," she says softly. "I always hated going to the doctor. Kept putting it off. By the time I went, it was too late."

"You still should've told us."

"So you'd spend my last few months worrying about me?" Her wrinkled hand pats mine gently. "I didn't want anyone fussing over me. You and your sister were both on tour. Bailey is so busy with her internet, and I didn't want to upset Phoebe."

"I would've come home sooner."

"I know you would've. That's why I didn't tell you."

I squeeze her hand. "What did—"

"Oh, I'm so sorry," a feminine voice says. My eyes dart over to Layla standing in the doorway, dressed in ripped jeans, an off the shoulder cream sweater, and brown leather boots since it's cold as hell in New York. "I didn't know you were here with her. I'll come back later." Before I can get a word in, she backs out and closes the door behind her.

"Such a sweet girl," Nanna says. "Shame everything she's going through."

"What do you mean?"

"The divorce," she says like it's obvious. "I always knew that man she married wasn't any good for her. I never met him, but from the way he kept her from everyone all these years, a woman my age gets a feeling. At least he agreed to give her primary custody of that sweet little boy. She's been looking for a job but is having trouble finding one."

"Wait, what?" I say, my head spinning with all of this information. "Layla got a divorce?"

"Yes. I've spent some time with Felix while Patricia has watched him so she can look for a job. Such a good boy. Reminds me of you when you were little. Polite and funny. And he loves my French toast." She winks playfully, and I can't help but smile.

"I always thought it would be you two that ended up together. Then she met him…" She scrunches up her nose in disgust. "But he's gone now. Who knows? This could be your second chance."

"Maybe…"

"I heard the song." She smiles. "'Shattered.' Your mom always plays them for me on her phone. I'm so proud of you. Of whom you've become. But that song… it made me sad for you. I remember when your parents got together. Your mom found out she was pregnant with you, and she was so scared but strong. She had a wall built thirty feet high, but your dad busted it down piece by piece. And once he did… well, their love was a beautiful sight to behold."

She takes her hand in mine and gently squeezes. "That boy… David… he hurt her, and I imagine her wall will be really high, but I have no doubt you'll be able to knock it down." She winks playfully. "And once you do, I bet your love will be just as beautiful."

I nod, unsure what to say in response. I came in here expecting to see her in bad shape, but instead, she's giving me relationship advice.

With a yawn, she removes her hand from mine and pats the top of it. "Thank you for coming. You'll be staying, right?"

"I'm not going anywhere, Nanna. Not until you're better."

She frowns. "Didn't you just hear me? You have a wall to take down, and you can't do that from across the country." Another yawn. "I'm feeling a little tired. It's been a helluva day. I think I'm going to rest my eyes for a few minutes." She closes her eyes. "I'll see you when I wake up, and we can come up with a plan of attack to tear down that wall and woo the hell out of your woman."

"I'll be here," I say with a laugh. Growing up, my grandpa and my dad always talked about how men have to woo the women they love. I always laughed at them, but now that I'm older, I get it.

I watch Nanna sleep for several minutes, trying to wrap my head around everything I've learned about her—about Layla. Once I know she's in a deep sleep, I head outside to see where my family is.

I find them in the waiting room with the guys… and Layla. Declan has his arm around her, and she's smiling up at him. He must say something funny because she throws her head back in a laugh, exposing her slim neck.

Declan lets go of her, and then Gage pulls her into his side, kissing her temple. It's been five and a half years since we've left, since they've spent any real time with her, so it should be awkward, but they're acting like no time has passed… and that's because despite her saying we're strangers, we're not. We never could be because those three years together—through good times and bad—cemented our friendships. Those guys care about her almost as much as I do. She became a part of us, and even though we had to walk away, we never stopped thinking about her. We just couldn't be with her. We had to let her go. And fuck if it wasn't the hardest thing we'd ever done.

Layla is the first to notice me. She dips out from under Gage's arm and walks over to me. "How is she?"

"She's sleeping. Thank you for coming. I'm sorry you didn't get to see her. Tomorrow—"

"Oh, no. I saw her. I've been here all morning. Felix insisted we make her a card. They won't let him visit because he's not family, and kids have tons of germs, so I brought it to her."

We stare at each other for several beats. There's so much I want to ask her, but then Declan comes over. "How's she doing?"

"She's okay. Aside from looking fatigued, you wouldn't know her body is giving up on her." I look at my dad. "There's nothing we can do?"

"I'm sorry, son." He puts his arm around me. "Her organs are shutting down. The doctors are shocked she's doing as well as she is and talking as much as she is. They said to prepare ourselves because it won't be like that for long."

"This fucking sucks."

"Yeah, it does," Mom agrees. "Why don't you go home and get situated? I know it was a long flight."

"I'm not going anywhere. I promised Nanna I'd be here when

she woke up. I just wanted to come out here and properly say hello." I give her a hug and a kiss on her cheek, then turn to the guys. "If you want to check in to a hotel…"

"Nonsense," Mom says. "You guys can stay with us."

"We appreciate that, Sophia," Declan says. "But you haven't lived with these assholes in a few years, and trust me, you don't want them stinking up your place."

In other words, the guys need their space to fuck, smoke, and do their own thing.

"I'm not sure how long I'll be here," I tell them. "If you want to head back…"

"Fuck that," Gage says, looking somewhat sober. "If you're here, we're here. Besides, I need to say hi to Nanna."

"I'll let you know when she wakes—"

"Excuse me," a female doctor cuts in. "Are you the family of Maria Garcia?"

"We are," Mom says, speaking for all of us.

"Maria went into cardiac arrest. Because she signed a DNR, we weren't able to resuscitate her. I'm sorry, but she didn't make it."

And just like that, my heart implodes inside my chest.

"THIS SUCKS."

I glance over and find Layla sitting next to me. The funeral has ended, and Maria's casket has been lowered into the ground.

"Are you going to your parents'?" she asks when I don't say anything. There's a repast taking place at my parents' house, but I can't find it in me to move.

When I stay quiet, she reaches over and threads our fingers

together. I look down at our joined hands, noticing her left hand is missing her wedding ring. In its place is a pale strip where the ring once was.

"The last time I was home, she made me French toast. I told her not to, said she should be relaxing, but she insisted. She said she would make them every time I came home as long as I keep returning." My voice chokes up on the last word, tears filling my eyes.

"She made them for Felix a couple of weeks ago. He said they were his favorite, so I tried to make them for him the other morning." She laughs softly. "He said they were good, but they weren't as special as the ones she made him." I laugh at that, knowing exactly what he means. Nothing compares to her French toast.

"Going home will make it real," I say, answering her earlier question. "And I'm just not ready for it to feel real yet. She won't be there to offer to make me food or do my laundry when I'm not home. She won't leave me a snack when I sneak in after curfew or gripe about the guys leaving a mess even though she insists they come over… because she's gone, and she'll never be back."

Layla squeezes my hand. "She is. I can't say I completely understand because my dad and I were never that close. He worked far too much and wasn't around enough. But it still hurt when he died. Every morning on his way into the office, he would call me to say hi. The first day he didn't call, it was hard. My heart hurt, and I cried. The next day, though, I was ready for the heartbreak. Each day got easier, my heart healing more and more. It still hurts, and I miss him, but it's bearable now."

She looks at me, her brown eyes shining. "It won't be today or tomorrow or the next day, but eventually, your heart will heal."

When she squeezes my hand again, I look down at our hands, remembering the last conversation Nanna and I had. I've never been the type of person to believe in fate. But right now, while I would give anything to have Nanna back, I'm wondering if maybe, as her last gift to me, she brought Layla and me together. Because had she not passed away, I'd still be across the country instead of sitting right here holding hands with the only woman I've ever loved.

"I think you're right," I tell Layla. "I think my heart will eventually heal."

Twelve

Camden

Declan looks up from the paper where he's scribbling lyrics, Braxton stops strumming his bass, and Gage removes the joint from his lips.

"What's up?" Declan asks, reaching over and taking the joint from Gage so he can take a hit.

"We've done everything together from day one," I begin, nervous at what I need to speak to them about. "Every decision, every show, when we decided to move to LA—"

"Just get to the damn point," Braxton cuts in, snatching the joint from Declan. "You want to stay in New York, and you need us to agree."

I open my mouth, shocked as shit that he hit the nail on the head. "How did you know?"

"It doesn't take a brain surgeon," Declan says. "We saw you walk in with her after the funeral, holding hands."

"It's not like that," I start.

"Of course it's not," Declan replies. "Because it's too soon. She's only just gotten a divorce. She needs time to get over whatever that fucker did."

"But this time, how about you *not* wait until she's moved on and found someone else, yeah?" Braxton hands me the joint, and I take a hit. "I hate this fucking city, so if I'm going to be stuck here for the foreseeable future, you better fucking man up and do something this time."

"Do what?" Bailey asks, strolling into the studio. Her nose scrunches up in disgust at the smell of weed, and she steals the joint from me, dropping it into my can of soda.

"Get the girl," Declan says with a smirk.

"What girl?" she asks, confused.

"Layla… duh." Declan rolls his eyes. "Is there any other girl for your brother?"

"Does this mean you're staying?" she asks, her voice rising several octaves in excitement.

"Yeah," Braxton tells her.

"But you guys hate New York," she points out.

"Camden doesn't," Gage says, speaking for the first time. "Camden never had his shot. When shit went down"—he swallows thickly—"he got on that plane for us. Now, regardless of how much we hate this city, it's our turn to stay for him."

Fuck, these guys.

Gage glances at me, taking another joint from behind his ear and lighting it, despite knowing Bailey will grab it and snuff it out. "This time, get the fucking girl. Don't make us being here a waste."

Bailey does just as I thought and snatches the joint, dropping it into Gage's beer. "Have you told Dad? You're supposed to be working on your next album. We're going to have to make adjustments." I can see her brain shifting into work mode as she pulls out her phone and starts typing. "Shit, Cade has to stay in LA. Now, I'm going to have to find someone else to film the web series."

"Hire Layla," I say.

Her head pops up. "What?"

"Hire Layla to film the series. We'll also have music videos we have to do. She can do those as well."

"She's never worked in the music industry," Bailey says.

"I don't care." I shrug, propping my feet up on the table. "She has natural talent. I want her. Cade can work with someone else in LA, and we can record our album here."

"THANK YOU FOR MEETING WITH US," BAILEY SAYS TWO DAYS LATER IN THE CONFERENCE room in Blackwood Records's office.

"I'm not sure what I'm doing here," Layla says, glancing around at everyone sitting at the table. Because everything is done through Blackwood, my dad—our manager—and my mom—Blackwood's attorney—are here, along with me, Bailey, since she's in charge of all media, and the guys, who I brought in as reinforcements because she likes them and has always had trouble telling them no.

"Raging Chaos has decided to relocate to New York for the foreseeable future," Bailey says.

Layla's eyes dart over to me in shock. "You're… You're moving back here?"

"Figured it was time I came home. Missed my family."

The guys chuckle but keep their mouths closed as Layla nods slowly. "Okay, what does that have to do with me being here? I actually have an interview at Picture Perfect soon." She glances at her phone to look at the time. "I told Bailey, but she said she just needed to speak to me for a moment."

"We want to hire you," I say, cutting to the chase. "Cade, the videographer you covered for at the charity concert, has to stay in LA, so we need someone to document us. Since we have a few shows to attend, there will be some travel, but mostly it will be here, at the place we're renting, at the studio. We're doing a web series for the fans to get a behind-the-scenes look at what goes down when we're recording an album, from us writing the songs to recording them. We're also going to need to do a couple of music videos. One of them will be fan-based, the footage from over the years… from the beginning, spanning over various tours, meet and greets, etcetera."

Layla slow blinks several times before she finally speaks. "Why me?"

I knew she would ask that, especially since she hasn't done shit in the music industry, so I'm prepared to answer her. "Because you're talented. We're picky about who we let into our world, and we're extremely private. Cade has been with us for years, but he can't be here. So we talked, and we want you."

"I don't know what I'm doing."

"Yes, you do," Declan says, joining in as backup. "You did it for us before we became who we are. The hits on those YouTube videos are why we blew up so quickly. They're still huge. You're real and raw, and you know us. The real us. We don't want to bring some fake person in who has no idea who we are."

"I… I can't," Layla says softly. "I appreciate the offer, even though I'm ninety-nine percent sure this is out of pity since Bailey knows I'm jobless. I have Felix, and David—" Her phone rings, cutting her off. She glances down at it, her lips turning down into a frown. "I need to get this." She answers the call and steps away from us. "Yes, this is Felix's mom… Is he okay? No, absolutely. I'll be right there. Okay, thank you."

She hangs up, pockets her phone, and darts her eyes around at each of us. "That was Felix's school. He's not feeling well and has a slight fever. I need to go pick him up."

"Oh, no," Mom says. "We can continue this another day."

"That's okay," Layla rasps. "There's nothing to continue. One day, I would love to work with musicians. I would love to make documentaries and music videos, but that can't be right now. Being a newly single mom means having to put my son first. Like now… going to pick him up from school because he's sick.

"My life, my priorities, doesn't meld with that of a rock star's." She looks at me, and I feel the double meaning in her words: our lives, even though she knows I'm here for her, knows I'm in love with her, would never work because we're two different people. She's a mom, and I'm a musician. Well, fuck that.

"My mom was a single mom when she met my dad. She was putting herself through college when she got pregnant with me. She got through law school with the help of my dad and my aunt Naomi. She didn't allow being a mom to stop her from doing what she wanted. She and my dad worked it out. She traveled when she could, stayed home when she had to. They handled it. Everyone in this room is your support system. You don't want to work at Picture Perfect, taking family portraits all day. That's not who you are. You're interviewing there because you think that's what you're supposed to do. That's the safe route."

"I'm doing what's best for my family," she says. "I'm sorry. I have to go." And with a small, sad smile, she walks out the door.

"Well, that didn't go as planned," Bailey says. "I honestly thought she would go for it. She had a blast videoing you guys at the concert. I thought we would offer her the job, she would say okay, and we'd sign the papers."

Dad laughs. "Nothing with women is ever that easy." He puts

his arm around my mom and kisses her temple. "I had to work hard to get this woman to be with me." He glances at me. "But the best women are usually the hardest to rein in."

"This isn't over," I tell them. "Not by a long shot. I'm only just getting started."

KNOCK. KNOCK. KNOCK.

I stand at Layla's front door, waiting for her to answer. Bailey said to give her time, but I can't do it. Every time I give her time, she slips through my fingers. I can't let that happen again.

"Who is it?" a tiny voice says on the other side of the door—her son.

"Camden."

"Who?"

I chuckle. "Camden Blackwood. We played *Sonic* together at your grandma's."

A second later, the lock clicks, and the door opens, exposing Felix in his pajamas, his brown hair wet like he just took a bath. "Hey, Cam! Are you here to play with me?"

"Felix!" Layla gasps, running down the stairs… in nothing but a damn towel. "Did you just open the door?"

"It's Cam, Mom. He's here to play with me."

"You know better than to open the door for anyone," she says, kneeling in front of her son. "Only adults can answer the door."

"But…" He frowns.

"No buts. It's different here than in Boston. Anybody can knock on the door. You can't open it unless I say you can."

"What if it's Dad?" he asks.

"You don't open it for anybody," she says again. "Now, please go lie down."

"But I'm not sick anymore. I feel good."

Layla rolls her eyes. "That's because you just threw up everywhere, so your belly doesn't hurt right now. But you're still sick. Go lie down. You can watch a show."

"Fine." He sighs, then glances at me. "Can we play when I'm not sick?"

"Sure, bud," I tell him. "Feel better."

"I already do," he grumbles, dragging his feet over to the couch.

"What are you doing here?" Layla asks. When I glance back at her, I'm able to get a good look at her up close. Her hair is up in a loose bun, and her towel is wrapped around her body, being held together with a tight knot that's nestled in the middle of her breasts. The towel covers all the important parts but stops short, showing off her tanned, creamy thighs.

"Camden!" she hisses, making my eyes rise. On my way up to her face, I catch sight of something I've never seen before.

"I brought Felix some chicken soup," I say, lifting the brown bag up and setting it on the table. "Is that…?" I step closer, taking in the black ink etched into her skin between her collarbone and shoulder. It's a camera, similar to the one she used to carry with her everywhere she went. Only instead of it being put together, the lens is broken, and pieces of it ascend up and over her shoulder. "Holy shit," I breathe when I see the single word that's scribbled across the front of the camera, where the brand name should go. "You got a tattoo of the song I wrote about you."

Her eyes go wide, and then she drops her gaze to her towel-covered chest. Her hands fly across her body as if just realizing she's been standing here this entire time in nothing but a towel.

"Oh my God!" she gasps. She's about to run away, but before

she can, I reach out and grab her arm, pulling her into the kitchen, where Felix can't see us, but we're close enough to hear him.

"Let me see it," I insist, once I've backed her against the edge of the counter.

"No! Let go of me," she hisses. "I need to get dressed."

"Not until I see it." I place my hands over hers on either side of her body and get a good look at the tattoo, shocked as shit that she actually inked herself permanently with the title of my song.

"When did you do this?" I ask, looking up and meeting her eyes, our faces only a few inches apart.

"The night of the concert. I had too much to drink. It was a drunken—"

"No." I press my fingers to her lips to silence her. "Don't you dare blame drinking on this. You never do shit without thinking it through. You're the most levelheaded person I know."

"I—" she breathes, but I cut her off.

"We'll talk about your tattoo later… when we're alone. What I want to discuss right now is the job offer."

Her eyes go wide, confused as to why I'm changing the subject. What she doesn't understand is that I plan to have my chance with her, but it won't be until she's ready—and based on that tattoo, it's clear she has some kind of feelings for me—but her lame excuse of being drunk tells me she's not ready to pursue those feelings yet. So I'll wait until she's ready. Because I'm a patient guy.

"The job pays six figures and requires light travel. It would start as a ninety-day trial period, and once the ninety days are up, if both sides are happy, we'll sign a one-year contract."

"Six figures?" she chokes out. "But I have Felix…"

"We know you have a son and that he'll always come first. You don't think my parents know a thing or two about raising kids while working in the music industry? You've got this, Shutterbug, and we all have your back."

Thirteen

Layla

"MOMMY! LOOK WHAT I MADE FOR DADDY'S BIRTHDAY." FELIX THRUSTS A CARD AND A drawing at me. "It says Happy Birthday, Daddy. I love you, and I hope you have yummy cake and share it with me."

I look at the random letters that most definitely do *not* spell any of those words and then smile down at Felix. "This is beautiful. Your dad is going to love it. And I bet he'll share his cake with you."

Felix beams. "I wanna give it to him now."

"Oh, umm," I say, unsure what to do. David hasn't taken Felix overnight with the excuse that he's getting everything together. We've met a few times at the park and a couple of times for dinner, but every time, it ends with him begging me to work things out and him getting mad when I tell him it's not happening. I'm starting to wonder if maybe he's hoping if he prolongs getting his own place long enough, I'll give in and take him back, even though I've made it clear that's not going to happen. Simply looking at him disgusts me, and if I could have it my way, he would drop off the face of the planet and leave Felix and me alone, but that's not how real life works. David is Felix's dad, and by law, he gets to see him every other weekend and every Wednesday until he's eighteen.

"Please." Felix looks up at me with puppy dog eyes that I have a hard time saying no to.

"Okay, sure. We can go by his office."

"And bring him cake?"

Oh, Lord. "Sure, we can pick one up on the way."

"Yay!" He jumps up and down in excitement.

We take the train downtown and then stop by the bakery across from the building David works in. When we arrive at his office, no one is at the receptionist's desk, so we walk past it and head straight to David's office.

In Felix's excitement, he runs ahead and, without stopping to knock, crashes right into his father's office. "Happy Birthday, Daddy!" he yells.

There's a screech and then a hiss. When I catch up, entering the office, I find David's assistant pulling her skirt down while David blocks her the best he can. It's obvious from the bulge in David's pants that they were in a compromising position.

"Layla, get him out of here," David barks when neither of us moves.

"Felix, c'mon, sweetie. Daddy's busy."

"But I made him a birthday card!" Felix whines, confused.

"You can give it to him another time," I tell him.

"But… But…" Tears fill his eyes. "I got him a cake."

When he refuses to move, I drop the cake onto the table and pick him up. "I know, but we have to go."

"Wait, please," David calls out as I stalk out of the room. "Shit, Layla, wait!"

"Nope, not going there," I tell him.

"Stop!" He grabs my shoulder and whirls me around. Memories

of him forcing himself on me resurface, and I jump back as if I've been burned.

"Don't you dare touch me," I hiss. "We're divorced. You're free to do as you want. But maybe you can stop begging me to take you—" I stop myself, remembering Felix is in my arms. He deserves better than this. Better than to listen to his parents go at it in front of him.

"Begging you?" the woman screeches. "He hasn't been with you in over a year."

"Not now, Vanessa," David barks.

I snort out a laugh. "We've only been divorced for a couple of weeks." We haven't been living together for two months, but it took six weeks to finalize the divorce.

"You said you haven't been together in over a year," she continues. "Are you telling me you were with me while you were with her?" Her eyes turn into thin slits.

"We moved here together," I point out because c'mon, she can't be that stupid.

"He said you moved here so he could see his son, but that you guys weren't together." She stalks toward him as he yells at her to shut up, and I use that as my cue to get my son and me out of here.

I don't put Felix down until we're on the train heading home. He's quiet for the entire ride, and while I doubt he knows all that happened, kids can sense moods, and I'm sure he knows something is wrong.

Afraid that David will try to show up, I text my mom, asking if she's up for company. When she doesn't respond, I assume she left her phone somewhere and head to her house. But when we get there, she's not home.

"Looking for your mom?" a masculine voice says.

I glance over and see Camden standing on the front porch steps of his parents' house.

"I want cake, but Mommy left it with Daddy." Felix huffs in frustration, his only concern the abandoned cake. Thankfully, he isn't aware of what he walked in on, nor does he understand what we argued about.

"What kind is your favorite?" Camden asks, walking over.

"Vanilla. Mommy loves chocolate, so she buys cakes with both, and I give her my chocolate, and she gives me her vanilla."

"That sounds like the perfect way to eat a cake," Camden says, smiling at Felix before he looks at me. "Our moms are at their book club."

"Oh, shoot." I knew that. It just slipped my mind in all the craziness. Every month, the ladies meet and discuss a new book they read while they get drunk on wine and gossip.

"Juniors has some delicious cake," Camden says with a knowing smirk.

Damn him. He knows Juniors is my favorite restaurant. At his words, Felix perks up. "I wanna go! I love delicious cake! Can we go, Mom?"

"Fine, but you have to eat first." I give him a playful side-eye. "Then we can have cake." I glance back at Camden. "Have a good night."

"Damn, so I bring up the restaurant, and I'm not even invited." He pouts, his lips curving down and making him look hella sexy. Ever since I heard that song and learned how he felt about me, I can't stop thinking about him. I was always attracted to Camden, but the truth is, I never knew he felt that way about me. He and the other guys always had girls surrounding them. It comes with the territory of making beautiful music. I always assumed he just saw me as the girl with a camera attached to her face, tagging along.

But now that I know he wanted more, I can't help but wonder how different things could've been had he told me… until I think about the fact that I wouldn't have Felix. Then I have to tell myself that everything happens for a reason. While the teenage Camden was sweet and sexy, albeit a little cocky, the older version of Camden is gorgeous, slightly harder, and a hell of a lot more confident. He left for LA trying to find his place in this chaotic world and found it in his music.

"I didn't think you'd want to spend your Friday night eating chicken fingers and cake," I say with a laugh. "Surely, a famous rock star like yourself has other, more interesting plans."

"I thought I heard you out here," my mom says, stepping outside.

"I thought you were at your book club." I glance at Camden.

"We were. Sophia held it here this week." She envelops Felix in a hug. "This is such a pleasant surprise. Sophia made brownies. Would you like one?"

"Yes!" Felix lights up.

"Oh, actually, we were going to go to Juniors," I tell her.

"Nonsense. We have tons of sweets here," she says as the other women in the book club file out, saying goodbye to all of us. "I feel like I haven't seen my grandbaby all week. Have you been hiding?" she asks Felix playfully.

"I made Daddy a card for his birthday, and Mommy got him a cake, but he yelled at Mommy and made us leave."

Mom's eyes fling over to me as my heart sinks. Guess he understood a bit more than I thought.

"Daddy's just having a bad day," I explain, the defense of David's disgusting actions tasting like sour lemons on my tongue.

"There he is!" Gage booms, stepping out of a Town Car, followed by Declan and Braxton. "We've been blowing your phone up. Lush. Tonight."

"Did you say Lush?" Bailey asks, rushing out the door. "I've been dying to check out that club. It's hard as hell to get into, but of course you got an invite. I'm in."

Declan snorts. "Who said you're invited?" He pulls Bailey into a side hug and ruffles her hair.

"Me," Bailey sasses. "What time are we leaving?" She glances at me. "Layla and I need time to get ready, and I need to let Cynthia know. She's been dying to check out that club."

"Wait… what?" I say, confused at the turn of events.

"Not sure," Declan says. "Camden, what time do you want to head out?"

"Eh…" He shrugs. "I think I'm going to sit this one out."

The guys, all at once, start giving him shit.

"You should go," Mom says to me. "You haven't been out in a while. I can spend the evening with Felix."

"We were supposed to go to Juniors," I say again.

"I wanna stay with Grandma. Please." Felix hits me with his damn puppy eyes. "I'll go with you to Juniors tomorrow. C'mon, Grandma, let's go eat brownies. Bye, Mom!" he yells, dragging my mom inside the Blackwoods'.

"You in?" Declan asks me.

"Sure, why not."

"Nice. Now, what time are we leaving, Pretty Boy?" Declan asks, calling Camden by his nickname the guys dubbed him years ago because he doesn't look like your typical rocker. He's, well, pretty. With gorgeous emerald eyes, soft, wavy hair, a natural tan that women would kill for, and a face that looks way too innocent and sweet to be singing the crude words he sings on a nightly basis, Camden is the face of Raging Chaos. He's also, without a doubt, the *prettiest* of the four guys, who are in contrast rough and dark and exactly what you'd imagine a bad boy rock star to look like—covered in tattoos with piercings in various places. Camden, on the other hand, has no tattoos or piercings… as far as I know.

"I thought you said you weren't going," I say to Camden, whose eyes are locked on me.

"I am now." He glances at the guys. "Let's leave around nine."

"Oh, should I be filming this?" I ask, switching into work mode.

"No," Camden says. "You should focus on having a good time."

IT'S MY FIRST TIME AT A NIGHTCLUB, AND I'M HAVING A BLAST. THE LIQUOR IS FLOWING, THE music is thumping, and Bailey, Cynthia, and I are dancing our hearts out on the dance floor. Cynthia is sweet and totally has googly eyes for Bailey. They're so cute together, and I hope it works out between them.

When I stepped out of Bailey's room, dressed in one of her strapless mini dresses, I could feel Camden's heated stare. My tattoo was on full display, and if the way his eyes seared into me was anything to go by, he was thinking about when he saw it peeking out from under my towel the other day—when I lied and told him it was a drunken mistake.

Because it's November in New York and cold as hell outside, I covered up with a thick coat, hiding it away. But the second I removed it at the club, he was back to staring at it. If the other guys noticed it, they didn't comment.

We were escorted straight to VIP with the guys' security, where we've spent the night drinking and dancing. Camden hasn't said much, but the way his eyes haven't left me almost all night feels like he has a lot to say—only I'm too chicken to find out what.

"Oh, check out that guy eyeing you," Bailey says, her words coming out a bit slurred. I don't even bother to look.

"He totally is," Cynthia agrees, waggling her brows.

"Nope, not happening." I shake my head to emphasize my point. "I'm on a hiatus from men."

"Oh, fuck," Gage says. "Again?"

"What's that supposed to mean?"

"It means you did that shit our junior year, right before you chose to go out with David the Dick."

"Huh… I did, didn't I?" I shrug. "Well, at least I didn't get cheated on during that year."

"David cheated?" Bailey gasps.

"Yep," I say, choosing not to elaborate. "I've only seriously dated two guys in my life, and both cheated on me." My eyes drop to the shots of liquor. I grab one, down it, and slam the empty glass on the table. "What does that say about me?"

"It says absolutely nothing about you and everything about them." Camden twirls me around so we're facing each other, our chests almost touching. "You're perfect, Layla. You're smart and sweet, and those assholes cheating on you is their issue, not yours."

"Maybe." I shrug, suddenly feeling kind of sorry for myself.

"No, not maybe." His large hand covers mine, and he pulls me over to a more secluded area, pushing me gently against the wall. "Do you have any idea how fucking beautiful you are?" He drags his knuckles down the side of my cheek and neck, landing on the spot where my tattoo is. "And this tattoo? It's the sexiest thing I've ever seen."

His touch causes chills to race up my spine, and my entire body visibly shivers.

"Tell me the truth, Shutterbug." He leans in and whispers into my ear. "Why did you get this tattoo? And don't you dare say it was a drunken mistake."

"I… I never knew you felt that way," I admit, not quite answering his question but also kind of answering it. "I was shocked, confused…

Bailey and Kaylee knew. Hell, even David knew, but I didn't. I drank… a lot, and then I got the tattoo. But… no," I murmur. "It wasn't a mistake."

He leans back slightly, his face only inches from mine.

"Nanna saw it," I continue. "It peeked out of my top one night when I was picking up Felix from my mom's. She loved it. Said she always knew you had feelings for me, and it was about time you admitted it." I laugh softly, shaking my head.

"When we spoke in the hospital, she mentioned you got divorced," he admits. "We were supposed to come up with a plan of attack."

"For what?"

"To break down your wall and get you to fall in love with me."

Holy shit… He's not holding back at all.

"Why didn't you ever tell me how you felt?"

"Isn't that the million-dollar question…?" He rests one hand against the wall next to my head, and the other goes back to my face, dusting several strands of sweaty hair out of my eyes. "It never felt like the right time. You were either taken or on an anti-boyfriend kick." He playfully rolls his eyes, making me laugh. "And then, before you were about to leave for college, I was going to. I was gonna throw it all on the table… And then all that shit went down at the party, and you posted that David proposed, and I… *fuck*, I just felt like maybe it wasn't meant to be. Gage and Brax needed me, so I left."

"Without even saying goodbye."

"It was too damn hard. You needed to focus on your future, and I needed to be with my band."

"And now that I'm divorced, you're back?" I tilt my head up slightly, and our mouths are so close. If Camden just moved a little closer, they would touch.

"This is my second chance," he says, shocking me. "I let you go once, but I can't do it again without telling you how I feel. I'm in love with you. I probably have been since the day I saw you crying on your front steps. I know you need time to get over David, and I'm going to give you that time."

"Cam," I gasp. "I don't know—"

"You don't need to know anything right now except that I'll be waiting for you to be ready, and once you are, I want my chance with you."

"I can't jump into something again. I have Felix now, and… I barely know you. Yeah, I knew you years ago, but we've both changed, and this time, I need to be careful. It's not just my heart that's at stake but also my little boy's too. We haven't hung out or talked in five years. I might not even be the same girl you once loved. I meant what I said before… we're practically strangers."

"I get it," he says, smiling softly. "And the fact that you're protecting your heart and your son's only makes me love you that much more."

"So then what do we do? Where does that leave us?"

"We get to know each other all over again," Camden says, rubbing his thumb across my bottom lip before he steps back, breaking all contact. "Starting right now." He extends his hand. "I'm Camden Rocco Blackwood, lead singer of Raging Chaos. It's nice to meet you."

I snort out a laugh at his introduction and accept his hand. "I'm Layla Isabella Kessler. Can I have your autograph?" I flip my hair playfully, making him laugh.

"Oh, Shutterbug, you can have way more than that."

"Oh, yeah?" I play along. "Like what?"

"Me," he says, using my hand to tug me toward him. "You can have me."

Fourteen

Layla

"I'M THANKFUL FOR MY MOMMY BECAUSE SHE LETS ME STAY UP PAST MY BEDTIME sometimes and because she signed me up for dance classes, and Grandma because she lets me have another cupcake when Mommy says no…" Felix looks around the table and stops on Camden. "My friend Cam for buying me the new *Sonic* game."

Everyone laughs under their breath as he continues to thank everyone he can think of for doing something for him or letting him do something he shouldn't do. It's Thanksgiving, and we're all at the Blackwoods for lunch. We've finished eating dessert, and Sophia insisted we continue Nanna's tradition of everyone going around and saying what they're thankful for. Normally, we would eat later, but with my custody agreement, David gets Felix at two o'clock, so everyone agreed to eat earlier so Felix and I could join.

It's going to be the first time Felix spends the night with David, and I'm not looking forward to it. After the craziness at his office, he showed up at my house the next day, begging to talk, but I refused. I think he's finally gotten the message because he texted me to let me know he rented a condo near his work and would like to take Felix for the weekend starting on Thanksgiving. It'll probably be the most time they've spent together since he was born, since David always works. He assured me he would spend the weekend with him and not pawn him off onto his parents—although that might not be a bad thing since his parents are actually good grandparents—or drag him into the office, so hopefully he's telling the truth because I officially start my job for Raging Chaos this weekend.

I've signed the contract and am going away with them early tomorrow morning for the weekend to LA for Escape, a music festival that takes place all weekend. The guys will be performing on Saturday night, but they will also attend meet and greets and panels, where they'll be asked questions about their music and band. Since David is taking Felix for the weekend, I'm able to go. It will be my first weekend away from Felix, so at least I'll be busy instead of wallowing by myself.

And then there's the fact that I haven't seen or heard from Camden since our conversation at Lush, where I allowed the alcohol flowing through me to speak honestly and even flirt with him. After he made it crystal clear that he wanted me, we spent the rest of the night dancing, and then we headed back home when the club closed. They had the car drop me off first, and after Camden made sure I was in safely, he kissed me on my forehead and wished me a good night, leaving me to spend the rest of the night thinking about everything he said.

"Camden, it's your turn," Sophia says, snapping me out of my thoughts. "What are you thankful for?"

Everyone turns their attention to Camden.

"Hmm…" he says as if thinking about what he wants to say. "Despite losing one of my favorite people, I have a lot to be thankful for this year. It's the first time in a few years that we've been able to be home." His gaze skates over to Declan, Braxton, and Gage. "I'm thankful for another year of success with Raging Chaos. It's been a wild ride thus far, and I can't imagine being on it with anyone but you guys." The guys raise their glasses and tip their chins up, silently agreeing.

"I'm thankful for the home-cooked meal," he continues, glancing at my mom and then his. "It's been a tough few weeks without Nanna. I miss her daily phone calls and her reminders to do my laundry." He looks at his sisters and chuckles under his breath. "I'm thankful my sisters have stepped up to call me every day. Now, if they could just do my laundry, I'd be set." He shrugs, and everyone laughs. "And…" His eyes meet mine. "I'm thankful for opportunities I never thought possible."

Everyone goes quiet, waiting for him to elaborate, but instead, he takes his glass and raises it, his eyes never leaving mine. "Happy Thanksgiving, everyone."

As everyone raises their glasses, I notice my mom is smirking, her gaze darting back and forth between Camden and me. Dammit. She totally knows.

"SO I HEARD YOU'RE TAKING DANCE LESSONS?" CAMDEN ASKS FELIX, COMING OVER AND sitting next to him. Lunch is over, and everyone is relaxing before dessert since we all just pigged out on way too much food.

Felix looks up from his iPad, where he's probably bulldozing some crops or building a house out of blocks. "Yeah," he says softly. "Mommy signed me up."

"That's cool. I took dance lessons when I was younger too."

Felix's eyes light up. "You did? Daddy said it's only for girls, but

Mommy and I went there, and the lady said there will be other boys too."

Camden's jaw ticks in anger, and I hold my breath, waiting for him to say something rude about David. Instead, he says, "Well, I'm a boy, and I can dance better than a lot of girls. As a matter of fact, I was in a music video once."

Felix gasps. "Really? Was it Justin Bieber's?"

Camden laughs. "No, it was my sister Kendall's, but she's big like Justin. Want to see the video?"

"Yeah!" Felix yells, practically bouncing in his seat.

Camden hooks his phone up to the television, and a minute later, an older music video of Kendall's pops up. I smile as we watch it, and Camden points out where he is, remembering this music video like it was yesterday. Camden was a fill-in for a dancer who got food poisoning, and they wanted a certain number of dancers. Since he had taken dance lessons growing up, he had no problem filling in. I spent the day watching the production and fell even more in love with the music industry, cementing that I wanted to do that one day.

"That's so cool!" Felix says, jumping up at the part when they break into a hip-hop type of dance. "Can you show me how to do that?"

"Sure," Camden says, standing. He does the move, and Felix watches, his eyes wide with excitement. "Need me to show you again?" Camden asks when he's done.

"Nope. I got it!" Felix busts into the same moves Camden just did, mimicking move for move. Granted, they're not as fluid since he's only four, but he gets every one right. When he finishes, he looks at Camden nervously, waiting for him to tell him how he did.

"Holy shit, little man," Braxton says from the couch. "You can bust some moves."

"Yeah, you can," Camden adds, raising his hand for a high five.

With the biggest grin on his face, Felix slaps his hand, soaking up the praise.

"Maybe one day you'll be dancing in a music video," Camden says.

"Yeah," Felix says. "And my mommy is going to make it."

Camden smiles at me. "I have no doubt, bud. And I bet it will be one awesome video."

"WHAT'S WITH THE FROWN?" MOM ASKS, COMING UP BEHIND ME. I WAS IN THE KITCHEN helping with the dessert dishes, but when my phone went off with a text from David, letting me know he's running late, I excused myself outside to call him. Of course, he didn't answer. Instead, he texted me that he had to run into the office for an emergency.

"David won't be picking up Felix until later." I glance up and force a smile. "I think we're going to head home. I'm pretty sure more cake ended up on Felix's clothes than in his mouth."

Mom nods. "I know this is hard on you, but you're handling it all very well. I'm proud of you."

"Yeah?" I laugh humorlessly. "Because it feels like my entire life has completely spun out of control."

"Oh, Layla…" Mom sits next to me and pats my thigh. "It's just a bad moment. It will pass."

"A bad moment?" I scoff. "It feels like a bad life." I lay my head on her shoulder, and she wraps her arms around me.

"Not all bad," she says. "I saw the way Camden has been looking at you all day. That boy always had a crush on you."

"Of course you knew," I mutter. "Because apparently everyone knew but me."

Mom chuckles. "Any chance of something happening between you two?"

"I don't know. He wants there to be, but…" I close my eyes and release a harsh breath. "I feel broken. I know I shouldn't. I know what David did to me wasn't my fault, and it's on him. He allowed his anger and jealousy to steer his decisions. I know… I know I didn't do anything wrong… at least not that warranted to be raped."

"But?" she prompts.

"But setting the rape aside, he's been cheating on me with his assistant for God knows how long." She knew about David raping me, but I haven't told her about him cheating. "And it wasn't the first time. I don't even care that he cheated. We're over, and after what he did, I lost every ounce of love and respect I had for him. It's just… I can't help but wonder if it's me. I keep thinking, why wasn't I enough? Am I not pretty enough? Sexy enough? Am I not good enough in bed?" I choke out, a ball of emotion clogging my throat.

"And then I think about Camden and how he wants me to give him a chance. The other night when I mentioned that I was cheated on by the only two guys I've been with, he said it's them, not me, but how can it be them and not me, when both of them cheated on me? And if I couldn't keep them satisfied and only wanting me, how the hell would I ever keep a man like Camden satisfied? He's a rock star, for God's sake. He has beautiful women throwing themselves at him every damn day. What do I possibly have to offer him that he can't get from all those other women?"

I glance up at my mom, needing her motherly wisdom, but my eyes lock on Camden, who is standing just behind us.

"Felix was looking for you," he says. "I thought I saw you come out here. I wasn't trying to eavesdrop." He swallows thickly, his Adam's apple bobbing. "I only heard the end of what you were saying."

"Great," I mutter, dropping my head into my hands.

My mom's arm leaves me just as a strong hand grips my hand and gently tugs it. I'm forced to look at Camden, who's now crouching in front of me. I look for my mom to save me, but she's already disappeared inside. Damn traitor.

"But I'm glad I did," he says, palming the side of my face. "I don't know all that went on in your marriage, but what I do know is that I'd give anything to be able to come home to you every day. Your boyfriend from high school cheated on you because you moved away, and he was young and not thinking about forever, and your husband… he cheated on you because he's a damn fool. But neither of those circumstances were because of you."

I start to argue, but he presses two fingers against my lips. "Sex is sex, Layles. Guys can get off with anyone. Give them a warm hole to sink into, and they're good to go. But what a guy *can't* get just anywhere is a good woman. Someone who supports and loves him. Who is there, day in and day out, making sure their family is taken care of. And all of those things are found *in the home*, not outside of it. David made the same mistake many men make. He was too busy looking outside to pay attention to what was inside."

"What if…?" I sniffle, hating that I'm crying in front of Camden. "What if what's outside is better than what's inside?" I ask, tears filling my eyes and falling without my permission.

"If *you're* inside, that's impossible."

"David didn't think so," I murmur.

"And we've already concluded that he's a fool. David didn't deserve you. He didn't appreciate you. Because if he did, he would've been too busy looking inside to notice anything beyond those walls. He had everything. The beautiful wife, the adorable kid. A loving home. And he lost it all because he chose to look outside instead of cherishing and appreciating what he had on the inside. But that's on him, not you, and it's sure as hell not fair to throw his dumbass choices on me."

His emerald eyes sear into me. "If I had you, I know I'd never look outside. Them fucking blinds would stay closed." He smirks, and I find myself laughing. "You're beautiful and smart and sexy as fuck, and if I'm ever lucky enough to get you inside my four walls, I will prove to you every damn day that you're all I see… all I want. That there's nothing worth looking outside for.

"I hate that he hurt you. I hate that he ruined your family, and Felix will be affected. But selfishly, I'm so fucking thankful he showed his true colors, and because of his stupidity, I was able to tell you how I feel. I missed my chance all those years ago, but I'll be damned if I let you slip through my fingers again."

"I need a little bit of time," I tell him, needing to be honest. "I heard everything you said, but the truth is, I never knew you felt that way. Right now, I'm trying to wade through my mess of a life, and I don't think I'm in a place where I can be what you need. I know you said you'd never cheat on me, but I don't want to enter into a relationship feeling insecure. And I know that's not fair to you because you haven't done anything wrong, but I can't help how I feel."

Camden nods, his lips turning into a sad smile. "I get it. I heard you. When I shook your hand at the club, it was us starting over… as friends. I'm here, as your friend, and hopefully, one day when you're ready, I can be more. But just know that I'm here, no matter what. I fucked up when I walked away five years ago. I did what I had to at the time for Gage and Brax, and even myself, but I still fucked up. And to be given a second chance… I won't fuck it up again. Even if it's only as your friend."

I sigh in relief and wrap my arms around Camden, needing to

hug him. "Thank you," I tell him, breathing in his warm, comforting scent. "I don't know what the future holds, but I can tell you that right now, I can definitely use a friend."

"THIS IS ALL THE INFORMATION YOU NEED IN CASE OF AN EMERGENCY." I HAND DAVID A folder that contains copies of Felix's insurance card, birth certificate, social security card, his pediatrician's number and address, the local hospital's information, my phone number (I know, I know, I'm acting crazy), my mom's information, and a bunch of other numbers he might need.

"Poison control?" he asks, glancing up at me and raising a brow. "Do you really think all of this is necessary? I'm his dad. I can handle things. I don't need a file on my own kid."

"Please take it, just in case," I insist, my heart pounding against my rib cage at the thought of my little boy leaving for the weekend. Of him possibly needing me and me not being there. This is why so many women stay in bad relationships—for their kids, so they can be there for their kids. Because the worst part of being divorced is having to let your child walk out the door without you over and over again. What if he gets hurt? What if he has a nightmare and calls out to me in the middle of the night? What if…? What if…? What if…?

"If there's an issue, which I doubt there will be, I can just call you." He closes the folder and drops it onto the table.

"Yeah… I know," I say, picking it back up and handing it to him again. "But just in case. Please." I debated whether to tell him that I'll be in California this weekend but decided against it. For one, he'll give me tons of shit for it, which will sour Felix's first weekend at his dad's. He's already been acting off since we moved here and got divorced. I don't need to add to his craziness right before I leave our son in his care for seventy-two hours. And also, I don't want to deal with him. He'll eventually find out, but for now, I'm okay with him not knowing. It's not even his business, but I'm sure when he finds out, he'll try to make it so, as well as try to make my life a living hell.

The problem is, by not telling him, he thinks I'm going to be here in New York, so he doesn't understand my need to make sure Felix is taken care of. It will be my first time without my little boy for longer than one night, and on top of it, I'm going to be across the damn country, where I can't just jump into an Uber and get to him in minutes.

"Whatever," he grumbles, shoving it into the front pocket of the suitcase Felix packed. David and I explained to him that he'll be getting his own room, but he's only four and doesn't get it, so he insisted on packing his favorite stuff to take with him.

"I'm ready!" Felix yells, running down the stairs. When he stops in front of us, he glances at me. "Mommy, you have to put on your shoes so we can go to our new house."

Oh, jeez… Because I didn't already feel like the worst mother in the world for ripping my son's family apart—even though it needed to happen and is for the best.

I get down on my knees, so Felix and I are at eye level. "The new house is only for you and Daddy," I explain. "This house is still mine and yours. You have two houses and two rooms. Sometimes, like right now, you'll go with your dad, and I'll stay here by myself until you come back here."

Felix's brows knit together. "But… I wanna stay with you. I don't want you to be lonely."

Be still my heart.

"I love you so much," I tell him, pulling him into a hug. "And I'm going to miss you, but you're going to have fun with your dad. I won't be lonely, I promise."

"Hey, Felix," David says. "I was thinking we could go to the park this weekend. Maybe we can convince your mom to join us."

"David," I hiss, knowing exactly what he's up to. The guy switches between hot and cold like a drunken Mother Nature. He's either pissed at me or apologizing to me. He either tells me I'm a shitty person for ending our marriage or begs me to take him back. And just when I think he's finally accepting where we stand, he pulls this shit.

"The park sounds like so much fun," I tell Felix in an upbeat voice so he doesn't catch on to the stifling tension between his parents. David might disgust me on a deep level, and I might've lost all love and respect for him, but he's still Felix's dad, which means I have to deal with him for the rest of our damn lives. His *only* saving grace is that his son absolutely adores his father, and I can't simply take Felix away from his dad because of what went down between us. But one wrong move on David's part, and I won't hesitate to strike against him.

"Can you go?" Felix asks before I can finish my sentence.

"I can't," I tell him, hating the heartbroken look on his face. "This weekend is all about you and your daddy. I want you to have tons of fun and call me every night before bed to tell me how your day went, okay?"

"Okay," he says, nodding.

"I love you, and I'll miss you." I pull him into a hug and inhale the scent of his shampoo.

"Love you, Mommy."

The moment David and Felix take off, I break down sobbing and call my best friend, needing her.

"Did they leave?" she asks, already knowing what was going down tonight.

"Yeah. I know this is what I wanted, but…"

"No," she says in a stern voice. "This is not what you wanted. You wanted a husband who would love and cherish you, who would treat you with respect and honor the vows he made. Unfortunately, David turned out to be a rapist asshole. Now, you're doing what you have to do, not what you *wanted* to do, and if it means you cry, then fucking cry, and I'll sit on the phone with you while you do."

And that's exactly what I do. I cry over the phone and to Kaylee until the tears dry up, and I fall asleep with the phone to my ear, wishing I could fix my broken life.

Fifteen

Camden

Cadillac SUV. She's dressed in a pair of dark wash skinny jeans, a thick coat since it's cold as shit, and boots that almost reach her knees. Her brown hair is up in a loose ponytail, and her makeup is a bit on the heavier side—almost like she's trying to cover something up. It doesn't look bad. It's just not how I've seen her wear it since we've reconnected.

"Is that your way of telling me I look like shit?" she grumbles. "Thanks."

Declan snorts from inside the SUV. "Sounds like operation *Get Layla* is going smoothly."

I reach in and punch him in the arm, then round the vehicle so I can open the door for Layla. She hands our driver her suitcase, and he throws it into the trunk. As she's getting in, her eyes land on the other vehicle.

"What's that?"

"Our security team. We don't really need them much in New

York since the people here are too busy to give a shit about us. But LA is another story. We have a team of four, and they have to go everywhere we go when we're in LA. Two of them were actually with us at Lush, but they make it a point to blend in unless we need them."

She nods and gets in, scooting to the other side, so I can sit next to her. Declan's already moved to the second row to sit next to Braxton, and Gage is sleeping in the front seat. Since the vehicle is warm inside, she unzips her coat and shrugs out of it, exposing a tight long-sleeved shirt that shows off the swells of her perfect round breasts.

"What's wrong?" I ask her when the vehicle lurches forward to head to the airport.

"I couldn't sleep. Felix is with David for the weekend. It's our first time away from each other for this long." Tears well in her eyes, and my heart shatters at her voice's broken tone.

Without thinking, I pull her into my arms and kiss her temple. "I'm so sorry you're going through this." I can understand on a certain level because of my parents being in the music industry. They had to travel a lot, and oftentimes, we couldn't go. But I've never been on the other side of it. When I have kids one day, I'll be where she is, only it won't always be for just a weekend but for weeks at a time. It's the downside of the business we're in. Touring is where we make the majority of our money. It's why so many artists go on tour every year. Why we've been going on tour every year. My dad's advice was to hit the iron while it's hot, so later, when we're ready to settle down, we can travel less like he did.

"I'll get through it," she says. I expect her to pull away since she's so hell-bent on taking shit slow, so I'm a bit surprised when she snuggles against me and sighs into my chest. A few minutes later, the soft sound of her snoring tells me she's fallen asleep. She stays like this for the entire ride. I use my available hand to go through my phone, double-checking the agenda Jill sent us. While my dad is our band manager, we also have a tour manager—Jill—who handles everything we do on the road, whether it's a tour or a festival like the one we're attending this weekend.

Since we're not performing until tomorrow, she left today open for us to do what we want. The guys already know I've made plans for Layla and me for the day. My goal is to reconnect with her and remind her of the friendship we once had while wooing the hell out of her. I only get one day alone with her, so I'm determined to make the most out of it.

A few minutes into the drive, my phone goes off with a text from Kendall. When I click on it, I see she actually texted Gage, Braxton, Declan, and me.

Kendall: Hey! Mom said you guys are flying in. Let's meet up. I miss you!

One of the nice things about living in LA for the past five years is that, even though the majority of my family lives in New York, Kendall owns a home just up the street from us in Calabasas. With us both touring like crazy, we don't see each other often. But during the rare occasion we're both in LA at the same time, we hang out. Kendall loves her house and loves to throw pool parties, which leaves me to man the grill.

Me: You're back?

Kendall: About to land. I was thinking I could fly home with you guys on Sunday since I couldn't make it home yesterday for Thanksgiving. I'm going to surprise Mom and Dad and chill in New York for a while. I'm exhausted.

In other words, she and her latest boyfriend broke up, and she's going to New York to hide out. My sister is what you'd call a serial dater. No matter who she's with, she finds something wrong with him. And when they break up, she writes a shit ton of songs about him. Ever heard what people say about Taylor Swift's exes? They've been *Swifted*. Well, my sister's exes… they get *Stiffed*. It's a play off the wood in Blackwood. Lame, I know. But it doesn't change the fact that, like Taylor, my sister has developed quite the reputation for luring men in, making them fall in love, and then kicking them to the curb. I love my sister, she's one of my best friends, but I pity the men she hooks. I honestly don't think she does it to be cruel. I think my sister loves the idea of being in love. She has it in her head what it should look like, feel like, sound like, and when the guy she's with does something she doesn't like, she drops him quicker than a bad habit. Hell, she has yet to bring a single guy home with her to meet our parents.

> **Me: I can do breakfast. Layla's with us. She's our new videographer. I made plans with her for the rest of the day.**

> **Kendall: I heard… and of course you did. I need to shower and get some shut-eye, so breakfast is a no-go, bro.**

> **Braxton: Sleeping all fucking day. Club LA tonight.**

Club LA is our go-to place to chill. It's owned by a good friend of ours, so whenever we go, we get VIP, which allows us to party without all the craziness that comes with being who we are.

Gage responds next—guess he woke up: **Same**

I'm about to put my phone away when another text comes through from Declan: **I'm down for lunch or dinner.**

I mentally roll my eyes. Of course he is. The guy has had a crush on my sister since we first met. Normally, a brother would be worried about his friends hooking up with his sister, but in my case, if Kendall ever gave in to Declan, I'd be more concerned about him. Because Declan is a hopeless romantic. He's the sweet to Braxton's jaded. The light to Gage's dark. And the optimistic to my—until recently—pessimistic ass. He keeps us all grounded. Never allowing the scales to tip too much one way.

Kendall: Sounds good! I'll text you when I wake up.

When we arrive at the airport, we're taken straight to the Blackwood jet that's waiting for us. Layla walks on board with wide eyes, checking it all out. It reminds me of the first time the guys came on board. I was raised in this lifestyle, so for me, it's a normal occurrence. Don't get me wrong, I don't for a second take it for granted or not appreciate what I have, but the wow factor just isn't there.

We take off, and the guys find a place to crash, leaving Layla and me on the couch. "Any plans for today?" she asks, constantly glancing at her phone. "I didn't see anything on the agenda." When I made the plans for us today, it was to reconnect, but now I'm hoping they'll take her mind off the fact that she's away from her son all weekend. Because of her divorce, she'd be in the same position she's in now, but I'm sure it's harder knowing she's hours away from him.

"Actually, yeah. I was hoping we could spend the day together."

Her gaze pops up. "Like all of us or just the two of us?"

"Just the two of us… if that's okay with you. I thought it could be a good way to get things back to a starting point with us. See if the adult us still connects like the teenage us used to."

She sucks in her bottom lip, then slowly releases it, and I wonder how she tastes, and if one day I'll get a chance to find out. I have no doubt the adult me still wants the adult her, but I know that since she hasn't shared the same feelings I have all these years, I need to show her how good things can be between us.

"Yeah, that's okay with me." She slides a bit closer. "Things have been crazy since I returned to New York. Between the move, the divorce, and finding out that after all this time, you wanted more, and I had no idea, I think spending some alone time together is a good idea."

I pull her into my side and kiss the top of her head. "I'm going to woo the hell out of you, Layles."

She laughs, shaking her head. She isn't a stranger to that term. My family's used it as long as she's been around.

"I think… I think I'm okay with that," she says softly, shocking the hell out of me. She lays her head back on my chest, and a few minutes later, she's fallen back asleep.

Sixteen

Camden

Declan chuckles. "More like six of your houses. But yeah, this is home."

"We figured sharing a house would be better than living separately," I explain. "Last year, we had a studio built so we don't have to go to the Blackwood studio every time we want to work on our music. Traffic in LA is a bitch. Not as bad as New York, but still pretty bad."

The guys all go their separate ways to their rooms while I give Layla a quick tour, leading her to the guest room. "This is your room. It has an en suite bathroom, and the balcony overlooks the infinity pool, rolling hills, and a bit farther out, the stadium."

"This is perfect. Thank you." She pulls the French doors open, leading to the outside. We picked this house because it's in a gated community but on a good-sized piece of property. It's our very own sanctuary.

"Wow, it's so warm." She laughs. "A weekend here and I might be convinced to move the hell out of frigid New York City."

"If you think the weather will convince you, wait until you see what I have planned."

She twirls around. "What are you up to?"

"You'll see," I say, giving her a playful wink. "I'll give you a few minutes to freshen up if you need to and change into something cooler. Oh, and make sure you're wearing comfortable shoes. We'll be doing a good amount of walking. I'll meet you downstairs."

When she enters the living room about twenty minutes later, she's in the same jeans and shirt, but in place of her boots are sneakers. When I glance up at her, I find her eyes are rimmed red, and her nose and cheeks are splotchy.

"What's wrong?"

She shakes her head, but the second I'm off my seat and over to her, palming her face, she breaks. "David is being a dick. I tried to call to talk to Felix, but he said they're busy. I should've known he would act like this."

"Because you're with me?"

"No, he doesn't know I'm here or that I work for Blackwood. I didn't want to chance him freaking out. I'll have to tell him eventually, but…"

"I get it. But why is he acting like this?" I didn't want to pry. I was hoping she would eventually tell me all that went down, but I can't be there for her if I don't know what's going on.

Layla flinches, and my hackles rise. "Layles," I say gently. "You know you can trust me, right?"

"I know," she says softly. "I really just want to spend the day with you without bringing David into the mix. Can we please just enjoy our day? I promise I'll tell you everything soon. I'm just not ready to right now."

"Okay," I concede, hearing the pleading in her voice. "We can do that. And when you're ready to talk, I'll be here."

"Thank you," she says, sagging in visible relief.

Since we won't require any security where we're going, we take off in my Mercedes C-Series Coup. It's not often I get to actually drive it, and since it's nice out, I ask Layla if she's okay with rolling the windows down. Of course she is.

The ride is made in comfortable silence with Layla sticking her hand out the window and reveling in the cool breeze. I can't help but constantly glance at her. She's so fucking beautiful, and despite everything going on, she actually looks almost content right now.

Twenty minutes later, when we arrive at the heliport, her eyes swing over to me. "We're going in a helicopter?" she squeaks. "Are you freaking serious?"

"It's the quickest way to get around." I shrug, loving that she's obviously excited.

"Oh, shit," she says when she meets me around the front of the car. I take her hand, leading her to the one we're taking.

"What?"

"I knew you were going to woo me, but this… You're pulling out all the stops, aren't you?"

I have to laugh at that. "Damn right." I tug on her hand so she's forced to spin around into my arms. "I'm not taking any chances this time. I've wanted you for eight years. When you got pregnant and then married David, I thought I'd lost my shot. I'm not gonna lie, a part of me kept holding on to hope, which makes me sound like a dick because that means I was banking on you eventually getting a divorce, and I shouldn't have wanted that for you. You deserve to be happy, even if it's not with me. But still, here we are, and as I said before, I'm not taking this second chance lightly. If we don't end up together, it's because you don't want to be with me. And if that's the case, it is what it is. No matter what you decide, unless you walk away, I'll never go another five years without talking to you again."

She smiles softly. "That makes me happy because I really did miss you." She wraps her arms around me and places a chaste kiss on my neck. "I'm sorry I didn't know how you felt."

"It's not your fault. I should've made it clear. But now I am."

While I knew she'd be wowed by the helicopter, I wasn't lying when I said it's the quickest way to get around. Within fifteen minutes after taking off, we're landing on Catalina Island and stepping off the helicopter. A taxi is waiting for us, and a few minutes later, he drops us off at the Avalon Resort.

During the entire trip so far, Layla's been taking picture after picture with her camera hanging around her neck. It reminds me so much of the girl from high school. I'm glad she's back in my life and that I get to spend so much time with her since she's working with us.

"Wow," she breathes when we make our walk out to the beach. "This is amazing. Do you come here a lot?"

"Actually, I've never been here," I admit.

"What?"

"I considered showing you around LA since that's what I'm familiar with, but the thought of being recognized and fans getting crazy… I just wanted some time with you. So I did some research and found this place. I think it's a lot like New York. When you're a tourist, you visit everywhere, but when you live there, you forget to actually enjoy it."

"I get that," she agrees.

Threading our fingers together, I guide her over to the private picnic the resort set up for us inside the cabana I booked ahead of time. There's an assortment of meats and cheeses on a charcuterie board, a pitcher of sangria, and several other plates of food for us to snack on.

I fix us each a plate while she pours us a couple of drinks, and then we take them over to the double lounger, where we can lie down and enjoy the nice weather and view.

Layla's the first to speak. Between bites, she says, "How are Brax and Gage doing? Like really doing. We've kind of kept in touch over the years, but it was mostly commenting and liking each other's pics."

"They're okay." When she glances at me, raising a single knowing brow, I sigh. "Brax's okay. I mean, he's turned into a bit of a slut, but I think he's just trying to move forward."

Layla nods. "Kaylee kind of did the same thing right after. She lashed out, got caught up in some bad stuff, and failed out of Boston."

Damn, I had no idea. Not that I feel too bad for her. She chose to do what she did. But if I'm going to have a shot at being with Layla, I have to be accepting of all the parts of her life, including Kaylee… and David.

"She's graduating in December from NYU," she adds.

"That's good," I say evenly.

"And Gage?" she prompts.

"He's…not so good," I admit truthfully. "My dad has mentioned rehab a few times but hasn't pushed because he's not a danger to himself. He's just always kind of high."

"I just want to hug him and never let go," she says with a sigh.

I look over at her. "I know they've missed you. They don't talk about you much since they knew how I felt… how I *feel*. But I've caught them talking about Felix a few times. Checking out his birthday pictures. Commenting on when you graduated from college. We were so proud of you."

Her eyes fill with liquid. "I did the same thing with all of you. I hated seeing everything as an outsider, but I loved getting glimpses of you guys. You did what you dreamed of, and I'm so happy for you guys." She laughs softly. "Of course, now every time I hear a song, I wonder if you're singing about me."

I chuckle at that, glancing at the tattoo of the camera peeking out of the top of her shirt. "If they were written by me, and they're about love, they're about you."

She shakes her head, an adorable light blush creeping up her neck and cheeks. "I can't believe I had no idea. Everyone knew…"

I have to laugh at that because she isn't lying. Literally, everyone knew but her.

"You had no clue at all?"

"No. I always thought you were good looking, so had I known…" She shrugs. "Ever since I found out, I can't stop thinking about it. Analyzing everything, questioning my feelings." She frowns. "David knew. He hated anyone even mentioning you. But I just thought he was being crazy."

"He is crazy."

"Yeah," she says solemnly. Then she takes a deep breath and releases a harsh sigh. "Sorry, I said no bringing him up, and then I did."

"He's your ex, and he's Felix's dad. I know that in order for us to have a real chance at being in a relationship, I have to be open to hearing about him."

"Thank you." She leans over and kisses my cheek. "That means a lot to me."

We spend the rest of the day exploring the island. We don't bring up David or the guys anymore and instead focus on getting to know each other again. At one point during our hike, she starts a game of twenty questions, which leads to *would you rather*. I don't know if it's being away from the city or everyone, but she opens up, allowing me into her adult thoughts, feelings, goals, and dreams.

She's light and playful, laughing and making jokes. I already knew I wanted her, but by the time we're climbing back into the helicopter, I can say with certainty that I'm still in love with her. She might be a few years older and a mom, but she's still the same person I fell in love with on the steps of her family's home all those years ago.

"Too bad we didn't leave a little later," she says once we're situated in our seats and buckled in. "I bet the sunset from up here is beautiful."

"Actually," I say, feeling on top of the world. "I booked a tour for on the way back. We're going to see all of LA from above, along with the sunset."

She shakes her head and smiles, those damn dimples popping out. "Oh, Camden, your wooing game is seriously on point."

We put on our headsets, and the rotors start spinning. A few minutes later, we're on top of California, listening to the pilot tell us about what we're flying over. Layla stares outside the window, mesmerized, while I stare at her.

When she glances over at me with a gorgeous smile splayed across her face, my heart stutters in my chest, and without thinking, I thread my fingers through the back of her hair and pull her to me for a kiss.

Seventeen

Layla

TODAY HAS BEEN ONE OF THE BEST DAYS OF MY LIFE. BETWEEN THE HELICOPTER RIDES, exploring the island, and spending time with Camden, getting to know him all over again, I'm in heaven. The past several years have consisted of me being a student and becoming a mom and a wife. Don't get me wrong, I love my son, but it means my days have been spent watching children's shows and having conversations with someone who thinks it's funny to fart in the tub and make bubbles.

And I hadn't realized until today just how off David and I were. He worked and provided for us, but we never actually spent time together, and because I was so busy going to school and taking care of Felix, I never stopped to question it. We didn't go away or have date nights. He worked, and I took care of our home and Felix. But spending the day with Camden made me see that I want more. I learned more about him today than I think I ever learned about David in our years together.

And if I was worried about picking up where we left off five years later, it was a waste of a worry because Camden made it so easy. Our conversations flowed. We laughed and joked, and for the first time, I felt like more than a caregiver. I felt a lot like me. And sadly, it made me realize that somewhere along the way, I forgot who I was.

We're on the helicopter, on our way back to LA, and when I turn to thank Camden for today, our gazes clash. Before I know what he's doing, he tugs me toward him, our mouths colliding in the sweetest yet most intense kiss I've ever experienced in my life.

Our lips caress, our tongues stroke. He tastes like the beer he was drinking earlier and something uniquely Camden. I sigh into him, wishing we were alone so I could climb into his lap and burrow myself into him. I want to deepen the kiss, to feel him everywhere and get lost in him.

And then his fist tightens in my hair, and without my permission, my brain goes back there… Instantly, I jump back, smacking the back of my head on the glass.

Camden's eyes widen. "Are you okay? I'm sorry… I shouldn't… I should've asked."

"I'm okay," I tell him as traitorous tears fill my lids. "It's okay." I nod emphatically, trying to convince myself.

He doesn't take his eyes off me. "Layles," he begins as if he can see through me. He knows something is wrong, and I'm going to have to explain because before those memories popped up, I was immensely enjoying that kiss. Butterflies were attacking my belly, and sparks were flying behind my lids. And I knew at that moment I wanted Camden. I want to try. I don't care that I've only been divorced for a short time. I've spent the past five years alone while David was cheating on me. He was living two lives while I was barely living, and now it's my turn to live.

"Can we talk when we get back to your place?"

"Of course," he says. I can feel him mentally taking a step back because he thinks I didn't want the kiss, but in a helicopter isn't the place to have this conversation. Hopefully, when we're done talking, he'll know how I feel and what I want.

"YOU GUYS COMING?" BRAXTON ASKS WHEN WE WALK THROUGH THE DOOR. HE'S DRESSED IN a pair of skinny jeans, a shirt taut across his chest that reads: *My other shirt is at your mom's house*, showing off several tattoos up and down his arms, a pair of Vans, and a matching Vans hat. One thing I've noticed about all four of the guys is that while they've spent the past five years playing their heart out, they've also spent a lot of time working out.

"You checking me out, Layla?" Braxton says, lifting a playful brow.

"What? No!" I say with a laugh. "I was… well, kind of." I shrug. "In my defense, you guys are all tattooed and buff now. Except Cam. He's just buff."

Braxton throws his head back with a laugh. "Buff?"

"You know…" I squeeze his forearm. "Hard and muscular."

"Quit touching my boy," Camden says with a mock glare as he pulls me away from Braxton and drops his arm around my waist. "If you want to feel something hard and muscular, you can touch me."

I reach over and make a show of squeezing his bicep. "Damn, Cam, you are hard."

"Oh jeez, please don't stroke his ego anymore," Declan says, entering the room. "The guy already thinks he's God's gift to… well, the entire human race."

"Shut the hell up," Camden says without any conviction in his tone.

"What? It's the truth." Declan shrugs. "And it doesn't help that women fawn all over your pretty boy face." Declan reaches out to stroke Camden's face, but Camden smacks his hand away.

"You leaving soon?" Camden asks.

Declan laughs. "Yes, don't worry, we're getting out of here so you can continue your wooing in a few minutes. We're just waiting on Gage."

"Where are you guys going?" I ask. While Braxton is dressed all wannabe grunge, Declan's wearing nice denim jeans, a button-down collared shirt, and clean white Nikes. He's not wearing a hat, and his long hair is tied neatly in a bun.

"The club," Declan says just as Gage walks out from wherever he was. His bright blue eyes are bloodshot, and when he gets closer, the scent of cannabis fills the air. Like Braxton, he's dressed like he's going to a skate park instead of a club with his shoulder-length curly hair down and still wet from his shower.

"Hey, you," Gage says, pulling me out of Camden's arms and giving me a side hug. "Glad to see you coming around again."

"I'm glad to be back around," I tell him, snaking my arm around his back.

"You guys joining us?" he asks.

I glance at Camden. I was hoping we could talk, but I won't stop him if he wants to go out.

As if he can read my mind, he shakes his head. "Nah, we're gonna stay in, order some grub, and make it a Netflix and chill kind of night," he says, winking at me.

I laugh at the same time Declan snorts. "Yeah, okay. You gonna watch *Friends*?"

"Funny," Camden says dryly. "Speaking of *Friends*… How was lunch with my sister?"

Declan clears his throat, his demeanor going serious. "Good.

We went to La Grande. She mentioned meeting us at the club."

"That's good. Well, you guys have fun. Make sure you're ready to go in the morning by nine. We have the panel at eleven and the meet and greet afterward."

"Yes, Dad," Braxton says, mock saluting him.

Gage kisses my temple, then leans in and whispers, "Go easy on our boy, yeah? He's been waiting for you for a long-ass time." Then he releases me and follows Declan and Braxton out, leaving Camden and me alone.

Once the guys are gone, Camden turns his attention on me. "What would you like to order in? We have pretty much anything available."

"Chinese?" I suggest since I know we both love it.

"Sure, I know a good place," he says, pulling out his phone and then handing it to me so I can see the menu. After I tell him what I want, I excuse myself to try to call David again so I can talk to Felix.

"Mommy!" Felix shouts, answering the phone.

My heart swells, and I release a breath of relief at his voice. "Hey, sweetie. How are you?"

"I'm good."

"Yeah? What are you doing?"

"Talking to you." He giggles, making me laugh as well. "Are you having a good time with Daddy?"

"I'm bored. When can I come home?"

My heart falls. "Did you guys go to the park?"

"No, Daddy had to work. We're at his office. It's borinnnnnggggg. He let me watch videos on his phone."

That must be why he answered it when I called.

"Where is your dad now?"

"He's…" There's shuffling, and then Felix says, "It's Mommy!" He must be talking to David.

"Hello?" David says.

"Are you seriously at the office?"

He sighs. "I know you don't understand this since you've never worked a day in your life, but some of us have responsibilities. Something came up, and I needed to handle it."

"You told Felix you were going to take him to the park."

"And I'm going to… tomorrow. Is this what you called for, to nag the hell out of me? If you're so concerned, how about you stop acting stubborn and let me put our family back together?"

"I'm not having this conversation with you again. Let me talk to Felix so I can say goodbye."

"Mommy!"

"It's me. I love you, sweetie, and I'll see you in two days. Okay?"

"Okay. Love you. Bye."

The call ends, and I sigh in frustration.

"Everything okay?" Camden asks.

"Not really," I say honestly. "There's some stuff I need to talk to you about. The reason I abruptly ended our kiss."

"Then let's talk." He guides us over to the couch and sits down, pulling me with him, so I'm sitting up against him.

"I'm a little nervous," I admit, pulling back slightly. "I know you say you like me, and while you might think I'm still the same person I was five years ago, a lot has changed. I'm a mom now, and with that comes a lot of responsibility."

"Layles, I know you're a mom, and I know you've changed. We both have. But that doesn't hinder my feelings for you. Spending the day with you showed me that we're still as compatible as we were before, and if anything, seeing you be an amazing mom to Felix the few times I've been around you guys only adds to your appeal."

I can't help but smile at his admission. "Thank you. But thinking I'm a good mom is different from being part of our lives. And unfortunately, that also will include David. And after what I tell you, you might want to kill him, but you won't be able to because he's Felix's dad and… yeah."

I exhale a harsh breath and then just say what I need to say. "The reason I ended our kiss, which I was enjoying, is because when you pulled my hair, it brought back horrific memories of when"—I clear my throat—"David raped me."

Camden's eyes bug out, and his jaw ticks. "He did what?"

"It's why we got divorced. He found out that I saw you at the concert. A picture went around of us."

"Yeah, I saw it. When I briefly spoke to you as I was walking off the stage."

"He's always been jealous of you. Even in high school, we would constantly argue about me spending too much time with you. Anyway, between the picture and the tattoo, he flipped his shit. He spat at me and slapped me and then forced himself on me. Today, when we were kissing, you tugged on my hair, and without meaning to, that day flashed in my mind. When he was forcing me to give him head and then raping me, he kept pulling on my hair. I have nightmares sometimes about it, but I didn't realize being sexual with someone would trigger a flashback."

"What in the actual fuck," he says slowly. "Your husband raped you?"

I nod, choking up at the pained expression on his face. "Yeah. He hurt me… bad."

"Why the fuck isn't he in jail?"

"Because I searched *proving your husband raped you,* and it scared the hell out of me because most women said they couldn't prove it. It'd be a messy battle, and I was afraid if I was accused of lying, he could somehow take Felix away from me. I believe in the judicial system, but it's not without flaws, and I couldn't risk it. So instead,

I hired an attorney and divorced him."

"I'm going to kill him." Camden's body visibly vibrates in anger. "When Nanna said David hurt you, I thought she meant emotionally. I had no idea she meant literally."

"One, you're not going to kill him because that will end with you in prison, and that would make David all too happy." I palm his cheek. "And while physically he did hurt me, it hurt just as bad emotionally. I felt violated on many levels."

"Fine, I won't kill him," he relents. "But I'm not throwing *destroying him* off the table. He's going to pay," he says in a tone that brooks no argument. I won't let him make good on his threats, but for right now, since he's thousands of miles away, I'll let him make his warnings. Kaylee and my mom did the same thing.

I stroke his cheek, and he seems to calm down somewhat.

"What can I do?" he says, leaning into my touch. He brings his hand up to mine and holds it against his face for a second before he turns slightly and kisses the inside of my palm. "How do I fix this for you?"

My heart warms. "You're doing it. This weekend away, despite missing Felix, is exactly what I needed. I feel like I have a small piece of me back for the first time in a long time. Being with you feels good, feels right. And the truth is, things haven't felt right for a long time."

He grabs my hips and pulls me onto his lap to straddle his thighs. "I feel the same way. Since the day I got on the plane to California, it's felt like a piece of me was missing, and being with you, spending time with you, it's as though the pieces have clicked into place. We can take things slow—"

"I don't want to take things slow or fast. I just want to be with you and see where it leads. We take it at our pace, do whatever feels *right*." I lower my top, exposing the tattoo. "The night I got this tattoo, I think I already knew I had feelings for you. I've never permanently marked my body before, but when I heard that song, I did it without even thinking twice." My eyes descend in shame. "At the time, when David confronted me, I was in denial, but he wasn't wrong in his accusations. I was married and got a tattoo to represent you and the way you feel about me."

"Hey." Camden lifts my chin. "I happen to love that tattoo."

"Yeah, but you wouldn't have if I were with you and got one about another guy."

"That's true, but maybe everything happens for a reason. I wrote that song years ago, but I couldn't find it in me to actually sing it. At the last second, without knowing you'd be there, I decided to, and that song led to you finally hearing my words and in turn getting that tattoo."

"And was the reason for my divorce."

"No," he says. "David forcing himself on you was the reason for your divorce. If my wife came home with a tattoo of a song by another man, I wouldn't be happy, and I'd definitely question our relationship and where we stand, but I sure as fuck wouldn't rape her."

"I know you're right, and it's for the best… the divorce, not the rape. But I think what has me feeling guilty is that I don't feel guilty about getting the tattoo, but I feel like I should. Does that make sense?" I ask with a laugh.

Camden smiles. "I get it, but everything that happened led us to right here, so I say fuck feeling what you think you should feel. It's over and done with, and I love seeing that tattoo on your body."

"I do too. Although, I think you should rewrite the ending… the part about finally moving on."

Camden's mouth quirks into a sexy grin. "How about we leave that song the way it is and instead write our own song?" He tugs on the front of my shirt, pulling me toward him, and my heart swells, knowing he did that so he wouldn't use the back of my head. His lips brush softly against mine, once, twice, then he coaxes my lips open, slipping his tongue into my mouth.

My hands glide over his shoulders, up his neck, and land on the back of his head, my fingers threading through his soft, messy hair. Camden's tongue wraps around my own, and he sucks it into his mouth. I find myself grinding against him, deepening the kiss and needing to be closer to him.

And then a buzzer goes off, breaking the moment.

"That would be the food," he groans, resting his forehead against mine.

Eighteen

Camden

MY HEAD IS ALL OVER THE PLACE, MY THOUGHTS SWIRLING AROUND LIKE A DAMN TORNADO. On the one hand, I'm ecstatic that Layla is willing to give us a chance and see where things go. She admitted to my feelings not being completely one-sided and the tattoo meaning more than she was willing to admit at the time. On the other hand, it feels like every admission has been blanketed with a dark cloud thanks to David. I always knew he was an asshole, good at hiding who he really was. He had everyone fooled, but not me. I should've pushed harder back then and convinced Layla he wasn't the one for her, but I pussied out and let her walk away, and in the end, he hurt her on so many damn levels.

I tried to be positive, telling her everything happens for a reason, and to an extent, I believe that, but on the other side of the coin, I'll always wonder if what happened could've been prevented had I stepped in years ago. I know… It's pointless to live with what-ifs, but I can't help it.

All I can do at this point is make sure I'm there for Layla and her son and keep a close eye on that rapist fucker. One wrong move, and he's going down.

After bringing the food in, Layla and I spend the next couple of hours chowing down and watching some Horny Housewives in England show. That's not what it's called, but the show is about some British folks who spend their days trying to hook up with each other.

When the main chick's brother pushes his woman against the tree and starts fucking her like a savage, I notice Layla squirm in her seat. She's turned on. And while I want nothing more than to tend to her needs, I also want to let her lead at her own pace. Knowing the last time she had sex was when her ex-husband raped her changes shit.

"Is the show boring you?" Layla asks when she catches me staring at her instead of watching the show.

"What show?" I joke.

She rolls her eyes and swats my chest playfully. "It's still kind of early. If you want to go to the club—"

"Hell no." I pull her into my arms. "The only thing I want to do is hang out with you."

A small smile curls on the edge of her lips as I lean in to press my mouth to hers. I still can't believe that I can finally kiss her whenever the hell I want after all these years. When our lips touch, she sighs into the kiss, tugging on my shirt so I'm forced closer, deepening the kiss.

Layla edges backward until she's on her back, her head resting on the arm of the couch, and then she reaches out for me, but I don't go. Not yet. Because I need a moment to look at her, to appreciate what I finally have in front of me.

"What?" she asks, her voice coming out breathy and impatient.

"You're beautiful."

Her nose scrunches up, and her cheeks turn a gorgeous shade of pink. "Cam…" she whines. "Come here."

I pull my phone out, needing a picture, and her eyes go wide. "You're always the one taking the pictures," I explain. "I want one of you. On my couch, looking relaxed, with a bit of a tan from our day on the island, with your hair fanned out, and a slight blush on your cheeks." I snap a photo of her, and I'm about to put my phone away when she leans forward slightly and removes her top, exposing a sexy as fuck pink lacy bra. It's slightly see-through, and her hard nipples are poking through it.

With her eyes on me, she reaches down and unbuttons and unzips her pants. "Help me take them off."

I do as she says and peel them down her hips and thighs. Underneath is matching lacy underwear. All see-through, showing off her trimmed pussy underneath.

"You always wear matching bras and underwear?" I ask curiously.

The corner of her lips quirks up, knowing exactly where I'm going with this. "Only when I think there's a chance someone might see."

I absorb her words, my insides lighting off fireworks that she came here thinking there'd be a chance I'd see. This was before we talked, which means she was thinking about me.

"Take a picture," she says. "I want to see myself through your eyes."

I do as she says, taking a few pictures. But when I click on them to show her, my attention strays back to her because she's arching her back now, unclipping her bra and taking it all the way off. Her perfect round tits are paler than the rest of her from wearing a bathing suit, and my mouth waters, wanting to take her rose-dusted nipples into my mouth.

As if she can hear my thoughts, she drags her hands down her chest slowly, seductively, landing on her nipples. She tweaks them, making them even harder than what they already were, before she continues downward to her underwear. She hooks her fingers into the sides and drags them down her creamy thighs. She has the perfect triangle of neatly trimmed hair between her legs, and all I can think about is burying my face in her pussy.

"Are you going to take a picture?" she asks softly.

"No, I wouldn't risk it." Too many celebrities have gotten their phones hacked, their private pictures stolen. I shouldn't have even taken the ones I did.

"Here," she says, reaching forward and grabbing her camera. "Use this."

I take it from her and turn it on. I have no idea how the hell to use this thing, but I'm assuming I can just point and click. I do as such and take several pictures of Layla sprawled out on my couch, naked and fucking gorgeous.

I'm taking a picture of her when I notice through the lens that she's spread her legs, exposing her pussy. Pictures forgotten, I drop the camera onto the coffee table and give her my full attention.

"We were supposed to take things slow. If you don't want—"

She presses two fingers against my lips, silencing me the same way I've done to her in the past. "Our pace… not fast or slow. We do what we want, and tonight, I want to be with you. Some would say it's too fast since we've only just decided to give this thing between us a go. And some, our friends and probably you, would say this has been a long time coming." She laughs softly. "So we do what we want because I want this. I want you."

I stare into her eyes for several seconds, looking for any sign that she's not sure, but all I see is a beautiful, confident woman lying on the couch, wanting to be with me. But still, I have to ask.

"This isn't…" I clear my throat, hating to bring that asshole into my home, into this moment. "This isn't to try to rid what happened with *him,* right?"

I don't have to say his name for her to know who and what I'm talking about. "No," she says with conviction in her tone. "I will admit, I'm looking forward to having a new experience to fill my head, but I'm not using you to make what he did go away. Nothing we do will make what he did go away. Also…" She releases a harsh breath. "I don't think…" She flinches, suddenly looking nervous, maybe embarrassed, for the first time.

"What? Tell me."

"He… He did it in my… butt." She whispers the last word, her face flushing in embarrassment. "We'd never had sex like that before, and when he forced me, it was back there. So maybe we don't…"

"I won't touch you there," I promise while mentally counting backward from ten to calm myself. If we were in New York, I'm not sure I'd be able to hold back from going after him. No, that's not true. I *know* I wouldn't be able to because what the fuck is wrong with him to not only rape Layla, but there? Knowing it would hurt her worse. He's going to pay. I don't care what it takes. I will *make* him pay for what he's done to her.

"Maybe one day," she continues, her voice small.

"Layles…" I pull her legs toward me, so I can get closer to her face, and her legs hug my waist. "Everything we do or don't do is up to you. You're leading, baby. I'm just following. Okay? You tell me what you want, and I'll make it happen. You tell me there's something you don't like, and it goes into the no pile."

She nods, a tiny smile appearing. "Well, if that's the case, I would like for you to fuck me now."

A short laugh shoots out of me. "Oh, yeah? Is that what you want?"

"Uh-huh."

"Your wish is my command. But first…" I scoop her up into my arms, making her squeal in shock. "I'm going to make you come several times."

"What are you doing?" she asks as I carry her down the hall.

"Taking you to my room. There's no way I'm risking anyone seeing you like this."

Once we're in my room, I slam the door closed, then walk us over to my bed. I set her down in the middle, loving her here, in my bed, in my home. She's naked and on display and so goddamn beautiful.

"What are you thinking about?" she asks, raising a single brow.

"That I can't believe you're actually here, naked in my bed." I reach down and stroke her soft cheek. "I dreamed of this so many times."

"Well, believe it." She beams up at me, her brown eyes twinkling with happiness. "You know what would make this even better?"

"What?"

"You taking off your clothes." She grips the edge of my shirt and lifts it over my head. When her gaze lands on my naked upper body, her eyes turn molten with lust. "Sometimes, when I would watch your concerts online, I would pause it on the parts after you took your shirt off."

"You used to watch us?" I smirk, loving her admission.

She grabs the necklace, the one she gave me years ago, and tugs on it gently, bringing me close to her. "The first time I saw you wearing this necklace, I thought I was seeing things. I zoomed in and couldn't believe it. Every concert I would watch, I'd check. As soon as your shirt would come off, I'd look for it. And every time you were wearing it."

She shakes her head. "I thought maybe it was a sign not to give up on our friendship. I wanted so badly to call or text you, but I didn't know what to do. So I just kept watching, telling myself the day I saw you without it on would mean you'd moved on from our friendship. But you never took it off."

"Never." I brush my lips against hers. "It was my only connection to you. I never took it off. When we were doing a cover for *Rolling Stone*, they tried to make me, but I refused." I move to her neck, and she tilts her head, giving me better access to trail kisses along her heated flesh. She visibly shivers, and I chuckle softly, loving the way I affect her.

"I love that," she breathes, her fingers dragging through my hair as I kiss my way downward, stopping every couple of inches to suck on her flesh. Layla moans, her legs tightening around me. "I missed you so much. Every day... I hate that—"

"Stop," I tell her, pressing my lips to hers. "What's done is done. All that matters is that we're here, right here, right now, together." I kiss along her jawline, then work my way down to her chest, inhaling the sexy as fuck vanilla scent she slathers all over her damn body. When I get to her nipple, I wrap my lips around it, darting my tongue out and slowly licking the hardened peak until she's squirming under me. Then I switch to her other breast, giving it the same attention. Layla gasps and moans, grinding against me.

"Cam, please," she begs, wanting more.

"Shh." I kiss my way down her torso. "Stop rushing me."

"But—" she whines.

"No," I say firmly, spreading her legs and planting a kiss on the top of her pussy. "I've waited too damn long for this." I glance up and find her looking down at me with hooded eyes. "I'm not going to rush. I'm going to explore every..." I part her lips. "Single..." I run my finger along her seam, finding it dripping wet and ready for me. "Inch of you." I dip down and dart my tongue out, licking up her center and stopping at her clit. One taste and I'm already addicted.

I eat Layla's pussy, listening to her moans of pleasure, learning what she likes and what turns her on. I work her up higher and higher until she screams out my name, coming so hard, her body arches off the mattress, her legs shake, and she leaves a wet spot on my sheets. Goddamn, I'm never washing these fucking sheets.

"Come fuck me," she says, her voice soft and sated. Her eyes are barely open, and she looks like she's flying on a damn cloud. Mentally, I thump my chest with my fist because I did that. I brought her pleasure. And I'm nowhere near done.

Shucking off my pants and briefs, I crawl up her body, kissing her flesh. When I get up to her face, I palm it with one hand, using the other to hold myself up, and look into her eyes.

"I need you inside me," she says, wrapping her legs around me, causing my dick to stroke her pussy lips.

"Soon," I tell her, pressing my lips to hers. "But first, I need to make sure we're on the same page." Her brows furrow, and I drop a kiss to the middle of them. "This isn't a one-time thing or just two friends reconnecting. I want you in every way that matters. I want all of your days and your nights. Your happiness and your sadness. I want your tears and your laughter. I want your body...and your heart."

A small gasp escapes past her lips. "You have me. I don't know how this will all work, but you have me. All of me. I'm all in."

The surety in her words and the way her eyes bore into mine have me pushing inside her. Our mouths collide, our tongues caress. I get lost in her perfect warmth. In the way her pussy tightens around my shaft. She feels so damn good. We fit perfectly together. When I open my eyes, needing to see her, to remind myself that I finally get to have her, I find her eyes already open, looking at me.

"You okay?" I murmur against her lips, fucking her slow and deep.

"Yeah," she breathes, smiling at me. "It feels so good... *this* feels so good."

She finds her release first—moaning so loudly if the guys were here, they'd hear her through the walls. Her perfect pussy chokes the hell out of my dick, coaxing my own release out of me. I nuzzle my face into the crook of her neck, suckling on her hot flesh, and I come harder than I've ever come in my life.

We lay like this for several minutes, our sweaty bodies wrapped around each other. When we've both caught our breath, I pull out of her, noting the way my cum seeps out of her hole.

"We didn't use protection," I voice.

Her eyes go wide. "I'm on the pill."

"I'm clean. I haven't been with anyone in... a while."

She nods. "I got tested after *him*."

Sensing the mood darkening at the mention of her ex-husband, I jump off the bed and pull her into my arms.

"What are you doing?" she asks with a laugh.

"*We're* going to shower." I drop a chaste kiss to her lips. "I'm going to clean you, every part of you, so I can dirty you up all over again."

"Ohhh." She grins. "I like that plan."

Nineteen

Layla

"Nope." Camden shakes his head, pinching his lips tightly together.

"C'mon… one bite." I playfully push the food toward his mouth.

"No," he insists, the word coming out muffled since he's not chancing opening it and me shoving the snack in.

"I promise, it's delicious." I'm straddling his lap in the living room, the movie we were watching long forgotten. After Camden gave me another orgasm in the bathroom, followed by a round of shower sex, my stomach rumbled in hunger, so we got dressed and went to the kitchen in search of something to eat. He warned me that because they're only in town for the weekend, their stock of food is limited.

He was right. But upon inspection, I found they had bananas, raisin bread, and mayonnaise. And everyone knows banana and mayo sandwiches are the shit. Well, everyone except Camden. When we used to hang out, I'd make them all the time, and he'd refuse to even try them. Damn man is so stubborn.

"If you take one bite, I'll…" I lower my hand and rub it against his groin, then lean in and whisper, "give you the best blowjob of your life."

Camden groans, and I can tell he's about to give in because he's eyeing the banana-and-mayo-covered bread when the alarm chimes, indicating the door has been opened, and a few seconds later, Braxton, Gage, and Declan saunter in with a few scantily clad women. The way they're all talking and laughing loudly, their words slightly slurred, tells me they've had a good amount to drink.

The women are draped over them and giggling like they're five, and when the guys see us, they stop. Gage smirks, and Braxton grins. And that's when I remember I'm on Camden's lap in nothing but his shirt.

"About time," Braxton says, extending his fist to bump it against Camden's. When Camden doesn't react, he drops his fist and shrugs. "Damn, I thought once you finally got laid, you'd loosen up."

Camden continues to glare, so I jump in. "Did you have a good night?"

Braxton's grin grows. "Night's just getting started." He waggles his brows, and I stifle my gag, looking at Gage, who's resting against the wall with one of the women groping him like they're not in front of other people.

His eyes meet mine, and I notice they're bloodshot and sad. Unlike Braxton, who's drunk and happy.

"C'mon, Brax," one of the women says. "Show me your room."

"Specifically your bed," another woman adds with a giggle that has my ears bleeding.

"Gotta go," Braxton says. "And before you go all parental on us…" He looks at Camden. "We're taking them out to the pool house. We would've gone around back, but we forgot our keys."

"Remember we have to leave tomorrow at nine," Camden reminds him.

"Yes, Dad." Braxton mock salutes him, then wraps his arms around two women, yelling out, "Night!" while Gage and the other two women follow.

As they leave, I count how many women there are: two brunettes, a redhead, a blonde…

"That's four women for three guys," I point out. "Someone's going to feel left out."

Declan barks out a laugh. "That's four women for two guys, and trust me, none of them are going to feel left out."

It takes me a second, but once I put together what he's saying, I actually do gag this time. "They're sleeping with two women *each*?"

Declan chuckles, and Camden shakes his head.

"Won't be the first time," Declan says. "I'm off to bed. See ya in the morning."

Once he disappears down the hall, I turn my attention back on Camden. "You better have that pool house bleached." I mock shiver. "I can't even imagine the fluids that are getting swapped in there."

Camden rolls his eyes playfully. "Forget them. What I want to focus on is that blow job you were talking about before we were interrupted."

"Oh yes, in exchange for trying this." I pick up the bread I had placed on the plate and lift it to his mouth. Just as he's opening to take a bite, my phone vibrates, reminding me—for the second time, since I clicked ignore earlier when we were busy in the bedroom—to take my birth control and iron pills.

"Be right back." I drop the bread, kiss him quickly, and run to his bedroom to grab my pills, swallowing them with a mouth full of water.

"Okay, now where were we?" I say when I sit back on the couch.

"Oh, right! You're going to take a bite of this delicious sandwich." I'm bringing it to his mouth when an alarm sounds, indicating a door somewhere in the house has been opened.

I give Camden a look, silently asking who's coming in, but he shakes his head and bites down. He chews slowly, making a face similar to the face Felix makes when I force him to eat his vegetables, then audibly swallows.

"Fuck, that was horrible."

"What? It's yummy. Maybe you need one more—"

"Nope!" He snatches the bread from me, drops it onto the plate, and tosses the plate onto the coffee table. "One bite is what I agreed to." He scoops me up into his arms and stands. "Now it's time to pay up."

As he's walking us out of the living room, there's a clatter from the direction of the kitchen, and then a "Fuck!" Braxton pops his head out of the kitchen. "I need condoms and lube. Who the fuck used the last of it in the pool house and didn't restock?"

"You're looking in the kitchen for condoms?" I ask, confused.

"And lube," Braxton adds.

"Why—"

Camden shuts me up by kissing me and continues walking us to his bedroom, ignoring Braxton. Once we're inside and the door is shut, he sets me on the bed and steps between my legs, then goes about kissing my face and neck, but I can't get my question out of my head.

"Why would he be looking for condoms and lube in the kitchen?"

"Because there's usually some in the kitchen drawer," he says, peppering kisses along my neck.

His answer leads to another question. "Do you guys have sex a lot in the kitchen?"

He shrugs, then gently pushes me down so I'm on my back and

he's hovering over me. His mouth lands on my ear, and he tugs on the lobe.

I should be focusing on him, but now I'm wondering… "Have you had sex in the kitchen?"

This makes him stop in place. His eyes meet mine. "We're not having this conversation."

"What conversation?"

"The one where you ask me how many women I've slept with, and my number will undoubtedly be higher than yours because you've only been with one guy…well, now two, with me. That'll lead to you asking questions you don't really want the answers to, which will end with you becoming insecure and getting upset."

"Wow, you just had an entire conversation for us both *and* told me my feelings."

Camden sighs and rolls off me, landing on his side. "I just got you. The last thing I want is for you to run scared."

"That bad, huh?" I joke. Camden doesn't laugh, though, and that makes my stomach roil. I know he hasn't been a saint all these years. He's in a rock band. The sex and drugs are expected to go along with the rock and roll. But he's right… Now that I'm thinking about it, I can't help the insecurity from rearing its ugly head. It's one thing to speculate, but it's another to actually see Braxton and Gage walk in with multiple women.

"Have you had sex with multiple women?" I blurt out.

Camden's eyes roll up to the ceiling. "I guess we're going to have this conversation anyway." He sighs and flops onto his back, and I hate that I've just ruined the moment, but I can't help my curiosity.

"Have I had sex? Of course," he says, glancing over at me. "With more than one woman? Yeah. But not as often as you're thinking and not in a long time. When the fame first hit, women flocked to us. I was heartbroken, learning you were getting married and then you got pregnant, and I lost myself in a few women. But it got old real quick. The fake women, the fake emotions. It's not for me."

I nod in understanding, hating that I hurt Camden when I didn't even know I was.

"I can't take back what I've done, but I can tell you, none of the women I was with compare to being with you."

I roll my eyes playfully and he palms the side of my face. "I'm serious, Shutterbug. Being with you…it's incomparable. I told you before, for a guy, sex is usually just sex, but with you, it's so much more. I always knew it would be like this, but I never imagined it would actually happen."

I wrap my arms around his neck, and he pulls me on top of him so he's leaning against the headboard, and I'm straddling his waist. "I get it. I appreciate you explaining it to me, and I won't ask how many or anything like that. Am I a bit self-conscious after seeing those women? Yeah." I shrug. "Those women from earlier were nothing like me. They were dressed in tight, sexy dresses, faces full of makeup, fake breasts, and based on how tiny they were, I doubt they've had any kids."

"They're fake. Fake hair, fake makeup, fake tits. Fake tan. All fake." He squeezes my hips. "You're all real, and no man wants fake over real."

"You said you did. And Brax and Gage obviously do."

"I didn't *want* fake. I went for fake because it was easy. Brax's heart is fucked, and Gage…" He shakes his head. "In their own time, they'll come around. They'll find someone real, like you, and it will be a game changer, just like you are for me, but right now, the fake is what's getting them through each day. Not having to think too hard, not having to feel. The fake is how those who can't have the real survive."

His words burrow into my chest and squeeze my heart. I never thought of it like that, but he's right because looking back, what I had with David wasn't real—it was fake. It was how I got by. Only I didn't know it until Camden came back into my life and showed me the real.

I edge down and lay my head on his chest, wrapping my arms around him. "I hope one day Brax and Gage find the real because the fake really sucks."

Twenty

Layla

 CAMDEN YELLS OUT TO THE CROWD OF THOUSANDS OF PEOPLE. OF COURSE, they all scream back like he's a damn god. "Hell yeah! We just got done with a hundred and fifty–show tour, but I have to tell you, there's *nothing* like being home."

The crowd erupts in even louder cheers—if that's even possible—and I make sure to record their reaction. The festival has been going on all day, but not a single band has had the same response as Raging Chaos.

Gage starts drumming the beginning instrumentals to their first song, then Braxton and Declan join in. A few seconds later, Camden starts singing, and the crowd goes crazy.

I move my camera from the guys over to the crowd, zooming in on various fans. One woman is holding up a sign that reads: I <3 you Brax. MARRY ME! Several women are flashing the guys their breasts, and a few are even crying. It's insane. The charity concert I attended was tame because it was for a charity. But out here, anything goes. The smell of weed permeates the air, smoke creating a hazy fog across the area.

I shift my focus back to the guys as they get lost in song after song. Knowing how Camden has felt for me all these years gives every song, every lyric, new meaning. I can tell which songs Braxton and Gage wrote because they're all bitter and angry and filled with rage. But Camden's… they're filled with heart and love mixed with evident sadness.

At some point, Declan's hair falls out of its knot and his long hair curtains his face. Gage's shirt has come off, exposing his tattoos and six-pack abs. Braxton's eye-fucking several of the women in the front row, and Camden's hoodie is coated in sweat, sticking to his muscular torso and showing off the outlines of his shoulders and back.

The fans eat up every minute they're on stage, and I don't blame them because I can't take my eyes off them. This is nothing like watching it on the internet. The electricity, the spark. They're a force to be reckoned with when they're on stage like this and in their element. My gaze goes back to Camden, who's now singing about wanting what he can't have.

> *It should be me, kissing you, touching you, inside you*
> *But instead, it's him, getting you, every fuckin' piece of you*
> *Those pieces should be mine*

My heart swells at the words, at the implication behind them. I wonder if he'll write songs about us now that we're together.

When Camden announces the last song, they boo, and when it ends, they beg for more. Of course, Camden messes with them, asking if they deserve an extra song. They scream the place down, so with a panty-melting wink, he gives in, and the guys give them one last song before saying good night and walking off the stage.

Since they're done, I make my way to the back, handing over my equipment to the sound manager and crew. Then I head to the guys' private room for tonight. A few minutes later, I'm checking my phone when the door swings open, and the guys, along with their security and tour manager, enter.

Gage immediately lights up a joint, Braxton rips his shirt off, and Declan pulls his phone out. Camden's eyes find me, and his entire face lights up. He stalks across the room and pulls me into his arms, not giving a shit that he's covered in sweat or that we're not alone. My legs wrap around his waist at the same time as his mouth crashes against my own. The kiss is filled with heat and intensity. My back hits the wall, and his fingers squeeze my ass. As the kiss deepens, my fingers tug the strands of his hair, and I grind my center against him, needing more.

"Get a fucking room," Declan yells through a laugh.

"Or you can all get the hell out of this one," Camden fires back.

His beautiful green eyes, filled with a mixture of mirth and lust, stare into my own. "I loved having you here, standing only a few feet away, knowing I could kiss you, touch you, be inside you afterward." His confession that his words were about me has me wanting to get him alone and make good on every one of his wants.

"Do you have anything you have to do now?"

"Only you." He smirks.

We leave the crew to handle everything and are on our way back to Camden's house when my phone rings: David.

Since Felix is with him and it's late in New York, I immediately answer it.

"Hello."

"I need you to come over."

Before I can ask why, I hear the sound of my little boy crying in the background. "What happened?" I ask, my heart bottoming out in my stomach. I know that cry. He's hurt. Something is wrong.

"I don't know," David says, his tone dripping with impatience and frustration. "He was asleep and then woke up crying. He won't stop! I need you to come over here."

"I can't," I tell him, closing my eyes in pain. Felix's crying doesn't stop, and the sound has me wanting to reach through the phone and comfort him, but of course, I'm hours away. "I'm…not in New York. You need to ask him what hurts. If it's his stomach or—"

"Where the fuck are you?" David barks.

"It doesn't matter. Just focus on Felix. Ask him what hurts."

"He won't stop crying!"

"Because he's in pain. Is he holding his belly or maybe pulling on his ear?"

"His ear. He's pulling on his ear. Now, where are you?"

"David!" I snap. "Forget about me. I'm not there, and I can't be there right now. You need to give him Tylenol for kids."

"I don't have any."

Of course he doesn't. And I didn't think to pack any. Dammit. "You'll have to go buy some."

"I can't believe you're not here. What did you do? Go away? Our fucking son needs you, and you're not even here."

I know his accusation is super hypocritical since he's never been there for Felix a day in his damn life, but it still hurts knowing I'm not there.

"Look," I say with a sigh, not wanting to fight. "I'm going to get there as soon as I can." My eyes meet Camden's, who nods in understanding. "But it won't be for a few hours. I need you to get him Tylenol to help with the pain. If you can't do that, you need to take him to the ER, so they can. Ear infections hurt really bad. Hence, his crying. He's in a lot of pain."

"Fine."

"Also, make—" Before I can finish my sentence, I realize the crying has stopped in the background because David's hung up on me. I call him back, but he sends me to voicemail. I try again—same thing.

"I can't believe this." I drop my head into my hands, and Camden tucks me into his side.

"We're heading to the airport," he says.

My head pops up. "Right now?"

"I've already told Jill to schedule a pilot. The jet's been on standby, ready to go tomorrow."

"What about the guys and our stuff?"

"They'll grab it for us, and the jet will come back for them."

"That's such a waste, though," I say, feeling guilty.

"The only important thing right now is getting to your son. I have the means to do it, so it's being done." He kisses my temple, and I sink deeper into his side.

During the entire plane ride home, I try to call David, but he refuses to answer, sending me to voicemail or letting the phone ring every single time. Hours later, we land, and there's a car waiting for us. I try to tell Camden we should take separate vehicles so I can go straight to David's, but he insists on going with me.

When we pull up to the building David lives in, I turn toward him. "I appreciate you getting me here so quickly, and I get why you wanted to come with me because you're worried about what he'll do, but I don't think you should come in with me. It'll only rile him up and—"

"I get it," he assures me. "I'll be right here, waiting for you."

"Thank you." I plant a chaste kiss on his lips.

"I need you to do something for me before you go."

"What?"

He pulls his phone out and dials, and a second later, my phone is ringing. "Answer it."

I do as he says, confused, and his face shows up since it's a video call.

"Keep the phone in your pocket, so I can hear, just in case. I'm going to record the call… just in case."

I nod once in understanding. I hope nothing bad happens, but I love that Camden is looking out for me.

After walking up to David's complex, I press the number of his apartment to be buzzed in. Since he's on the first floor, I find his number quickly and knock. A few seconds later, the door opens, and with a look that could kill, David widens the opening, silently telling me to come in. My stomach drops at his cold demeanor, and I'm glad Camden can hear everything going on.

"Where's Felix?" I ask.

I'm glancing around at David's new place since I've yet to see it, so I'm taken aback when he shoves me against the wall, caging me in.

"Where's Felix? What the fuck do you care?" David hisses, slamming his palm against the wall. "I saw the pictures! You were in fucking LA with him! While your son was here, crying in pain, you were off with him!"

"David, you need to lower your voice and back up," I say slowly, trying to calm him down. "It's not what you think." It kind of is, but I'm not about to say that.

"Then what is it?"

"I got a job working for Blackwood as a videographer."

"You mean you got a job working for *him*! You're such a fucking slut. You've probably been fucking all of them for years. Haven't you?"

I knew him finding out I work for Blackwood would piss him off, which was why I hadn't told him yet. But now I'm wishing I would've because somehow, a picture must've leaked, and he found out anyway.

"I'm not having sex with them. I was given an opportunity," I explain calmly. "Now, please, before you do something you're going to regret, back up."

His eyes turn into thin slits, and a second later, his fingers wrap around my throat. The back of my head hits the wall hard, and I yelp out in pain. "The only opportunity that asshole is giving you is to suck his fucking dick!" He slaps me across the face and then squeezes my throat harder, making it difficult to suck in air. I claw at his arms, trying to get him to let go, but he ignores me.

"I would rather watch you take your last breath than to support you fucking that piece of shit." He tightens his hold on me, and my vision turns blurry. I'm scared he's actually going to kill me, and then the door swings open and in walks Camden.

"Get your hands off her!"

The shock of seeing him has David releasing me. "Fuck you!" he barks. "You always wanted my wife, didn't you?" He stalks over to Camden and punches him in the face. Camden stumbles back slightly but quickly gets himself together, refusing to take the bait. David's about to punch him again when Felix screams, "Mommy!" and runs down the hall and into my arms.

Camden glances at Felix, and David uses the moment to sucker punch him again.

"Stop it!" I yell.

"Get the fuck out of my house!" David barks at Camden.

"Mommy, my ear hurts," Felix cries.

"I know, baby. Did Daddy give you medicine?"

He shakes his head.

"Why didn't you give him medicine?"

"You're raising this kid to be a damn brat. He wouldn't stop crying all fucking night."

"Because he's in pain!" I hiss. "What the hell is wrong with you?"

"It was late. I wasn't running out with him in the middle of the night."

"I'm done with you," I say, knowing this conversation is pointless. I never should've left Felix with David. He's a selfish asshole and has no idea how to parent.

"You're not taking my son with that piece of shit!" David booms, trying to block me from leaving.

"Yes, I am. Now move. I need to get my son some medicine. He's got to be in excruciating pain right now."

"You're not—"

"Yes, she is," a masculine voice says. Camden's huge-ass bodyguard, along with two other guys, just as big, step in and surround David. "Go ahead, Layla. Take your boy home."

"Thank you," I say, scurrying out the door with Camden and Felix.

"Are you okay?" I ask Felix once we're in the car and Camden's driver has taken off. "How does your ear feel?"

"It hurts," he says softly. "Daddy yelled at me and wouldn't fix it. I wasn't trying to be a brat." His eyes turn watery, and he looks down in shame.

I glance at Camden for a moment. His jaw is locked, and his fists are clenched in his lap. I want to thank him for stopping David, for not fighting back, for having his security as backup, which I had no idea about, but right now, I need to focus on Felix.

"You are not a brat," I tell him, pulling him into my lap. "You're in pain, and your dad should've given you medicine. I'm so sorry I wasn't here." I hug him tightly. "I'm going to make you feel better." He nods into my neck and then rests his head on my shoulder.

Since it's Sunday, and his doctor's office isn't open, we go straight to the pediatric wing at the hospital. Thankfully, it's not too busy, and they can get us in quickly. Since he's being checked out, they have Felix change into a hospital gown, and then the nurse comes in to take his blood pressure and temperature.

When she lifts the sleeve, I notice a large purple mark on Felix's arm. "How did you get this?" I ask. I didn't notice it before because he was wearing a long-sleeved shirt.

"Daddy got mad at me."

I hear Camden curse under his breath.

"Are you saying Daddy did this to you?" I confirm.

"I was crying, and he got mad."

While the nurse finishes up, I pull my phone out and text Camden: **Can you find a police officer, please? I want to file charges, and I don't want to wait.**

I'm done. I never should've let David get away with raping me. I tried to take the easy way out, the route that wouldn't make waves and put Felix in the middle of a nasty custody battle. Never in a million years did I imagine he would hurt our son, but he has. And now I'm fucking done. I don't care what it takes. He's never taking Felix again. Not as long as I'm alive.

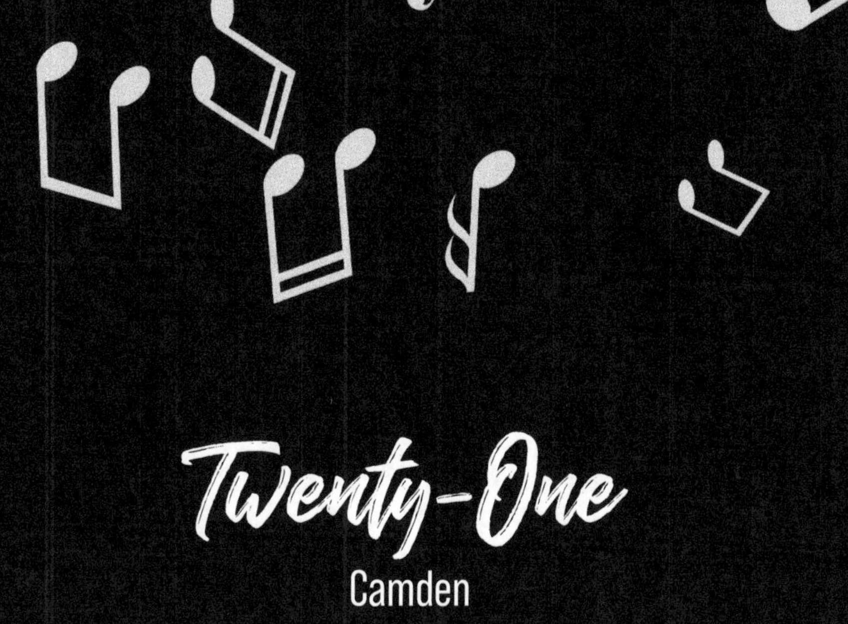

Twenty-One

Camden

Layla: SOS my house

IT'S BEEN YEARS SINCE I'VE GOTTEN AN SOS TEXT FROM LAYLA. I'M SITTING IN MY PARENTS' living room, talking to them about everything that's happened, but the second I see it, I shoot up, telling them I have to go. Since Layla's house is only a couple of blocks away, it doesn't take long to get there. When I do, I find her sitting on her front steps with her head in her hands, her body shaking.

"Hey, what happened?" I ask, sitting next to her. "Where's Felix?"

She looks up, her tear-filled eyes meeting mine. Her face is splotchy, and she has tear stains running down her cheeks. It's only been a few hours since I last saw her, and I already miss the hell out of her.

"He's in bed asleep. The attorney said he can file for emergency custody tomorrow morning, but he doesn't believe I'll get it. He said the judge usually needs more than that to take away a parent's rights. It's going to take time to build a case."

"More than someone leaving bruises on his son's body and his ex-wife's throat?"

"Apparently so," she chokes out. "I don't know what I'm going to do. Something is wrong with him. He's snapped. And I'm so afraid he's going to take it out on Felix. He already has! The bruise on his arm. The way he emotionally fucked with him." She looks over at me with such fear, I want to kill David with my bare hands.

"I can't let him take him," she says softly. "We have joint custody. He gets him every other weekend and every Wednesday. I can't let it happen."

"So what are you going to do?"

"I'm going to run."

"What?" I ask in shock. She can't just leave. Where would she go? What would she do? "You can't do that. You'd be committing a felony, and if he ever found you, he'd get Felix."

"Then I'll make sure he never finds me," she says, conviction stitched into every word. Her phone that's sitting on her lap beeps three times, but she ignores it. "I already fucked up once letting my son go with him. I should've run with him after David raped me. I was scared, and I fucked up, but I won't make that mistake again. I won't leave my son with that man ever again."

"You didn't fuck up. You made the best choice you could in a shitty-ass situation."

Wordlessly, she stands and heads inside her house, and I follow her in, my mind reeling with everything. While she goes about pulling out some luggage from a hall closet, I pull my phone out and text my dad. I don't want to say anything to her because I don't know for sure, but one of his best friends is actually a judge here, and if anyone can help us, it's him. I quickly explain what her attorney said and what she's planning to do since he already knows what happened with Layla and Felix earlier today—I told him when I went over there for dinner, needing to talk to someone about it all.

Dad: Give me a few minutes.

I put my phone away and follow Layla into her bedroom as she pulls clothes out from her drawers. I want to stop her, tell her to think about this, but I don't because I know she feels completely helpless and is in mama bear mode. I've seen my mom in it many times over the years, and there's no arguing with her when she's like that. Based on the determined look in Layla's features, I imagine it's the same for her.

Beep. Beep. Beep.

When her phone sounds again, Layla stops what she's doing and goes to the bathroom. I don't know why I follow her, but I do. It's not like she's going to disappear right this second. She presses a button on a gadget that's sitting on the sink, and a couple of pills drop into her hand.

"What's that?"

"My mom bought it for my birthday," she says. "I have a horrible memory and forget to take my pills, so it's synced with my phone to remind me. It'll keep going off every few minutes until I take them." She fills her cup with water and downs the pills. "It's my birth control and an iron supplement because I'm at risk for anemia."

I press the button, but nothing happens.

"It's not a candy dispenser," she says with a laugh. "It only dispenses when it's supposed to."

"What do you do when you're traveling?"

"You can select the days you're traveling, and it will dispense it ahead of time so you can take them with you. The app will still remind me."

"That's pretty cool. My grandma is always complaining about my grandpa forgetting to take his heart medication. I should buy him one."

My phone vibrates in my pocket, so I pull it out.

Dad: Daniel said to call him. I can't make any promises.

I click on the number he's included and walk out of the room, so Layla won't hear me. After a couple of rings, he answers. "Camden, how are you, son?"

Daniel Maxwell was my family's attorney in LA before he moved to the East Coast and eventually became one of the most powerful judges in New York. I'm not sure how it all works, but from what I've heard over the years, he's really high up there.

"I'm okay. Just… fuck. I'm assuming my dad filled you in?"

"He did. I normally don't do this sort of thing, but I have a soft spot for women in abusive relationships, especially when children are involved. Send me over the police reports filed and all of her information and give me twenty-four hours."

"I CAN'T BELIEVE YOU DID THIS," LAYLA SAYS TO ME, TEARS BRIMMING IN HER EYES. "THANK you!" She wraps her arms around me and hugs me tightly, and I breathe in her comforting scent. "I don't know how I'll ever repay you."

"There's nothing to repay." I tilt her chin up and kiss her supple lips. "I would do anything for you and Felix."

More tears fill her eyes. "Thank you."

I take her hand in mine, and we walk out of the courthouse. Daniel came through big time. Not only was Layla given emergency temporary custody, but David has to attend six months of anger management and therapy, and the only way he can see Felix is with a social worker for supervised visits, one day a week in a public place. The judge will reassess after the six months are up and he's met with a court-appointed psychologist to be reevaluated. He's also not allowed to go within five hundred feet of Layla. And all of that was done in seventy-two hours before David could pick up Felix for his scheduled night.

"I really hope David gets the help he needs," she says as we step outside and walk over to my waiting car. "We never had the perfect relationship, but he wasn't always like this."

I love and hate that she's defending him. The fact that she sees the best in everyone and, despite the shit he's pulled, wants him to get better shows what a good person she is. But it also makes me feel like a shitty person because I'd rather David be given a death sentence for what he's done to her than a second chance.

"I have to get Felix from school and take him to his first dance class, but do you want to come over for dinner afterward?"

"Sounds good to me." I give her a playful wink that has her lighting up. The past few days, while we waited to see how it would all pan out, were stressful for Layla. She wasn't her usual bubbly, carefree self, so it's good to see her smiling again.

"Actually, you should invite your parents too," she adds. "I really want to thank your dad for calling the judge."

"I'll see what they're up to."

"Oh! And I should invite my mom. She's been so worried."

I laugh. "Layles, you realize you have a four-person table, right?"

She pouts adorably.

"How about we go out to dinner? Invite everyone."

She gnaws on her lip for a second. "Should we be celebrating the fact that Felix won't see his dad but once a week for only two hours?"

God, I love this woman. "I wouldn't look at it like we're celebrating the downfall of David, but more of the fact that you've made it through this shitty, dark part of your life. You deserve to feel safe and not have to worry about what he'll do. This outcome doesn't happen often enough for women in your shoes, so it's okay for you to celebrate that you now feel safe once again."

"I hate that," she says. "That this happens to women and children every day, and they don't get the same outcome. If I were rich, I would pay to help every one of them I could."

Her words give me an idea… but I don't mention it out loud.

"So dinner?"

"Yeah, that sounds good."

After telling Layla I'll pick them up later, I go by my parents' place and tell them the outcome and invite them to dinner. Then I head to the hotel to get changed. The guys are there, hanging out and discussing their plans for the night. When I tell them about Layla, they take it as an invite and agree they want to see for themselves that she and Felix are okay.

"Can we discuss finding a place?" Declan asks. "I'm sick of living out of my suitcase. We're finally off tour, and I feel like we're still on the road."

I roll my eyes at his dramatics. We're currently residing in a hotel room that's bigger than most people's homes in New York, but I also get it.

"You guys are still good with living in New York?" If they're not, I'll figure it out, even if it means flying back and forth.

"I assumed this was a permanent decision," Braxton says. "Is there any chance Layla would be willing to move to LA?"

"Willing? Maybe. But can she? No. David still has rights to Felix. She has to be here for him to see Felix every week."

"Then it looks like we'll need to find a place to live." Braxton shrugs. "You still want to live together, or are you thinking about getting your own place since you're now a family man and all?"

I hadn't actually thought about that, but while we're on the subject… "Your shit in LA had Layla asking if I've had threesomes." Braxton barks out a laugh, but I don't join in. "Maybe it would be for the best if I find my own place."

"What?" Declan asks. "We've always lived together. We write together, make music together…"

"That won't change. But Brax isn't wrong. My endgame is Layla and Felix, and I don't want to cramp everyone's style by bringing them around. I guess I could go to her house, but…"

"We get it," Braxton says. "That was her house with her ex. No man wants to fuck a woman in the same bed she was fucking another man."

"I wasn't thinking about that, but now I am. Thanks," I say dryly. Braxton shrugs.

"I'm getting ahead of myself. If Layla and I decide to one day live together, we can discuss the details then. For now, there's no reason we can't get a place together."

"Whatever you want, man," Braxton says. "You know we have your back." Declan and Gage both nod in agreement.

"All right, then it's settled. We need to find a place to live here."

"It'll have to be after we get back, though," Declan points out. "We leave for Florida in two days."

"What?" And then I remember. "Shit, we have the Disney parade. I completely forgot." We were invited by Disney to be part of their yearly Christmas parade. Ride on the float and sing a mix of some of our kid-friendly songs and the few Christmas songs we put out last year. Since it's recorded prior to Christmas, it's taking place this coming weekend.

"You've been a little preoccupied, but yeah, Jill sent us the info this morning."

While the guys are sitting around bullshitting, I call the real estate agent my family uses in New York to let her know what we're looking for. She says she'll get working on it and have places for us to see when we get back from Florida.

As we're hanging up, I get a text from Layla: **Felix is refusing to go to dance class. His dad made him feel like shit about it when he was with him over the weekend, and the other boy who attends the class isn't here, so it's only girls. We'll be home whenever you're ready to pick us up.**

Like hell he's going to give up what he loves because of that asshole.

Me: Text me the address, and I'll be right there. Don't leave yet.

"Hey guys, how would you feel about going to dance class with Felix?"

They all glance up at me with different levels of confusion on their faces. "His dad gave him shit, and now he doesn't want to go."

"Fuck his dad," Gage says, standing. "I'm in."

"Same," Braxton and Declan both agree.

Since we don't know the situation we're heading into, we take security along with us. When we arrive at the studio, Felix and Layla are sitting inside, where the parents sit and watch.

"Hey, heard someone is starting dance classes today," I say, stepping in front of them.

Felix looks up, shocked to see me here. "I don't know," he says with a frown marring his features. "My dad said boys don't—"

"Your dad is wrong," Gage cuts in, making his presence known. Felix glances over and sees Gage, Braxton, and Declan all standing in front of him. "There's nothing wrong with a man dancing, and this class looks fun as hell. So if you don't want to go, fine. But we're going."

Layla's eyes go wide.

"You guys are going to dance class?" Felix asks.

"Yep, you coming or what?" Braxton asks, extending his fist.

Felix pops off the chair and fist-bumps him. "Yeah, I'm coming."

When the five of us walk into the studio, we garner the attention of everyone, including the instructor, who eyes us curiously. "Are you in a band?" she asks.

"Yep. Raging Chaos," I tell her. "My friend Felix here is new, and since he's the only boy, he asked us to join. Would you mind?"

She smiles softly. "Not at all. Welcome to beginners hip-hop dance."

"HOLY SHIT," DECLAN SAYS, WIPING THE BEADS OF SWEAT FROM HIS FOREHEAD WITH A paper towel. "That was a damn workout."

"Yeah, it was," Gage agrees, still panting like he just ran cross-country.

"I had no idea dancing could use so many damn muscles," Braxton adds, flinching in pain.

"That was so much fun!" Felix says, completely unaffected. "Can we do it again?"

Layla laughs. "Yes, next week."

Since we came in separate vehicles, Layla and Felix head home, and the guys and I go back to our place so we can shower and get ready. When five o'clock rolls around, I head back out to pick them up. We're meeting everyone at Maya's, a Mexican restaurant Layla said Felix loves. I offered to pick up her mom as well, but she said she's riding with my parents.

It's nice going out to dinner in New York. Almost no security is needed. We get a private room since there's a shit ton of us, but it's not like in LA, where you need one so people will leave you alone.

It's a different vibe here, and I can see why my dad moved here years ago, leaving LA for good.

"Where are we all sitting?" Mom asks as the guys walk in.

"Oh, shit," Layla mutters.

"What?" I ask, confused.

"I didn't know they were coming to dinner. I didn't even—" Before she can finish what she's saying, Kaylee strolls through the door, running straight into Braxton.

"Oh, shit," I mimic.

"Oh," Kaylee gasps, her eyes going wide. Everyone turns to face them, no doubt holding their breath and waiting to see what'll happen. They haven't been in the same room in years, not since everything went down.

Kaylee's eyes meet Layla's, and Layla cuts across the room. "I didn't know. I'm sorry."

"It's okay. I can go," Kaylee says.

"Or you can stay," Layla offers.

"I can go," Braxton jumps in, refusing to look at Kaylee.

"Or you both can stay," Layla says.

"No, seriously, I can go," Kaylee insists. "I actually need to get home and pack."

"Where are you going?" Layla asks in shock.

"LA."

"What?" Layla shrieks. "Why?"

"The PR company that hired me has me going on tour with Sam York as his publicist." Sam York is a huge musician, sings mostly pop, and he's also a huge asshole with an even bigger ego.

Braxton snorts. "Of course they did."

Kaylee glares at Braxton, but as if remembering she's the reason for his bitterness, her features quickly soften, and she doesn't respond. "Anyway, I have like two days to pack, but I wanted to tell you in person and hug you." She wraps her arms around Layla, who sniffles in response.

"I'm going to miss you so much."

"I'll only be gone for a few months, and then I'll be back."

"You're going to be amazing!" Layla hugs her again.

"Thank you."

After Kaylee gives Felix and Layla's mom a quick hug, she takes off, and everyone finds their seats, none of us mentioning the huge elephant that still seems to be in the room, despite Kaylee leaving. Braxton is quiet for the entire dinner, drinking way too many beers, but everyone else is in good spirits. Layla thanks my dad several times for calling Daniel while he brushes it off like it wasn't a big deal.

"When do you guys leave?" Mom asks while we're eating dessert.

"Friday morning," Declan answers. "I've got my Mickey Mouse ears ready."

Mom snickers.

"Where are you going?" Layla asks me.

"*We're* going to Disney."

She frowns. "We? I can't...Oh, the parade. I forgot about that. I can't go. I actually need to talk to your parents about working for Blackwood."

"What? Why?"

"With David's visitation going down to two hours a week, that leaves me as Felix's only parent."

"And? Single parents work..."

"Yes, but I can't travel. Not without leaving him with my mom, and it's not fair to her to have to watch him all the time."

"*She* would love to watch him any time," Patricia cuts in, raising a single brow.

"And I was actually thinking we could take Felix with us to

Disney," I add.

"Disney?" Felix screeches, overhearing. Shit, I thought I was talking low. Note to self: kids have bionic hearing. "I want to go!"

"I would be working," Layla points out.

"And when you're not, we have passes to all the parks."

"I can keep him with me," Bailey offers. "He can watch the parade with me."

"Perfect," I say before Layla can argue.

"And in the future," my mom says, "if Patricia can't keep Felix, he's always welcome at our house. Between Easton and Bailey and me…"

"And me," Phoebe, my younger sister, says.

"You have an entire room of support," I tell Layla, draping my arm around the back of her chair. "We got this."

Twenty-Two

Layla

"MY GOD, WOMAN, YOU'RE A WALKING, BREATHING TEMPTATION." CAMDEN EDGES ONTO THE bed, circling his arms around me and pulling me into his front. "I've been waiting all damn day to be able to touch you." His hand skates down my hip and goes between my legs, spreading my thighs.

We've been in Orlando for three days, and this is the first time we've been alone. The last fifty-plus hours have been a whirlwind of activity. Between the Disney parade on Friday and spending the last two days exploring four parks with a four-year-old who's never been to Disney—along with four grown-ass men who you'd think were four-year-olds—it's been nonstop. Friday night, the guys had a couple of radio interviews to do and got back late, then last night, we got back late from the parks because everyone wanted to watch the fireworks. Felix was tired and cranky from overstimulation and ended up falling asleep in my bed with me both nights. Tonight, though, he's in his own bed, and Camden has apparently snuck into mine.

"Does it bother you that you can't touch me all day because of

Felix?" I ask, my insecurities of being a mom sneaking up on me.

"What? No." He turns me over to face him. "Your kid is fucking awesome, Layles. A mini you. I feel like I've gotten to experience my childhood all over again through him."

"Through him, huh?" I laugh. "I'm pretty sure you and the guys have experienced it through yourselves."

He grins, not arguing. "What I'd really like to do right now is experience *you*." He waggles his brows and cups my ass cheeks, pulling me close. His mouth seals over mine, and I groan in need. We've taken up an entire floor at the Disney resort we're staying in, each room having multiple bedrooms. Camden insisted Felix and I have our own room, not wanting to rush him seeing anything between us, for which I appreciate. Felix is going through a lot, and I love that Camden is aware and patient. But right now, I really want to experience him as well.

I turn over onto my back, and Camden climbs over me, deepening the kiss. His tongue delves past my parted lips, and his knees separate my legs, giving him access to my center.

"Fuck, you taste good," he murmurs against my mouth before moving to my ear. "I need to be inside you now." Our clothes come off, and once we're both naked, he dips his fingers into me to make sure I'm wet and ready—spoiler alert: I am.

Getting up on his haunches, he spreads my thighs wider, his thumb finding the spot that will bring me pleasure. He massages it with slow strokes while his other hand palms my breast, pinching my nipple.

When I moan in pleasure, he stops what he's doing. "I need a picture," he says, grabbing my camera from the nightstand and turning it on me. The camera clicks on, and he takes several pictures of me. "Do you have any idea how sexy you look like this? Your hair splayed out across your pillow, your cheeks flush. Your nipples hard and begging to be touched." He reaches out with the hand not holding the camera and pinches one. "I'm the luckiest guy in the fucking world." His words are like liquid heat straight to my core. I've never had a guy look at me like Camden does, like I'm everything he could ever want or need.

He sets the camera back down and then continues to stroke my clit and play with my breasts until I'm screaming out his name in pure ecstasy as my orgasm rips through me, sending shock waves through my body.

"Fuck, I love when you scream my name," he murmurs. Gripping the backs of my thighs, he enters me, his thick, hard length filling me to the hilt. His palms land on either side of my head, and his mouth crashes down on mine in a bruising kiss as he pulls back and thrusts roughly into me.

When I gasp into his mouth, he stills in place, removing his mouth from mine. "I'm sorry, shit. I didn't mean to be that rough. I wasn't thinking."

He's about to pull out, but before he can, I wrap my legs around him, holding him to me.

"Stop. You're good," I tell him. "I won't break."

He nods once, but he's obviously not convinced because instead of continuing the way he was, he's now slowed down.

"Cam, please," I beg, palming his face so he looks at me. He shakes his head, and I sigh, hating that he's holding back. Not wanting to ruin the moment, though, I let it go.

His mouth closes over mine, and he makes love to me slow and sweet. My climax builds higher and higher, and only once I've found my release does he let go, spilling himself into me.

"I can't get enough of you," he says, dropping kisses onto my lips, chin, neck… "Every time I look at you, I can't believe I finally get you all to myself, all the time."

"Well, not all the time," I joke. "Tomorrow morning, we have to go home to separate places."

"For now," he murmurs, locking his mouth with mine before I can ask what he means by that. Our kiss quickly turns heated, which results in us doing it all over again, leaving me sated and boneless and so damn happy.

"CAN WE GET A BIG TREE LIKE AT DISNEY?" FELIX ASKS, STRETCHING HIS HANDS OUT AS FAR as they can go.

"We can get a tree that fits in our living room."

He pouts. "We need a bigger living room."

Declan laughs from his seat on the plane. "Yeah, Layla, next time, make sure the living room fits a Disney-sized Christmas tree."

"We're looking at places," Braxton adds. "We'll make sure the living room is big enough, then you can have two trees."

"Yes!" Felix whoops. "Can we put a million candy canes on it?"

"Of course, little dude," Declan says.

From the second the guys met Felix, they've taken on the role of pseudo uncles. Anything he wants, they give him, and Felix has quickly caught on. I've had to stop them from being had by my four-year-old on several occasions.

"We'll see," I cut in, giving them a side-eye that they ignore. "I didn't know you were looking for a place," I say to Camden.

"Can't live in a hotel forever." He shrugs.

"So you're going to be living here?"

"Where else would I be?" he asks, giving me a confused look.

"I don't know… LA."

He quirks a brow. "Are you moving there?"

"You know I can't," I mutter. While the court didn't mandate me to live in New York, I have to be available every Wednesday evening for David to meet with Felix so they can have dinner together.

"Then this is where we'll be living," Camden says like it's a done deal.

"And the guys are okay with it?"

"Yep, it's home. We still have our house over there for when we need to be there, but we can do everything we need to do here."

"Can we get a tree when we get home?" Felix asks. "It's almost Christmas. They're all going to be gone."

"We'll see," I say.

"That means no." He pouts, making the guys laugh.

"No, it doesn't," I argue.

"You always say it when you mean no." He crosses his arms over his chest and sinks into his seat, his sad face deepening.

"Well, if you act like that, it *will* be a no."

With a huff, he pulls out his iPad and sticks his earbuds in to watch something. Within minutes, his eyes close.

"Thank you for this weekend." I lean in and kiss the crook of Camden's neck. He smells like the comfort of home, and I wish I could bottle it up and keep it with me for when he's not around.

"You don't have to thank me." He tilts my face and kisses me on the lips. "Since Felix is off school today and we'll be home in the early afternoon, why don't we take the SUV and get you guys a tree?"

My heart skips a beat. "That would be amazing. Thank—"

"No thanking me," he says, silencing me with a kiss.

When we get home, the guys go back to the hotel while Camden joins Felix and me. Felix doesn't know we're stopping to get a tree, so when we pull up to the tree lot, he squeals in excitement.

"Can I get one for my room too?" he asks, eyeing the small trees that are only like two feet tall.

"Let's focus on getting the one for the living room first."

"Fine." He runs through the trees, stopping at each one and explaining why it's the best tree. When we finally decide on one—and Camden sneaks in the mini tree—the lot guys load it up so we can take it home. Since it needs a few days to drop before we can decorate it, we order in and put a movie on to watch after Camden sets it up.

Felix is out halfway through the movie, and Camden and I spend the remainder of the movie cuddling and flirting. I want to invite him to spend the night, but I also know we need to take things slow when it comes to that, for Felix's sake.

"We're going to be working on a couple of songs tomorrow in the studio," Camden says when I walk him out. "Can you come by?"

"Of course." I give him a chaste kiss. "Text me when you get home."

About twenty minutes later, my phone dings. When I open it, I expect to find a text from Camden, but instead, it's from unknown. There's a picture of Camden, Felix, and me bringing in the Christmas tree. Only the picture has been marked up with a huge red X over Camden.

Only one person would send something like this, so instead of responding, I save the picture and block the text. I'll show it to Camden tomorrow to see if we should report it so it's documented. At the courthouse, David was glaring daggers at me but was smart enough to keep his mouth shut. I knew he wouldn't stay quiet for long.

I'm about to click out of my messages when it dings again... another picture. Only this one has me smiling as I take in a bare-chested, smirking Camden. **One day, instead of sending you pics of me in bed, you'll be next to me. Sweet dreams, Shutterbug.**

And with the image of him in my head, I fall asleep, pushing the thought of David from my mind—even if deep down my gut tells me this isn't close to being over.

She's like taking a hit of the strongest drug
She enters my veins, there to stay
I'm addicted, can't stay away

I STAND IN THE CORNER OF THE STUDIO, MY CAMERA IN MY HAND, FROZEN IN PLACE, AS I listen to Camden belt the words to a new song in the sound room. He told me he wrote a new song, but he didn't mention it was about me. And as I watch, with Camden's eyes locked on mine, heat radiating off his every word, the apex of my legs throbs in want, in need. If we were alone, I would be on him, begging him to be in me.

Earl—their producer who has flown to New York to work with them on recording their next album—presses a button and says, "Fuck yeah, that's what I'm talking about," but Camden isn't looking at him or really paying him any attention because he's zoned in on me, eye-fucking me. Liquid desire pools between my legs, and my blood boils like I'm on fire. My heart thrums in my chest.

"You wrote that about me," I breathe when he stalks over and pulls me into his arms.

"Damn near everything I do is about you," Camden murmurs, capturing my lower lip between his teeth. "Do you like it… the song?" He swipes his tongue along the seam of my mouth, sending a bolt of electricity straight to my core.

"I love it." I run my fingers through his hair and brush my lips against his. "And… I love you."

His eyes go wide at my confession. I didn't plan to say those words, but I one-hundred-percent mean them.

"Need ten," Camden chokes out, lifting me into his arms. My legs wrap around his torso, and his strong, supple lips collide with my own. I faintly hear one of the guys laughing, and I think Braxton makes a joke about being a minute-man, but I'm too caught up in Camden to really know.

The second we're alone, our clothes come flying off, both of us with one goal in mind: Camden inside me. Once we're both naked, he pushes me against the wall and devours my mouth. His hands go to my breasts, caressing them. Mine go to his dick, stroking it.

But that's not enough. I need more.

Without thought, I drop to my knees, ready to take him in my mouth, but before I can, he steps back.

"What's wrong?" I ask, glancing up at him.

"We should wait… until we're at your place… or mine."

"What?" I reach for him, but he shakes his head and pulls me up.

"We only have a few more hours. Afterward, we can go to your place before you have to pick up Felix."

I'm so confused. We were just ripping each other's clothes off, and now he's practically pushing me away.

And then it hits me… Every time we've had sex, it's been with him on top, or the one time in the shower, he let me ride him. He never lets me go down on him, and he never takes me from behind… because I told him what David did to me.

"Is it because you don't want me the way David had me or because you're afraid I'll freak out?"

His eyes widen slightly before they go soft. "I want to make sure you're comfortable. I don't want anything we do to trigger what he did… like the day on the helicopter."

I close the distance between us and, with one hand, cup his face. The other, I palm his now semi-soft length. "I can't promise anything we do won't trigger what he did. I don't know how it all works in my head, but I don't want what he did to affect us. I want to taste you, feel you, *love you*. I want you to fuck me every way possible. I want every bad memory with him to be erased and replaced with amazing memories with you. I want to be in the here and now with you. We already missed so much time. I just want to be with you."

"Fuck, I love you so damn much," Camden says before his mouth crashes down on mine. We kiss passionately for several minutes as I stroke his dick, getting it hard again. Then breaking the kiss, I drop back down onto my knees and take him into my mouth.

"Holy shit," he groans, his palm slapping the wall behind me as I go as deep as I can, licking and sucking on his velvety smooth flesh. His other hand goes to my hair, but instead of pulling it, he runs his fingers gently through it.

I have to admit, I was a little worried about how I would feel being in this position, but as I glance up at Camden, my mouth wrapped around his cock, and our eyes meet, I know I have nothing to be worried about because no matter what we're doing, Camden makes sure I'm comfortable.

"C'mere, baby," he says, pulling me up. My mouth pops off the head, and I pout because I didn't get to finish.

Camden chuckles. "I love your mouth on me, but I really want to be inside you." His lips capture my own, and he lifts me into his arms, pushing me against the wall. My legs wrap around his hips, and he enters me in one fluid motion. With his mouth never leaving mine, he works me over, hitting my clit in the most delicious way. That, combined with the way he's thrusting into me, hard and deep, sends me over the edge, taking Camden with me.

"Jesus," I mutter breathlessly, breaking our kiss and setting my forehead against his. "Every time I'm with you, I just want more and more."

"Well, that's good," he murmurs. "Because my hope is that you'll want me for the rest of our lives."

My eyes dart up, my head backing up slightly to meet his. "What… What do…?" I can't even finish my thoughts, my question. "The rest of our lives?" I finally say, swallowing the lump of emotion.

"That's my hope," he says, pressing his lips to mine. "Don't worry, Layles. I'm not proposing… yet. But yes, I want you forever."

His confession should scare me since I just got out of a crappy situation, but it doesn't. Instead, it feels as though the looming darkness has cracked open, exposing the most beautiful, bright light over us.

"Forever." I find myself smiling at the thought of spending every day for the rest of my life with Camden. "That sounds really freaking nice."

Twenty-Three

Layla

Camden: You, me, date tonight. Wear a dress.

Camden: And before you try to argue, your mom is keeping Felix overnight and taking him to school in the morning. She offered.

Me: Sounds good.

"WHAT HAS YOU SMILING?" BAILEY ASKS, TAKING A BITE OF HER SALAD. WE'VE BEEN working on the YouTube channel all day, so she ordered in lunch so we could eat and work.

"Your brother." I grin when she playfully scrunches her nose up in disgust. "He's apparently taking me on a date tonight."

"Nice. Where are you going?"

"I don't know." I shrug. "But Felix is staying with my mom overnight." I waggle my brows, and Bailey fake gags.

"You guys are so sweet, it makes me sick."

"Like you and Cynthia aren't sweet?"

"Not like that. She's chill."

"Whatever." I roll my eyes. "I need to pick up something to wear and new lingerie. Want to join me?"

"Sure." She tosses her empty salad bowl into the trash. "I'm always down to shop."

While we're at the store, Camden texts to let me know he'll pick me up at my mom's since I have to drop Felix off there.

I end up getting ready at my mom's—going with a long-sleeved olive-green sweater dress with the front cut low and buttons running down the sides, paired with high heeled boots. It's recently snowed, and while I want to look good, I don't want to die. My hair is down in long waves, and my makeup is on point. Underneath, I'm wearing a new bra and panty set that is going to have Camden drooling when he sees them on me later.

"You look gorgeous," Camden says, stepping around the corner and startling me. I hadn't realized he was already here. He's dressed in a pair of dark denim jeans and a long-sleeved beige sweater with brown leather boots. His hair is gelled back, taming his usual messy do, and his facial hair is trimmed short. My thighs clench, imagining what his face will feel like between my legs later.

"Hey, bud, doesn't your mom look beautiful?"

"Yeah," Felix agrees, nodding.

"But I think she's missing something. What do you think, Felix?"

"Yeah." He giggles. "She's missing something."

"I am?" I glance down. "My jacket's by the door…"

When I look up, Felix holds a black box wrapped with gold ribbon and a large shiny bow on top. "For you, Mommy. I helped Cam pick it out."

I take it from him and unwrap and open the box, and nestled inside is a thin white-gold necklace with two charms hanging from it. The first is a camera charm—inside the lens is a beautiful sparkling diamond—and the other is a circle charm with a quote on it that reads: *She believed she could, so she did.*

"You guys," I breathe, looking up at Camden and Felix. "You got this for me?" I ask Felix, who nods proudly.

"I told Cam your favorite thing is a camera."

"Thank you, sweetheart." I pull him into a hug and kiss his cheek. "I love it."

I stand, and Camden takes the necklace from me. Lifting my hair, he puts it on me, then leans in and whispers, "So you always remember what your dream is."

"Thank you." I turn around and kiss him on the corner of his mouth. "This is the most thoughtful gift I've ever been given."

After saying bye to my mom and reminding Felix to behave, we take off to dinner in the SUV with Camden's driver driving us. On the way there, Camden and I can't keep our hands off of each other. By the time we arrive at the restaurant, the only thing I'm hungry for is Camden, but apparently, he has a hell of a lot more restraint than me because when I mention that, he simply chuckles and tells me he's taking me to dinner.

We're escorted into the restaurant by his security and brought back to a private room, where there's a comfy-looking circular booth with a round metal grill-looking thing in the center. Camden helps me remove my coat, then hands mine and his to the hostess, thanking her.

He has me slide in first, and then he slides in next to me, his hand coming down on my thigh. Pushing my dress up, he glides his hand over my flesh while the server introduces herself and explains that this is Korean barbecue and we'll be cooking the food ourselves. I've never done this before, but Camden says he's had it a few times while they were on tour, so he orders for us both. The server lights the grill and then lets us know the food will be ready shortly. After she drops off our drinks, we're left alone.

"Thank you for my necklace," I say again, needing him to know how much the simple gift means to me.

"It looks perfect on you," he says, leaning over and kissing the crook of my neck. When he trails his nose along my flesh, I squirm in my seat.

"You can't do that." I groan. "I want you so badly, and you're making us eat instead."

When I pout half-playfully, Camden chuckles. "We have all night together, Shutterbug. I got us a room, and I plan to spend as much of the night as I can inside you."

The server drops off our food, explains each item, and then leaves us to ourselves.

"You're going to love this," Camden says, dropping a bunch of meat and veggies onto the grill. I watch as he cooks them, and once they're done, he captures a piece of meat between his chopsticks and brings it to my lips. The meat has a sweet taste to it and is full of flavor.

"What do you think?" he asks, taking a bite himself.

"Delicious."

The meal is spent with Camden feeding me, and once we've both had enough, he gets the check so we can move on to the next part of our evening.

Of course, the room he's booked is the penthouse suite, so we have the floor to ourselves. After he lets his security know we're good for the night, we head up to the room. Champagne and strawberries are waiting for us, and when I ask what the occasion is, he says, "There isn't one." He pops the top of the bottle and pours us each a glass. "My goal in life is to spoil you and Felix. To show you both every chance I get how special you are to me."

"If that's your goal, then you've already accomplished it," I tell him, taking a sip of my champagne.

"No, I haven't. I've only just gotten started." He sets our glasses down and encircles his arms around my waist. His mouth connects with mine, and the champagne and strawberries are forgotten as we get lost in each other.

When he unzips my dress, and I shrug out of it, letting it drop to the ground, Camden takes a step back, noticing my cream-color floral lace bra and panties complete with garters.

"Is this new?" he asks, licking his lips, his eyes locked on my body.

"Bought it today, just for you."

"Fuck yes," he growls, lifting and carrying me to the bed. He hovers above me, kissing along the seam of the delicate material. "Where did you buy these at?"

I quirk a brow. "Umm… why?"

"So I can buy you more because I'm about to rip these right off your fucking body."

Before I can protest, his mouth captures mine, the kiss so consuming that my mind goes blank. My only thought is that I don't care how Camden gets my lingerie off as long as he gets it off quick and gets inside me.

Twenty-Four

Camden

"WHAT IF HE'S MEAN TO FELIX?" LAYLA GNAWS ON HER LIP AS WE WATCH BEATRICE, THE court-appointed social worker, walk with Felix to her vehicle. Since David can't be near Layla, the social worker will be picking him up from the house and driving him to meet with David every Wednesday. He's allowed two hours with him at a restaurant or park… somewhere public, and then she'll drive Felix back home.

"The social worker will be with him the entire time," I assure her, massaging her shoulders to try to calm her down. Once they've driven off, she sighs and walks inside.

I imagine this will be the longest three hours of her life, so when we're inside, I order us dinner and ask her to show me some of the video footage she's gotten so far, knowing when she's discussing videography, she's in her element and will be thoroughly distracted.

We spend the entire time Felix is gone looking over the footage— and I have to say, I'm impressed. I knew she had raw talent, but her vision for the channel and music video already goes beyond my expectations. As we're discussing our upcoming schedule and some of the shots she'd like to get, the door swings open, and Felix runs inside, his smile bright and excited.

"Daddy got me the best present ever!" he yells. "A PlayStation!"

"Wow," Layla says, sighing in relief that it seemed to go okay. "Where is it?"

"At his house. He said I get it when I go over there."

Beatrice walks in just in time to hear what he says and frowns.

"When can I go to Dad's?" Felix asks, his eyes begging.

"I'm not sure," Layla says, glancing at Beatrice.

"Hey, little man. Why don't we go play in your room? You can show me your Nintendo Switch."

"Okay." He shrugs, easily distracted.

We hang out upstairs, playing a few different games until Layla joins us. She's quiet, not wanting to say anything in front of Felix. I know she's worried, though, because she gnaws on her lip constantly, and I get it. It's clear what David is doing. Felix is young and has a short memory. He's replacing the bad moments with the possibility of good ones while buying his trust. It's a shitty thing to do, and it doesn't surprise me that he's stooped to that level.

"Beatrice said she can't do anything about what David said," Layla says once Felix is asleep and we're on the couch, just the two of us. "He can tell him anything he wants as long as it isn't harmful. Saying he bought him something and that he'll get it once he can go over to his house isn't technically a lie. But she did say she'd add it to her report in case it's relevant later." She releases a harsh breath. "It just sucks because I know what he's doing, and there's nothing I can do about it. I feel so helpless."

"You're not helpless," I tell her, encircling my arms around her. "You're doing the best you can in a shitty situation. Many women in your shoes wouldn't have left him, filed for divorce, and then pressed charges. Every day, too many women stay in an abusive relationship out of fear of what will happen, scared for their kids. You're strong, and you have a good support system. All you can do is take it one day, one week at a time."

She nods against my chest, and I kiss the top of her head. "I was thinking about something you said before."

She looks up at me. "What is that?"

"About how many women have been hurt by their husbands, and more times than not, nothing happens to them. Every year, the guys and I donate to various charities, but I was thinking, what if we start one of our own instead of donating this year? One that focuses on helping women who have been in your situation but don't have the resources you have to get the help they need."

She sits up, her eyes locking with mine. "Are you serious? That would be amazing. You should've seen the horrible things I read when I was researching how many women every day are raped and abused by their husbands, and nothing happens."

"I was thinking you could be the spokesperson for it. Work with the organizer. We could host an annual charity benefit to raise money on top of what we donate."

Tears prick her eyes, and even though I know they're because she's happy, I still hate to see them. "I would love to," she says, wrapping her arms around me for a hug. "Thank you."

When she pulls back, she wipes her eyes and glances around the room.

"I'm thinking about moving," she says, shocking the hell out of me.

"Really?"

"Yeah, this place feels tainted." She means this is where David raped her, and it's hard to be here while trying to move on. "I think I'm going to look at some places. A fresh start of sorts."

She yawns and lays her head back on my chest, snuggling into my side. We stay like this for several minutes until I feel her breathing slow, telling me she's fallen asleep. Careful not to wake her, I carry her to her bed, then after checking on Felix, I head out. I'm almost to the door when Layla's phone vibrates on the coffee table. It lights up briefly, and the picture on the screen has me curious.

I tap on the screen to make it light up again and find a picture of us standing on the front steps of Layla's house as Felix leaves. There's a red X over me with an accompanying text: **He doesn't belong, and soon, he'll be removed.**

It's from a random email sent through iMessage, but it's obvious who it is. I look to see if there are any more and find one other from a blocked number. He must've switched to email, so he could make up as many as needed to threaten her… or, I guess, me. I forward both to myself and then send them to Daniel, asking his opinion on the matter. I block the email and bring her phone over to her, so she has it, then head out, setting the alarm and locking up behind me.

As I get into my SUV, I glance back at her place and wonder if maybe Layla would consider moving in with me. We've only been together for a short time, but I'm not about to let some ridiculous societal norm dictate how our relationship flows. I hate having to leave her every night and want the two of them under the same roof as me.

"HOW LONG DID IT TAKE BEFORE YOU AND MOM MOVED IN TOGETHER?"

My dad glances at me, a knowing smirk quirking at the corner of his mouth as he takes a sip of his morning coffee from across the table. "A few months. She was pregnant, and I had bought a place to be near her and Kendall, and you, once you were born. She needed to find a place to live, so I forced her to move in with me." He grins, clearly proud of himself. "Planning to ask Layla to move in with you?"

"Thinking about it." I take a bite of my eggs that Mom made this morning when I showed up. "I need to find a place to live. I was supposed to move with the guys, but she mentioned finding a new place and…" I shrug. "I hate being away from her."

Dad laughs. "I get it. I'm the same way with your mom."

"You going into the studio today?"

"Tomorrow. I have a meeting I need to attend today. Earl said you already have half the tracks recorded. He thinks it might be your best album to date."

I smile at that. Every song, every instrumental, is written by us. From the beginning, we've said we would never sing someone else's words. Our music bleeds through our veins, and every piece of it comes directly from us.

"Although," Dad adds, "he did mention you're getting kind of soft."

I shake my head but can't deny it. "He's not wrong," I admit. "I can't help it. I'm in love."

Mom walks in, her eyes twinkling, having heard what I just said. "And it looks good on you," she says, kissing my cheek and sitting down.

"Gage and Brax have a few tracks they're working on. I'm sure their bitterness and hostility will even my happiness out."

Dad chuckles. "I'm sure it will. I can't wait to hear it all. Jill is planning out your next tour. The goal is to release this album after the holidays and do a summer tour."

The thought of leaving Layla has my stomach knotting, and my dad can obviously sense it because he adds, "We're thinking a shorter tour this year. Two months and only in the US. Felix will be out of school in June, so he and Layla can join you in a few cities."

I nod at that, thankful as hell to have a manager—and a dad—who has my back. Two months might seem like a long time, but our last tour was just over four months long. And as much as I don't want to leave Layla, it's not fair to the guys. They've busted their ass right alongside me every day to make us what we are.

"We're going to be leaving for Big Bear the day after Christmas and spending New Year's there," Mom says. "Patricia is going. You should ask Layla if she and Felix would like to join. Invite the guys. Kendall was supposed to come home for Christmas, but she's met a guy…" She rolls her eyes playfully, used to my sister flitting from one man to another. "She's going to meet us there."

Big Bear Mountain has been a family tradition since my parents first got together. My dad took my mom and Kendall there when Kendall was little, and we have gone every year since. Eventually, they purchased their own cabin that's damn near big enough to fit everyone.

"I'll talk to Layla about it. I'd bet Felix would have a blast on the slopes."

After we finish up breakfast, I meet with the guys and discuss getting my own place with the hope of Layla and Felix joining me. Just as I suspected, they're cool with it.

"Dad mentioned Jill's scheduling our next tour."

Braxton nods. "Figured as much since we're about to put out a new album."

"You going to be okay with leaving Layla?" Declan asks.

"Yeah, I have to be. This is our life."

"True," Declan agrees. "Unless you're thinking maybe this isn't the life for you anymore," he adds, no malice or accusation in his tone.

"This is the life I want. Do I want Layla as well? Yeah, but I can have both. My grandparents and my parents both did. Dad said the tour would be two months instead of the usual four. Would that be okay?" The longer the tour, the more cities we stop in, and the more money we make. Not that we're hurting for cash, but I don't want to be the reason the guys make less.

"Sounds good to me," Declan says.

I glance at Braxton and Gage, who both nod.

"I can't stand being on the road for too long anyway," Braxton says. "Two months sounds good."

We bullshit for a little while, and then I take off to meet with the real estate agent and go over several places. I consider asking Layla first but decide it would be better if I asked her once I found a place. What I can afford and what she can afford are in two different brackets. I don't want her to see the prices. I just want her to see the place I find and hopefully agree to make a home with me.

It takes several hours and virtual tours, but I find it. The home I can see us in. The real estate agent makes a couple of calls, and I get the approval to see it in person this afternoon.

Me: Can your mom watch Felix after school? I need to show you something.

Layla: I can ask.

A few minutes later, she texts back that we're good to go, and I tell her I'll meet her at her mom's.

"Where are we going?" she asks as we walk down the street, our gloved hands threaded together. "It's kind of freaking cold out, you know."

"You'll see. It's not that much farther." We walk a couple more blocks, and once we get to the address the real estate agent gave me, we stop.

Layla glances at me in confusion. "Are we lost? It's going to snow soon." She scrunches her nose up like she always does when she doesn't like something. Layla has never loved the cold or the snow. If it weren't for her having to live near her ex or the fact that I know she loves being close to her mom, I could convince her without any effort to move to the West Coast.

"We're here," I tell her, guiding her up to the gate. It's one of the few homes on the street with an actual wrought-iron gate in the front yard that can be locked. I type in the code the real estate agent gave me and unlock it. The driveway isn't big, but there's a garage on the ground floor with two staircases ascending from each side and meeting in the middle where the front door is. We take the stairs on the left, and once we're at the door, I unlock and open it, exposing the open space.

"Whose house is this?" she asks, stepping inside.

I ignore her question and instead take her through the house. It's four stories, including the garage, with five bedrooms and four bathrooms. A living room and family room, a gym, and an office. There's also a room next to the garage that could easily be turned into a studio.

"This place is gorgeous," Layla says when we get back down to the living room. "Are you thinking about moving here?"

She has her back to me, so I don't answer. That way, she'll turn around. While I wait, I drop onto one knee and pull out the ring I purchased. Bailey thinks I should've taken one step at a time— either propose or ask her to move in—but here's the thing: I want it all. Every-fucking-thing. And I want it with her.

The second she turns around and sees where I am and what I'm holding, she gasps, her hands going to her mouth. "Camden... what are you doing?"

"Hopefully, I'm moving in here with you... as my fiancée. I mean, if you don't like this place, we can find somewhere else—"

Before I can finish my speech, she runs toward me, wraps her arms around my neck, and pulls me up, yelling, "Yes," over and over again. "I want to marry you and live here with you. Yes!"

I kiss her and then take her hand in mine, so I can slide the engagement ring onto her finger.

"I love it," she says, admiring the ring with happy eyes. "And I love you."

Twenty- Five

Layla

Santa.

"Maybe," I say noncommittally.

"What about the bike?" he asks, placing two carrots on the plate for the reindeer.

"I'm not sure," I say this time.

"What about the Legos? Do you think I'll get them?" Felix asks. "I think I've been good this year."

"You'll have to wait until Santa comes to find out," I tell him, ruffling his hair.

It's Christmas Eve, and we've just gotten back from Camden's parents' house, where we had dinner and watched *The Grinch*, a tradition that's been part of their family for several generations. Camden brought us home and is here for the Christmas story— at Felix's request—but will leave afterward, coming back in the morning for presents. We've decided to wait and not sleep under the same roof with Felix until we're married and move into the new house. It seems a bit traditional, but Felix has been through a lot, and I want him to have stability. We discussed us getting married and moving in with him, and he's as on board as a four-and-a-half-year-old can be.

"I've been good, right?" Felix says, helping me pour the milk in the glass. "I'm not a brat, right?" A sharp pain slices through my heart at his question, at his insecurity because of his father, and my eyes flit to Camden, whose jaw is now clenched tightly.

"You most definitely are not a brat," I tell him, kneeling in front of him so I can look him in the eyes, "and your dad never should've said that to you. He was mad that day but not at you. You are a smart, sweet, amazing little boy."

"I'm not so little." His brow dips as he shakes his head. "I'm big enough for a sled, right?"

"Yeah," I choke out, a bout of emotion hitting me hard over how much I love my son and how quickly he's growing up. In August, he'll be starting kindergarten. Sure, he's in preschool part-time now, but kindergarten feels so…official.

"You're definitely big enough for a sled," Camden adds, ruffling his hair. "And when Santa brings you one, we're going to take it to Big Bear Mountain and ride it up and down the hill a million times."

Felix's face splits into a grin. "I can't wait!"

"Felix," I add, "please remember that Santa has to bring presents to a lot of kids, so even though you asked for a lot of toys, that doesn't mean you'll get them all, but that's not because you weren't good. It just means he needs toys for other kids too."

Felix nods in understanding.

After I read him a Christmas story, I tuck him in and kiss him good night. He goes right to sleep since he knows Santa only comes when the kids are asleep.

"I can't wait to see Felix open his presents from Santa," Camden says, walking me to the door. "I'm not even getting shit from Santa, and I'm excited." Since my vehicle is small, Camden went Christmas shopping with me, and we used his SUV to bring home the sled I bought for Felix. His list was long, and I couldn't afford all of it—and I refused to let Camden pay for the rest—but he got enough to know he's been good, and he's *not* a brat like his dad said.

"I'll call you when he wakes up," I tell him with a laugh, loving that he's excited and wants to be part of Felix's Christmas. "It'll be early, so get some sleep."

"Can't wait."

A couple of hours later, all the presents are set out under the tree. I send a picture to Camden with a cheesy sticker that makes it look like Santa is in the picture, with a caption that reads: **You've been replaced by a jolly old man in a red suit.**

Within seconds, Camden replies: **I don't care how jolly he is. If he touches my fiancée, I'll kick his ass straight back to the North Pole.**

I smile at the word fiancée.

Me: I like being your fiancée.

Camden: I'd prefer you to be my wife.

Me: Soon...

Camden: Not soon enough.

Camden: I wish I were there with you. 7 more weeks is too long.

We decided on a Valentine's Day wedding—well, the weekend after Valentine's Day since it's on a Thursday this year. It only gives us a short amount of time to plan the wedding, but neither of us wanted to wait long. I wasted too much time on the wrong man.

Now that I've found the right one, I don't want to wait longer than I have to for us to start our lives together. I want to be Camden's in every way, as soon as possible, and he's completely on board with that. We both agreed on something intimate with just our friends and family, so it shouldn't be too hard to plan on short notice. My mom is also going to keep Felix while we go on a short honeymoon.

A knock on the door has me jumping out of bed, a huge grin on my face. It's just like Camden to text me that he's missing me while he's on his way over here. He's not supposed to come over until after Felix wakes up, but there's no harm in having a little Christmas Eve quickie. Maybe I can hide him and have him come out and pretend he just got here.

Only, when I open the door, prepared to kiss my fiancé and sneak him in, it's not Camden on the other side… it's David.

"What are you doing here?" I ask in shock. I haven't seen him since court because he meets with Felix and the social worker due to the restraining order I have on him.

"Fuck, sweetheart, you're so beautiful," he slurs, eye-fucking me. In my haste, I came down in my tiny pajamas since the heat was on and it's warm in here.

"You need to go now." I try to slam the door on David's clearly drunk ass, but before I can, he catches the door.

"Wait, please," he begs. "I know I fucked up, but it's Christmas… Please, Layla. I miss you and our son. Please. I just want to see him for Christmas."

"You know the rules," I tell him. "You need to leave, or I'm going to call the police." I extend my hand to push him out of the doorway.

"Are you fucking serious?" he hisses, tugging on my left hand. "You're engaged?"

I pull my hand back. "Yes, and you need to stop this. You're drunk, and if I call the police, you're going to be arrested for violating a court order. Go home, David."

"You're engaged to *him*, aren't you?" he slurs, his eyes filled with heat. "I knew it. I knew he'd steal my wife."

"That's enough." I push on his chest, and he stumbles back, so I use the opportunity to slam the door closed before he can slip back through the crack.

When he starts banging on the door and doesn't stop, I call Camden.

"Hey, baby," he says, not sounding sleepy at all.

"Hey, umm…I have a little problem, and I'm not sure what to do."

"What's wrong? And… what's that noise?"

"That would be my problem. David showed up drunk, begging to see Felix for Christmas. I thought it was you since we were texting, and you said you wished you were with me. Then he saw my ring and freaked out. I got him out and locked the door, but he's still here, banging on it."

"I'm on my way," he says. "Call the police."

Just as he says that, the noise stops. I peek through the peephole, and David is gone. "He left."

"Call the police," Camden repeats. When I'm quiet, he adds, "I know you feel bad for him because you have a huge-ass heart, but he knows the rules, and if he gets away with this, he'll keep doing it."

I sigh, knowing he's right. "Okay, you don't have to come over if you don't want to. It's late—"

"I'll be there soon."

An hour and a half later, a police report has been filed, and Camden and I are snuggling in my bed. Because there are no cameras, it'll have to be investigated, and that will take some time because it's Christmas.

"I'm having better security installed in here," he says.

"I won't even be living here soon."

"Not soon enough. And I need to make sure you and Felix are safe until I can protect you under my roof."

I nod into his chest, knowing that it's pointless to argue. Camden will do anything in his power to make sure Felix and I are safe.

"I really like being in bed with you," I tell him, running lines up and down his chest over his shirt. "But you know what I like more? You *in* me."

He chuckles softly but stops abruptly when I climb over him and straddle his waist.

"This isn't a good idea," he says, gripping the curves of my hips as I rub my center along his groin to wake his dick up.

"Why not?" I lean forward and pepper kisses along his jawline and down his neck. "You're here anyway, so we might as well make the most of it."

"Because you don't know how to be quiet." He taps the tip of my nose. "And if you wake Felix up, he's going to know Santa came, and he won't go back to bed."

"I can totally be quiet," I argue. "You're the one who moans loudly when you come."

Camden scoffs. "That's all you."

"Let's make a bet," I say. "Whoever makes a noise first loses."

His brows kiss his forehead. "What do I get if I win?" he asks, interested.

I tap my chin in thought. "If you win… I don't know," I say with a laugh. "What do you want?" I know what it is *I* want, something I've been wanting for a while now, and once I win it, he'll have no choice but to give it to me.

Camden sucks in his bottom lip, his eyes twinkling. "If I win, you have to go out on a romantic date with me for New Year's."

I roll my eyes. "That's a win/win. There's nothing *you* want?"

He shrugs. "I have everything I want."

"Aw, you're so sweet." I kiss the corner of his mouth. "Well, I'm not as selfless as you. There's something I want, and if I win, I'm getting it."

"Oh, yeah? What is that?" He squeezes my hips.

I feel myself flush once I have to actually say what I want out loud.

"Your face is all red," Camden points out. "What is it you want?"

"I want to…" I swallow down the lump of emotion clogged in my throat. "I want to have sex my way." He quirks a brow. "In different positions and rough… rougher than what we do… No holding back or treating me like glass and… I want anal."

His eyes go wide, then soften. "Layles…"

"It's what I want," I say, making sure my voice doesn't crack. "You treat me like I'm going to break. How can I ever move forward if every time we have sex, I'm reminded of what happened because of the gentle way you make it a point to treat me?"

He releases a harsh breath and sighs. "Fine, it doesn't matter because you're the loud one, and there's no way you'll stay quiet."

"I only have to stay quiet longer than you," I point out, dragging myself down his body. Before he realizes what I'm doing, I hook my fingers into his belt loops and pull his pants and briefs down, exposing his dick. "And the bet starts… now." I take his entire length into my mouth and deep throat him as far as I can go. He groans loudly, and I pop off, laughing.

"You weren't supposed to make a noise."

"That's not fair!" he whisper-yells. "I wasn't mentally prepared. You just stuck my entire cock down your fucking throat."

I shrug. "I warned you we were starting. You lose. I win."

He sits up and pulls me close to him, so we're face-to-face. "That's where you're wrong, Shutterbug. *Nothing* about what just happened or is going to happen makes me a loser."

Before I can argue, his lips fuse against mine, and his tongue lashes out past my parted lips, tasting me, stroking me. We shed our clothes, and I expect Camden to flip me over, fuck me on my back like he always does, so I'm momentarily taken aback when I end up on top of him with his dick deep inside me. My fingers dig into his shoulders while I ride him to orgasm.

When I've barely come down from my high, he lifts me off him and drops me onto the bed. "On your hands and knees," he demands. I scramble into position, shocked that he's actually going to do as I said. "That's right, baby." He massages one of the globes of my ass. "One day, I'm going to take you here…" He runs his fingers down the crack of my ass, sending a shiver of both fear and need through me. "But tonight, I want in your tight pussy." He spreads my ass. "You sure this is what you want?"

I nod emphatically. "Yes, fuck me like you mean it."

"You better hold on," he warns. I've only just gripped the sheets when he thrusts roughly into me from behind, making me moan.

"You have to be quiet," he says, smacking my ass lightly. "Can you do that?"

"Yes," I breathe.

"If you make any noise, I'm going to stop. Understand?"

I nod, and he rams into me from behind, pushing me forward. Thankfully, I'm holding on. A moan threatens to escape, but before it gets out, I drop my face into my pillow to muffle it.

Camden fucks me how I asked—hard and deep and so damn good. With every thrust, it feels like he's replacing my past with our present and making a promise for the future.

As we both find our release, his fingers dig deliciously into my hips, and once he's filled me with his warm seed, he leans over and trails kisses down the center of my spine.

I love the way he makes me feel wanted and cherished in everything he does. It doesn't matter if he makes love to me or fucks me hard because he does it with his heart every single time. He pulls out, and I flip onto my back, pulling him to me for a kiss.

"Was that what you wanted?" he asks, searching my face to make sure I'm okay.

"It's exactly what I wanted," I breathe, my body feeling like Jell-O from the two orgasms he's given me. "Thank you."

"You don't have to thank me, Layles." He kisses me lightly on my forehead. "You should know by now I'll give you anything you ask for."

"MOMMY! SANTA CAME!" FELIX SHOUTS, RUNNING INTO MY ROOM. I SPRING UP, READY TO explain why Camden is in bed with me. Only the spot where he was lying is empty. I glance around and wonder if I was dreaming, but when I move and feel the soreness between my legs, I know I wasn't.

"He did?" I ask Felix, focusing on him.

"Yep! And I was soooo good because he brought me a million presents."

I laugh at his exaggeration. "Wow, a million? You must've been the best kid in the world."

Felix nods, then runs out of the room. "C'mon, Mommy!"

"Give me a second," I call back, needing to go pee, brush my teeth, and make some coffee. I check the time on my phone and see it's only five thirty in the morning. It's going to be a long day.

Me: Where did you go?

When Camden doesn't respond right away, I assume he's back home and asleep. Once I'm done in the bathroom, I grab my robe to cover myself and pad downstairs to the living room.

I get to the bottom of the stairs and am halted in place by what I see. Presents… So many damn presents surrounding the tree and all over the floor. I blink several times in confusion. There's the sled I got him in one corner, but in the other is a… shit, there's a bike in the other.

"Mommy, this one has your name on it!" Felix shakes the box and runs it over to me. I read the tag, and sure enough, it's addressed to me, from Santa.

What the hell…

I pull my phone out and text Camden again: **What did you do?** He's the only one who could've done this. He's the only one with a key to my house and the alarm code. Well, my mom has one too, but this has Camden written all over it.

There's a knock on the door, so I put away my phone, checking the peephole to make sure it's not David. When I see it's Camden, I swing the door open, glaring. "What did you do?" I hiss.

"What?" he asks with a poker face.

"The presents… the millions of damn presents under the tree."

He steps inside and glances over at the presents, his brows furrowing. "Hey, Felix. Looks like you've been really good this year."

Felix nods, rummaging through all the wrapped presents. "I must've been so, so, so good."

Camden chuckles.

"When did you do this?" I ask, nodding toward the tree.

"Do what?"

"Bring all these presents over!" I whisper-yell so Felix doesn't hear.

Camden barks out a laugh. "The only thing I brought over are these donuts." He raises the box and then leans in and kisses my cheek. "Merry Christmas, baby."

With a smile on his face, he steps into the living room and sets the donuts on the table. "All right, Felix, which one of these presents are you tearing into first?"

Felix lifts a box—one I didn't wrap—and shakes it. "This one!"

"Oh, yeah," Camden says, winking at me. "I bet that's a good one."

Twenty-Six

Camden

"YOU READY?" DAD ASKS, PATTING MY SHOULDER WHILE I STRAIGHTEN MY BOW TIE IN THE dressing room mirror at the church where Layla and I are about to get married.

"More than ready."

"He better be," Declan says with a laugh. "He's been dreaming of this day for the past eight years."

I don't bother to argue because he's not lying. The past two months since Layla agreed to marry me have been spent getting the house ready so we can move in after our honeymoon and counting down the days until I can make Layla my wife and give her my last name.

When I get to the front, our friends and family sit and wait. My mom is in the front row, next to Layla's mom. Both women are dabbing their eyes. I'm the first to get married out of my sisters and me, so Mom has enjoyed helping get everything ready.

Since Layla doesn't have a bunch of girlfriends, she didn't do a wedding party. She has Kaylee as her maid of honor, and my dad is my best man. Since her dad passed away, she's asked my dad to walk her down the aisle. The music starts, and Felix comes out first since he's the ring bearer. He's dressed in a sharp little tux, looking adorable as he carefully carries the rings down the aisle, stopping when he gets to me.

"That was scary," he says, making everyone laugh.

"You did a good job." I fist-bump him, and then he runs over to sit with Patricia.

Next is Kaylee. She flew in this morning for the wedding since she's traveling with Sam York on his tour as his publicist. When she gets to the front, she nods once at me and smiles softly. I hate that she broke my best friend's heart, but she's still Layla's best friend, so I'm going to have to get used to her being around.

The music changes, and Layla and my dad appear a beat later. She's dressed in some off-the-shoulder white dress with beads and shit all over it. Her hair is down in loose waves, and her makeup looks professionally done because she never really wears a lot of makeup. She's fucking stunning and all damn mine.

When her eyes lock with mine, her grin widens, and I swear to God, my chest cracks open, and my heart leaves my body. My dad gives her to me, and it takes everything in me not to kiss her right now.

The officiant reads us his speech, and we recite our vows, and the second he says the words I've been waiting to hear—*I now pronounce you husband and wife, you may kiss the bride*—my mouth is on hers. She tastes sweet, and I want to devour her, but I'll save it for tonight. I release her, and she laughs softly, her face glowing with happiness.

"YOU LOOK BEAUTIFUL, MRS. BLACKWOOD," I TELL HER AS WE DANCE TO "PERFECT" BY ED Sheeran while everyone watches us. The reception is being held in the same hotel where we're spending the night before we take off tomorrow morning for our honeymoon. Layla hates the cold, and it's been a long winter, so I planned a week at an all-inclusive, adults-only resort in Mexico.

"I can't believe I'm Mrs. Blackwood." She shakes her head. "I can't remember the last time I was this happy. Thank you." She lifts up and kisses my lips. "How long until we can go to our room?"

I chuckle, loving that my wife is on the same page as me. "A few more hours."

The song ends, and the deejay welcomes everyone onto the dance floor. Layla seeks out Felix to dance with him while I ask my mom to dance.

"I'm so happy for you," she says, swaying to the music. "I always thought Kendall would be the first to marry." She laughs, glancing over at my sister, who's dancing with her newest boyfriend.

"She would have to stay with one guy long enough for him to propose and then for her to make it down the aisle," I joke. I love my sister, but she can't keep a man to save her life. And it's not them because she's the one always doing the dumping.

"One day, she'll meet the right guy, and she won't run," Mom says with a smile. "Not all of us meet the person we want to spend our lives with at fifteen."

I smile at that. "I didn't think it would ever happen."

"I know. But it did. Fate has a wonderful way of intervening. It's what brought your father and me together, and now you and Layla."

The song ends, and after kissing my mom on her cheek and thanking her for the dance, I find my way back to Layla. We spend the night dancing and socializing. The food is good, Felix loves the cake, and when it's socially acceptable, we thank everyone for coming and say good night. Layla tells Felix to be good for his grandma and that we'll be home in a week. She's nervous about not being there to hand him off to the social worker to see David, but her mom has assured her she'll make sure everything goes smoothly.

"Stop," I tell her when I open the door to our hotel room. "It's tradition, right? Good luck?" I scoop her up into my arms and carry her, bridal style, across the threshold.

"I think that's at the house," she says with a laugh.

"I'll do it then too." I shrug and place her on the floor in the center of the bedroom. Backing up, I take a good look at my wife before I walk up behind her and begin to undo the pearl buttons down her back. With each one I unfasten, her sexy back is exposed. When they're all undone, I flick the material, sending it into a pool on the floor.

"Jesus," I breathe, taking in her white silk corset and panty set. She steps out of the material, and my eyes go straight to her toned legs and fuck-me heels. I've got to be the luckiest motherfucker in the world. I want to send a thank-you note to David for being a dumbass and letting this perfect woman go, but he doesn't deserve shit.

Dusting her hair to the side, I press an open-mouthed kiss to the top of her shoulder, inhaling the vanilla and raspberry.

"I think I'm a bit underdressed compared to you," she says coyly, turning around and running her hands up my chest, then pushing my tux off my shoulders. Next, she unbuttons my shirt, kissing her way down my chest and torso. She bends down when she gets to my pants, squatting so she's eye level with my groin. The corset she's wearing plumps up her already full breasts, and I find myself running a finger across the swells of them.

She pushes my pants and boxers down and grips my shaft, stroking it up and down. It's already semi-hard from looking at her, so it doesn't take long for it to get as hard as granite. As much as I love her hands and mouth on me, the only way I'm coming with Layla as my wife is inside her.

"Come here, my beautiful wife." I pull her over to the bed, and she climbs onto it, giving me a show of her ass in the air, her heels still on her feet, and her tiny white lace underwear barely covering anything. When she stops and peeks over her shoulder through her lashes, I slap her ass playfully, making her moan.

"I've made a decision," she says, staying on her hands and knees.

I grip her hips and dip my head, giving the globe of her ass a kiss. "What's that?" I ask, massaging each round cheek.

"I want you to fuck my ass tonight."

Her words halt me in place. For most couples, a woman requesting that is simply kinky, but for Layla to ask is huge because the one and only time she's been taken there was when she was raped by her ex-husband.

I want to ask if she's sure, tell her there's no rush, we don't ever have to do it, but I know replacing the bad memories with the good is important to her, and if this is what she wants from me—*her husband*—I'll give it to her. I'll give her *any-fucking-thing* she wants if it makes her happy.

"You will, right?" she asks, her voice now shaky since I haven't said a word. "You said you would…"

I lean in and grip her chin, capturing her plump bottom lip with my teeth. "Baby, I'll fuck your ass so good that every horrible memory of that piece of shit will be wiped out." I kiss her hard, swallowing down the moan she releases.

"I brought lube," she says shyly. "In the luggage. I looked it up, and it said if you use it, it will hurt less."

My eyes stay trained on her for a few seconds, worried she's scared and doing this prematurely, but when she looks at me, I see the conviction in her gaze. She trusts me and knows I'll make sure anything we do together will be good for her.

"Go lie down on your stomach," I murmur, releasing my hold on her chin. She does as I say while I go to her luggage and pull out the lube she bought, along with the baby oil she uses when she gets out of the shower. I discard the last of my clothes, leaving me in only my boxer briefs, then pad back over to join her on the bed.

"You looked so damn perfect today," I tell her, straddling her legs and unclipping her corset that buttons down her back. "Walking down the aisle…standing at the altar… promising to love me for the rest of your life." I pull the straps off her arms, and she lifts slightly so I can remove the material from her.

I drop a kiss between her shoulder blades. "I swear I thought of a dozen love songs just watching you today, holding you, kissing you." I trail kisses down her spine, stopping at the sexy as fuck dimples just above her ass.

"The guys will think you've gone soft," she says with a laugh.

"They already know I have. You've heard our upcoming album." Damn near half the songs are about the way I love Layla.

I pull the silky material down her thighs and drop it onto the ground. "I can't help it, though. Every word, every lyric, is written with you in mind."

I squeeze some oil into my palm and rub my hands together to warm it up a bit. Layla is still on her stomach, her arms now above her head. Her face is to the side, her hair fanned out over her shoulder, and her eyes are closed. She looks like a damn angel. I'll never understand how anyone could ever want to hurt her, especially someone who claimed to love her. But I vow to make sure she's treated like she deserves every day for the rest of her life.

I start with her shoulders, massaging the tension out. She may trust me, but she's still nervous. He hurt her, and as strong as she is, she can't shake what he did. I knead her back and work my way to her peach of an ass, massaging the globes, working my way into the crack, but not yet going *there*. I skirt down, applying some oil to her thighs and giving them attention.

When I get to her heels, as much as I love the idea of fucking her with them on, I remove each one so she's comfortable, kissing the insteps of both of her feet.

"If you keep this up, you're going to put me to sleep." She sighs, clearly relaxed, just the way I want her.

"Then I'll just have to wake you up."

"We'll s—" Her words are cut off when I spread her cheeks and push a single oiled-up finger into her tight-ringed hole. "Ohhh," she half hisses, half groans.

"How does that feel, baby?" I ask, gently fingering her tight ass.

"It's… different."

I chuckle under my breath. "Get on your hands and knees." She pops up immediately, jutting her ass into the air. Reaching under her, I find her clit and massage it while working her ass with my finger. I can tell when the two combined begin to feel good because she starts to rock back and forth, helping me get her off.

"Oh, Oh… Cam," she groans. With a little more pressure on her clit, she explodes, her entire body shaking as she comes all over my fingers. I use the moment to add another finger to her ass, and she moans in pleasure.

"That's it," I murmur. "Fuck my fingers." I dribble a few drops of lube onto her ass, then add one more digit. Even though she's already come, she's turned the hell on, meeting my fingers thrust for thrust.

"It feels so good," she breathes, rocking back and forth. "More, please. I need more."

"So fucking polite. Begging me to fuck your ass."

"Please," she moans louder, taking my fingers deeper and harder. "Camden, please."

I pull my fingers out, and she whimpers, making me bite back a laugh. If that asshole had treated her right, she would've given him the damn world. Instead, he chose to hurt her. His fuckup is most definitely my gain. Because of his horrible choices, I'll get to spend the rest of my life loving and being with this woman. Something I never thought possible.

Grabbing the lube, I pour a generous amount on my shaft, then stroke it a few times, making sure to coat it nice and good.

"It might hurt a little," I warn her, lining my dick up to her entrance. "If at any point you want me to stop, tell me, and I will."

"Okay," she whispers, her voice shaky.

My fingers pull one of her ass cheeks to the side, and slowly, so fucking slowly, I breach the rim of her hole, watching as it swallows my dick inch by inch.

"Layles, you okay?" I ask when I glance up and find her face in the pillow, her body trembling. "Layla?"

"I… I don't—" The shakiness of her words has me pulling out and flipping her onto her back, not waiting for her to finish her sentence.

Twenty-Seven

Layla

I THOUGHT I COULD DO THIS, AND FOR A MINUTE, I WAS. HIS FINGERS IN ME FELT ODDLY GOOD. The way they stroked my insides had me coming apart at the seams. But then I got too brave, asked for too much, and the second his dick pushed into me, the flashbacks hit me hard. I tried to close my eyes and get past them, but of course, Camden noticed. He notices everything. He's so attuned to everything regarding me. My moods, my body, my emotions, and my expressions. He pays attention, real attention. It's one of the things I love about him.

"I'm right here," Camden says, parting my legs and hovering above me. "It's you and me, baby." His lips brush mine, sending a shiver up my spine. "We don't need to do this," he says softly. "I can make love to you just like this."

I shake my head, not wanting to let David win. He doesn't deserve to be in our honeymoon suite with my husband and me.

"Can we do it like this?" I ask. "I think it's the position. I want to see you."

Camden smiles gently. "Baby, we can do anything you want."

His mouth captures my own, and we kiss passionately. He tastes like the champagne from our final toast before we said good night, and it makes my stomach do a flip-flop. I married Camden today, my best friend, and I want our marriage to be free of David, of my past. And the only way that can happen is for us to replace this final bad memory with a good one.

"Lift up," he says when he breaks our kiss. I do as he says, and he places a pillow under my butt, propping my lower half up slightly before his mouth is back on mine.

I'm so lost in our kiss that I don't realize what's happening until the slight pain hits me. One of my legs is hooked on the crook of his arm, and he's pushing into me slowly, his mouth never leaving mine. Because we're oiled up, he goes in easily, the burning sensation lessening the deeper he goes.

"I'm all the way in," he murmurs against my lips. "Tell me when you're okay with me moving, or I can stay just like this."

"You can move."

"You sure?"

"Yes, please move."

He backs up slightly, gripping my thigh, and starts to move in and out of my ass. With every drive into me, the burn turns into pleasure. The hand not holding my leg finds my clit, and he massages it, his eyes never leaving mine. My orgasm builds slowly until I'm dangling over the edge, begging Camden to make me come.

With a flick of his thumb, he pushes me over the edge. I'm still screaming his name when he pulls out and comes all over my belly.

"Fuck, you're amazing," he groans, kissing me hard. "Let's go shower. I need to clean you, so I can fuck you, this time in your tight cunt."

"I'M NOT READY TO GO HOME, YET I'M EXCITED TO GO HOME," I SAY, MAKING CAMDEN LAUGH with my confusing statement. We've spent a week on the beaches of Mexico, and if it were up to me, we would stay forever. It's peaceful and sunny and relaxing, and did I mention it's peaceful? The only thing we're missing is Felix, who I've spoken to every day and has barely missed me since he's been too busy being spoiled by our moms.

"We can go back," Camden says, kissing my cheek. "Or we can go somewhere else. Aside from the next few weeks that are blocked off to finish this album and the tour that's scheduled, my calendar is wide open."

"When you're done with the album and we make the videos, my job will be done." I cuddle into Camden's side. "I was thinking of making a website and putting my name out there. Maybe get a few new artists to take a chance on me…"

I hold my breath, waiting for Camden to tell me there's no reason for me to work because he'll provide for us, the way David always did. Instead, he kisses the top of my head and says, "Baby, once our videos are out and your name is attached to them, opportunities will be flying in. You'll get your pick of who you want to work with."

I look up at him and smile, silently promising to stop comparing him to David and expecting the worst. Camden isn't David. He's already proven that over and over again.

"I know going on tour isn't the best situation for a kid, but I was thinking you guys can join us a few times. We'll be flying as well as using the tour bus, but we stay in hotels a lot. We can look at the schedule and see when I have days off, and we can explore the different cities."

"That sounds like fun," I tell him, leaning up and kissing his stubbled jaw. I'm going to miss the hell out of him while he's on tour for two months, but I knew going into this that touring is part of his life. And I'd never want to make him feel guilty for following his passions. I know firsthand how shitty that can feel.

When we pull up to the new house, I look at Camden in confusion. We haven't moved in yet, and he knows I'm dying to see Felix. The car must have a scanner on it that Camden told me about when discussing security because the gate opens automatically when we pull up. Not many homes in the city are gated, but Camden made sure ours is.

We get out, and he scoops me into his arms. "Love getting to carry my wife over the thresholds," he says, kissing me as he walks us to the front door. With one hand, he pushes the door open, setting me on my feet once we're inside. I expected the place to still be empty, so I'm shocked when I find it completely furnished with everything I've bookmarked.

"How did you—?"

My question is cut off when Felix's voice booms through the house, and seconds later, he's running into my arms. "You're home! Wait till you see my room!"

He grabs my hand and pulls me upstairs, Camden following. The walls—painted the color I picked out—are all empty, so it seems he only had the furniture I picked out brought in.

When we get to Felix's room, I'm stunned. He had requested a Sonic the Hedgehog room because he's still obsessed with the game, and Camden made it happen. The walls are painted like the game's background, and his comforter matches. The two large beanbags in the corner both have Sonic on them. Even the curtains have Sonic on them.

"This is my room," Felix says as if it's not obvious. "Grandma said I get to sleep here tonight."

Speaking of which… "Where is Grandma?"

"Right here," Mom says, walking in and giving me a kiss. "Look at that tan you've got. You look beautiful." She presses her palms to my face. "And happy."

"I am," I tell her, wrapping my arm around Camden's waist. "Did you do all this?"

"No," she says with a laugh. "That would be your husband. Felix and I just arrived so we were here when you got home." She pats my shoulder. "I'm going to take off. I have book club tonight. Welcome home. Come over soon so you can tell me all about your trip."

Once she's gone, Camden shows me the rest of the house, which is exactly how I envisioned it when I was picking out stuff online, and then we order a pizza and watch a movie with Felix. Tomorrow is Saturday so he doesn't have school, which means we get to spend the weekend in our new home as a family. Life can't get much better than this.

"SHIT," I HISS, PRESSING END ON THE CALL.

"What's the matter?" Camden asks, startling me. He wraps his arms around me from behind and nuzzles his face into the crook of my neck. For a moment, I'm distracted, basking in his touch.

"I have to go to the doctor for my yearly checkup, and I completely forgot. My mom just left to go to The Hamptons with your mom for a girls' weekend, so I can't have her pick up Felix from school."

"You have me," Camden says, turning me around to face him. "I'm your husband, and while Felix might not be my son, he's part of you, which by extension is part of me."

"I know, but—"

"No buts. We're a family and in this together. If you need something, all you have to do is ask."

"Thank you." I wrap my arms around him and kiss him. "I'll let his teacher know you're picking him up."

"Sounds good. We do need to talk before you go, though."

The look in his eyes has me worried. "Did something happen?" When he sighs, I know something has. "Camden…"

"I ran into David the other day. He knows you've moved and that we're married. Before Simon could stop him, he made some threats." Simon is one of his main bodyguards. Several of them rotate, but Simon is Camden's personal bodyguard and tends to go where he goes when it's needed.

"What kind of threats?"

"He said he's not going to let me take his family from him, and if I think this is over, I'm wrong."

A chill races up my spine, and I step back, needing some space. "He threatened you…?" My thoughts go back to the images he sent—Camden had sent them to Daniel, and he advised us to report them as threats so they're documented.

"Layles…"

"He's snapped. He's not the same guy he was when we first got together. Or maybe he is, and I just didn't realize it. We need to take his threats seriously."

"And we are," Camden says, taking my hands in his. "I've added to my security team, and Simon will accompany you everywhere you go."

"But he's yours…"

"He's part of my team, and I trust him more than anyone else to keep you safe. As my wife, you should have security with you anyway. New York is quiet, but the paparazzi are still around. We've been going everywhere together up until now, but if you're leaving on your own, I want you to take Simon with you, and you need to always take the SUV. No taking the subway, even if you feel it's faster."

Shortly after we got back, Camden insisted on replacing my little car with something safer. I wasn't thrilled, but I understood and let him because I've seen the way the photographers linger, especially when we leave the house. Sometimes, I don't even notice them there, but later, I'll see pictures of us all over the internet.

"Okay," I agree. "I need to get going so I'm not late." I give him a kiss on his cheek, then head out, Simon meeting me outside.

"Ma'am," he says with a smile, opening the door for me.

Once I arrive at the doctor's office, I'm seen quickly. After I give a urine sample, they check my blood pressure, and I get changed into a gown, then the doctor comes in.

"Good morning, Mrs. Blackwood. How are you feeling?"

"I'm good." I grin, loving my new last name.

"Any morning sickness or tender breasts?"

"I'm sorry, what?"

She looks at me, confused. "Aren't you here for your prenatal appointment?" She clicks on the tablet in her hand. "Oh, this is your wellness checkup? I'm so sorry. Your urine test showed a higher than normal level of HCG, only found in pregnancy, so I thought…"

"Wait," I gasp, my hand going to my stomach. "I'm pregnant?"

"We'll need to do an ultrasound to confirm. I'm assuming, based on your reaction, you didn't know?"

"No," I breathe. "I'm on birth control. I take it every single day."

"Unfortunately, no contraception is one-hundred-percent effective. When was your last menstrual cycle?"

I think back. I get it every month at the same time. That's the plus side to being on the pill, but… "Oh my God. I didn't get it last month. This doesn't make any sense. I haven't missed a single pill. I've been so busy with the wedding and our honeymoon, I didn't even think about it when it didn't show up."

"Could you have missed some days?"

"No. My alarm goes off to ensure I take it every day at the same time. I know you probably hear that a lot, but I'm telling you, I haven't missed it."

"It's okay, dear." She pats my leg. "Lie back, and we'll check things out before we assume anything."

A few minutes later, a *whoosh, whoosh, whoosh* comes over the screen. It's a sound I would recognize anywhere. A baby's heartbeat.

"Based on the measurements, you're roughly five weeks pregnant, which is why you might not have experienced any symptoms yet. We'll say you're due October twentieth, but that might change. Everything looks good." She takes some pictures of the tiny little blob and prints them out for me. "Stop taking your birth control immediately, and since you struggle with anemia, I'm going to have you up your iron intake in addition to adding a prenatal vitamin. I'll send the prescriptions to your pharmacy on file."

I'm still in shock as I walk out of the doctor's office, staring at the sonogram pics of the tiny little thing that's growing in me. A baby… created by Camden and me.

"Oh! I'm sorry," I blurt when I run straight into another person. My eyes ascend, and I instinctually take a step back. David. Towering over me. I look around for Simon but don't see him anywhere, and then it hits me: when I checked out, I went out a different door. I was so wrapped up in the news that I forgot he was with me.

"What are you doing here?" I ask because there's no way this is a coincidence.

"I knew you had an appointment today. It was on my calendar.

When you made it, you added it to our joint calendar."

"And you just took it upon yourself to show up?" I shriek. "You're not allowed to be near me. You know—"

"What the fuck is this?" David barks, cutting me off. He snatches the sonogram pictures out of my hand. "You're…" He glances down at my belly. "How far along are you?"

"Not that it's any of your business, but only five weeks." I grab the pictures back. "Now go away."

"No." He shakes his head. "No. No. No. Fuck!" His face turns red, and I take a step back in fear. We're on a crowded street, but it doesn't do anything to make me feel safe.

"This was not supposed to happen! You were supposed to get pregnant by me!" He stalks toward me. "It was supposed to be my baby! Not his! Of course he would take this away from me too. He's taken everything else! My wife, my son, and now he's taken my baby."

"David," I say slowly, my heart beating erratically in my chest. "This wasn't supposed to be your baby. We agreed to wait. I was on birth control." He isn't making any sense. This was an accident. When David and I were married, he asked me to have another baby, and I told him no repeatedly.

"Yes, it was! I knew once you were pregnant, you'd be okay. Just like you were with Felix. I just had to make it happen, and then you'd be on board." He now has me backed up against a wall and slams his hand against it in anger. "That baby was supposed to be mine, not his!"

An ice-cold chill flows through my veins at his words. He can't be saying what I think he's saying. There's no way he would… "David, what did you do?"

Before he can answer, he's ripped away from me by Simon, who shoves David against the wall. "Get away from her, now," Simon says, menace laced in his tone. "Let's go, Layla." He glares my way, and I go with him, feeling bad that I put myself in this situation because I didn't wait for him.

"I'm sorry," I tell him once we're in the SUV. "I left out a different door and completely forgot. David was outside waiting for me and… I'm so sorry."

He nods once. "I can't do my job if I'm not with you. Please remember that."

The ride home is quiet. I had planned to meet Camden at the studio, but I need to do something first. I have Simon wait for me in the vehicle while I run into the house and grab what I need. He takes me to the pharmacy I use, and once it's my turn, I hand the pharmacist the pills.

"Can you please confirm these are the pills for my birth control?"

A few minutes later, my suspicions are confirmed. "I'm sorry, ma'am, but these are placebo. They are not your birth control. Were you given these? I can investigate…"

"No," I say, shaking my head. "That's okay. Thank you."

There's nothing to investigate because I know exactly what happened. My ex-husband switched out my pills, not once but twice, to ensure I would get pregnant.

Twenty-Eight

Camden

The guys and I hold back our laughter while Felix sings the song he wrote for his mom. When we arrived at the studio, he was fascinated with the music equipment, so I told him if he wrote a song, he could sing it, and I'd record it for him. Since Layla's birthday is in a few days, he said he wanted to sing her a birthday song. The kid is completely tone deaf, but he's cute as hell.

"You're the best mom ever 'cause you let me stay up late and watch movies. Happy Birthday."

When he finishes singing, he takes off his headphones and grins at us. "Did I do good?"

"You fucking rocked it," Gage says.

"Watch your mouth." I punch him in the arm. "The last thing I need is him going home and using words like that around his mom. She'll never trust me with him again."

Gage ignores me, walking into the sound booth and fist-bumping Felix.

"Can I hear it?" Felix asks, hopping up onto the stool.

Earl snorts out a laugh, and I glare at the asshole.

"Soon," I tell him. "First, we have to edit it." And add a shit ton of Auto-Tune to it so it doesn't break his mother's eardrums.

"Okay, I'm hungry," Felix says.

"Let me see where your mom is at." I grab my phone and find several missed calls and texts from Layla. Shit, my phone's been on silent. The last one asks if Felix and I are okay, so I call her back.

"Hey," she breathes. "I've been trying to get ahold of you."

"Sorry, my phone was on silent. We're still at the studio."

"Okay, will you be home soon?" Something in her voice has my hackles rising.

"Yeah. Everything okay?" She hesitates, and I know something is wrong. "Layles…"

"I just need you to come home, please."

After we hang up, Felix and I say bye to the guys and head home, stopping at Layla's favorite restaurant to pick up food on the way—and then a drive-through for Felix since it's his least favorite.

When we get home, she pulls Felix into a tight hug, making him screech in surprise. "Mom, you're going to choke me to death," he says dramatically.

"I'm sorry, sweetie. I just love you so much."

"I brought food." I hold up the bag.

"Thanks." A fake smile stretches across her face, making my stomach sink.

"Can I go watch TV?" Felix asks. "I ate chicken nuggets."

"Yeah," Layla chokes out. "Go ahead."

Felix hightails it up the stairs, leaving Layla and me alone.

"You want to tell me what's going on?" I ask, laying the food out on the table.

Layla doesn't say anything right away, so I give her time and focus on my food even though I've pretty much lost my appetite. Layla pushes her food around her plate but doesn't actually take a bite.

Finally, she sets her fork down and speaks. "Our freshman year of college, David cheated on me." I set down my fork, giving her my full attention.

"We were living in separate dorms, and I was spending a lot of time with Kaylee. She was a mess after… everything. David was always complaining I wasn't paying enough attention to him. We were fighting all the time. He got drunk at a party one night and messed around with another girl. He swears they didn't have sex, but I didn't care. I broke up with him the second I found out."

She releases a harsh breath and shakes her head. "A few weeks later, I found out I was pregnant. I didn't understand how it happened. I was on birth control and never missed a day. I was eighteen and scared, and David begged me to stay with him. I took him back, and we got married, moved off campus into our own apartment his parents helped him pay for, and I never looked back."

She sucks her bottom lip into her mouth and rolls it out slowly before continuing. "I told the gynecologist, and after I gave birth to Felix, I got an IUD, but it caused a negative reaction so I went back on the pill. They gave me a different one, in case the one I was on didn't work with me for whatever reason."

I'm trying to follow what she's saying, but I'm not quite sure where she's going with this.

"Last year, David asked me for another baby, and I said no. From the beginning, our marriage was rocky, and it only got worse over the years. He worked a lot but was also controlling. He didn't pay attention to Felix and me but didn't want us around anyone else. I think, in a lot of ways, I stayed with him for Felix, and he knew that. Our marriage was barely hanging on by a thread when we moved here. With Felix going to school, it was only a matter of time until I got a job and became independent. That's why, even though I said no to having another baby, he went behind my back again and switched out my birth control pills for placebos."

Her eyes meet mine, and it takes me a second to wrap my head around everything she just said. "Wait, again?"

"Again." She nods. "I ran into him today. Well, not ran into him since he knew I had an appointment and made sure to *run* into me."

"What?" I bark. "Where the fuck was Simon?"

She holds up her hand. "I'm fine. It was my mistake. I left out the wrong door. When Simon realized I was gone, he found me and jumped in and got David away from me, but before he did, David confessed to messing with my pills then *and* now."

My head is spinning. "Now? What do you mean now?"

"I mean, David took it upon himself to switch out my pills without me knowing, so this entire time we've been having sex, thinking we're protected, I wasn't. And now, I'm pregnant."

She slides a black-and-white image over to me. I don't know what the hell I'm looking at, but I've seen it in enough movies and shit to know it's a sonogram photo. "You're… you're pregnant?"

"Five weeks." Tears fill her eyes. "I'm so, so sorry, Camden." She releases a harsh breath, and a couple of tears fall.

"You're pregnant," I breathe. "Holy shit." I pull my chair out and pull hers toward me, so I can see her belly. "You're pregnant with my baby?" She nods, and I lift her shirt, exposing her flesh. I drop to my knees and kiss just above her belly button. "Holy shit," I repeat. "I can't believe it. We're having a baby."

When I glance back up at her, she's looking at me with tears streaming down her cheeks. And then I remember the part about her not wanting to have another baby. David tricked her, and thankfully, she didn't get pregnant until we were together, but that doesn't change the fact that she wasn't given a choice. I'm almost positive that doing something like this is a crime, and he could be charged. Hell, if it's possible, I'm going to make sure he is charged.

I sit up and take her face in my hands. "Do you want to have this baby?" I ask slowly. If she says no, I'll be devastated, but I won't argue. What David did was fucked up. No woman should be tricked or forced into having a baby, so I sure as fuck won't guilt her into having this baby. If she decides not to keep it, I'll support her decision one hundred percent.

"I do," she says. "I really do want this baby."

I sag in relief. "Then why are you crying?"

"Besides feeling betrayed, I wasn't sure how you'd feel. I know you love me, but we're young, and this is still all new, and you're already taking on a stepson…"

"Whoa." I pull back slightly. "I'm not taking anything or anyone on. We're a family."

She nods. "I know but still…"

"We take it at our pace, do whatever feels *right*," I tell her, repeating the very words she said to me in California when she told me she wanted to be with me. "I don't care that we've only been married for a short time. I love you. And while I hate what David did, I fucking love that you're carrying my baby."

A smile cuts through the tears, exposing those twin dimples I love. "I do too."

I take the sonogram picture and glance at it. "I think it looks like a girl. What do you think?"

She laughs, the sound melodic. "I think it looks like one of Felix's drawings."

"YOU'RE HAVING A BABY?" MY MOM SQUEALS, THROWING HER ARMS AROUND ME AT THE same time Layla's mom hugs her. We're not announcing anything until she's in her second trimester, but we had to tell our families. She was worried they would feel like we're rushing, but of course, they're all ecstatic.

"How long until we find out the sex?" Patricia asks.

"Umm… a couple of months," Layla says.

"I can't wait to go shopping!" Mom adds.

"I hope it's a boy," Felix says. "Then he can play *Sonic* with me."

"If it's a girl, she can play too," Layla tells him.

He looks at her like she's crazy and shakes his head. "Is it time for birthday cake yet?"

"We have to eat dinner first," Layla says, ruffling his hair.

"We could eat cake for dinner." Felix shrugs.

"You know what?" Layla says. "That actually sounds like a really good idea."

Felix's face lights up. "Really?"

"Yeah, why not? It's my birthday, and cake sounds good."

"Yes!" He runs straight into the kitchen and jumps on a chair to check out the cake we bought for Layla's birthday. We're barbecuing outside since it's actually on the warmer side, and we've picked up a bounce house/water slide for Felix to play on.

I light the candles, and everyone sings "Happy Birthday," then Layla makes a wish, blowing them out. My mom cuts slices and dishes them out to everyone.

"Here, Mom." Felix scoops his chocolate cake onto her plate while Layla does the same with her vanilla. I watch them, feeling so damn blessed.

"Mom," Felix says, shoveling his cake into his mouth. "Is the baby in your belly?"

Layla smiles and nods. "Yep. That's where you were too when I was pregnant with you."

Felix's eyes go wide. "When I was in your belly, did you eat cake?"

Layla laughs. "A lot of cake. All chocolate."

Felix cringes. "That's not nice. You know I don't like chocolate cake."

Everyone listening to them laughs.

"Wait, Mom. Stop!" Felix drops his hand over hers before she can take another bite. "If the baby is in your belly, and you're eating cake…" He takes his finger and drags it from her throat down to her belly button. "Does the cake fall on the baby's head?"

Layla stifles her laughter when she sees he's dead serious. "It's a different part of my belly," she explains. "The baby is here…" She points at one area. "And the food goes here." She points at another area.

Felix nods. "Like when I'm full, and my belly still has room for dessert?"

"Yeah," Layla says with a laugh. "Just like that."

After eating the cake, Felix insists we give Layla her birthday present because apparently, we're not doing anything in order. So we pile into the living room since Bailey helped me turn it into a video. I went on to her social media accounts and saved a bunch of photos and videos of her and Felix over the years, and we made it into a digital collage of sorts.

"I made it for you because I love you," Felix says proudly.

The second the song starts and Felix comes on the screen, with his headphones on and grinning as he sings the lyrics he wrote himself, Layla's eyes water. I have to admit, with the Auto-Tune shit we did to the song, it doesn't sound half bad. Okay, I'm lying. The sound is cringeworthy, but it's still cute as hell. As the song continues, it switches from Felix to the various photos and videos of them. Layla starts to sob, and I notice her mom also tears up.

When it's done, Layla scoops her son into her arms and peppers kisses all over his face. "Best present ever," she tells him as he squirms and laughs, begging her to stop.

"Thank you," she says to me once she's set him down. "I love it."

"And I love you." I give her a hard and long kiss, not giving a shit that we have an audience. It might be Layla's birthday, but she's given me so damn much.

"AND... THAT'S A WRAP," LAYLA SAYS, BEAMING AT US AS THE FILM CREW STARTS SHUFFLING about, getting everything organized and cleaned up. For the past two days, we've been shooting a music video that Layla's producing. When she pitched it to us, we all agreed it was perfect. The song is called "Ghosted," and it was written by Declan. It's about unrequited love and will be the single we release as a teaser to our album. The video is about a guy following a woman around. He appears like a ghost to emphasize the fact that she doesn't return his feelings. She's going about her day and feels him around but can't actually see him. In the end, he vanishes into thin air, and she's left feeling unsettled as if his presence alone was enough to make her feel safe. It's sad as fuck, and our fans are going to eat it up. I can't help but wonder if it's about my sister, but I'm not going there.

"How soon can we have it finalized?" Dad asks Layla. "I'd like to get it released in the next couple of weeks.

"I think I can have it done by this weekend." She glances at her phone. "Shoot. I need to grab Felix and get him to Beatrice." She's referring to the social worker who takes Felix to meet with his dad.

"No worries. Go," Dad says. "I can't wait to see the finished product. You did a great job."

Layla blushes. "Thanks." She gives me a chaste kiss. "See you at home?"

"Yeah, I need to swing by the studio for a bit. Want me to pick up dinner on my way home?"

"Sounds perfect." She takes off with Simon while the guys and I head in the opposite direction. We're wrapping up the album today, and Earl asked us to come by to get it all finalized.

We're all deep in the music when my phone rings. "Give me a second," I tell everyone, hitting answer. "Hey, Shutter—"

"He's gone!" she cries over the phone.

"What? Who?"

"He's gone! David took him. He took Felix. Beatrice has called the police, but he's gone. He took him to the bathroom, and they never came back. Simon and I have looked everywhere, but we can't find him."

"I'm on my way," I tell her, jumping out of my seat. "Where are you?"

She gives me the name of the restaurant, and after telling the guys what's happened, they insist on going. More eyes can mean locating him quicker. On the way, I call our parents and fill them in. When we arrive at the restaurant, a few police cars are there, and an officer is talking to Layla. The second she sees me, she throws herself into my arms.

"I should've known he would do something like this. He's made so many threats." She sobs into my chest while I rub her back, wishing I could magically make Felix reappear. Of course he doesn't own any electronics like a phone, so there's no way to track him.

Because of the situation and the restaurant footage, we're able to get an emergency missing child alert sent out as well as file a missing person's report. The police promise to follow up on any leads, and then we're sent home since it's clear they're no longer in the restaurant.

A little while later, the police let us know David isn't at his house or at his parents'. Layla asks about his assistant, and they confirm she hasn't seen him.

"They have to be somewhere!" Layla cries. "I just don't know where to look." The look of helplessness in her features damn near kills me. She wants to be out scouring the streets, but we live in New York. They could be any-fucking-where.

I hold her all night until she finally cries herself to sleep. And then I hold her until I pass out, praying for Felix's safe return.

Twenty-Nine

Layla

IT'S BEEN TWO DAYS. TWO DAYS WITHOUT HEARING MY LITTLE BOY'S VOICE OR SEEING HIM smile. Since David walked him to the bathroom and they never returned, instead, going out the emergency exit. It's been two days of the police looking for leads, our family and friends searching anywhere we can think of. Even Kaylee came home to be with me.

But Felix and David are nowhere to be found. I've cried to the point that it feels as though my tear ducts have dried up. And of course morning sickness has decided to rear its ugly head, so between crying and searching, I've spent my time with my head in the toilet.

"Here, try this," Kaylee says, handing me a lollipop. "It's for morning sickness."

I'll try anything at this point, so I pop it into my mouth. "Thanks."

"We're going to find him," she says, her eyes meeting mine.

"I know." I nod, hoping my positive thinking will make a difference. "If you need to get back to work…"

"No." She shakes her head. "I don't need to be anywhere but right here with you."

"Thank you."

The day is spent with us being spoon-fed information on leads that don't seem to ever pan out. Camden suggests offering a cash reward for any leads, but the police are wary it will only make their job harder by causing a lot of false leads.

By day four, Camden insists we put out a cash reward, saying he's not leaving any stone unturned. He posts a picture of Felix on his social media and offers a million dollars to the person with the tip that leads to us finding him, along with a phone number they can call so we can weed them out.

It's late, three in the morning on day five, when I pass out from exhaustion, still not any closer to finding my son. I've tried calling and texting David, and Camden had a guy he knows try to track him, but his phone must be off or dead because it's untraceable.

I get up, groggy and in need of having to pee. When I glance at the time, I see it's seven in the morning. Camden left me a note that he's gone out to get breakfast. Through all of this, he's made sure I'm fed and taken care of, knowing I'm not in a place to do it myself.

I hear some shuffling, and assuming Camden is back, I go downstairs. Only it's not Camden… it's David and Felix.

"Oh my God!" I cry, running toward my son, but before I make it to him, David raises a gun, stopping me in my place. "What are you doing?" I screech. "Put that thing down!" Faintly, I hear my phone ringing upstairs, but I ignore it, focusing on David with a gun in one hand and my son, standing in front of him, sobs wracking his little body.

"He won't stop crying!" David yells. "The fucking kid won't stop crying for you." He shoves Felix forward, and he goes straight into my arms. I hold him tight, inhaling his scent.

"He can't have him," David barks. "And he can't have you! He took everything! My wife and my son and now he's having *my* baby!!" David says, his eyes manic while he waves the gun in the air. "If I can't have you, he doesn't get you either!"

His words seep into my pores like gasoline. "David…" He can't mean what I think he means.

"You're supposed to be mine!" he hisses. "Felix is supposed to be mine. That baby in your belly is mine! He took it all, and now he's going to lose everything."

"Please don't do this," I beg. "Please. I'll do anything!"

"It's too late." He takes a step forward, and instinctually, I take one back. "It's okay," he says, his voice now soft. "Because soon we'll all be together, happy again."

He raises his gun, aiming it directly at me, and I shove Felix behind me, hoping to at least save him. Then I close my eyes and do the only thing I can do: pray.

There's a scuffle, some shouting, and then a gun goes off. And when I glance up, what I see causes both relief and heartbreak deep inside me.

Thirty

Camden

"ANY NEWS?" I ASK MY CONTACT AT THE NYPD AS I GET INTO MY SUV AND PULL OUT OF THE garage.

"Nothing. Not a damn peep." I can hear it in his voice. He's concerned. It's been days, fucking days since they've disappeared. If David did it for money, he would've made contact by now. Every day they're gone means they have the chance to get farther away. At this point, they might not even be in the state. We know he hasn't left the country since Felix doesn't have a passport, but anywhere within driving distance is game. And every day we don't find him statistically decreases the chances of ever finding him. Daniel was able to get a warrant to search David's accounts, but nothing has been flagged, which means he's using cash.

"All right, thanks. If you hear anything…"

"Of course."

We hang up, and after making sure the gate is closed behind me, I head toward Layla's favorite deli so I can get us breakfast. Traffic is a bitch, like always, and it takes me a good twenty minutes to get there. As I'm parking in front of the deli, my phone pings with an alert: **gate access granted.** That can only happen if someone knows the code.

A few seconds later: **front door open.**

This can't be right. I click on the camera mode and damn near lose my shit when I see Felix…and David inside the house. Somehow, David must've found out the gate code, which wouldn't be hard since he's been stalking the hell out of us based on the threatening images he's sent. And Felix knows where we keep the spare key because he was with us when we hid it after Layla got locked out by accident.

There's no Layla, which means she's either upstairs sleeping or somewhere else other than the foyer since that's the only part of the house with a camera. I dial her number, but she doesn't answer. I call again. Still no answer. I send a quick text to Simon, letting him know the situation since he's closer, then call the police, giving them all the info I have—all while driving like a bat out of hell back to our house.

I'm almost home when I get a text from Simon: **deactivated all alarms. He's armed. Come around back.**

What the fuck. My heart pounds behind my rib cage the rest of the drive, praying to fucking God that David isn't crazy enough to actually use the gun. I park outside of the gate and jump it so I don't make any noise. The cops aren't here yet. When I spot Simon around back, he puts a single finger up to his lips, and I nod once in understanding.

He's got his gun in his hand, and I trust he knows what he's doing. He knows his only priority is to protect Layla and Felix—at all costs.

With the door cracked open, we can hear David speaking.

"You're supposed to be mine! Felix is supposed to be mine. That baby in your belly is mine! He took it all, and now he's going to lose everything."

"Please don't do this," Layla begs. "Please. I'll do anything!" The fear in her tone has me stepping forward, but Simon shakes his head, stopping me.

"It's too late," David says. "It's okay… because soon we'll all be together, happy again."

His words aren't just a threat. They're a promise. He's going to kill Layla and Felix and then end his own life, and there's no way I'm going to stand out here and wait for the fucking police to get here while that happens. They might be dead if we wait much longer.

Before I can make my move, Simon knocks the door open, making it bang against the wall. I'm not sure what the fuck he's thinking until I glance inside, and see that by doing so, he's distracted David, making him look this way. Without waiting, Simon aims and fires, hitting David in the chest. The force of the blow sends him flying onto his back.

I don't know if he's dead or not, and I don't care. Simon goes straight for him, making sure he's disarmed while I pull a shaking Layla and a crying Felix into my arms, needing to get them out of the room and out of the house.

As we're stepping outside, the police pull up, and I tell them where they can find David. A few officers head that way while two others stay with us, asking me what happened. I give them a quick overview, then ask if the details can wait, nodding toward my family in my arms, clearly distraught.

The officer insists they go to the hospital to get checked out, and thankfully, Layla agrees. Since neither needs immediate medical attention and I'm not about to let them out of my sight, I let them know I'll drive them myself. On the way, I call our parents, letting them know we have Felix back and they're okay. Layla and Felix are quiet for the entire drive, and I worry they've gone into shock. Layla sits in the back with Felix, holding him.

When we arrive, the nurse brings us back right away, having been told to expect us. Thankfully, they let them both stay together. The nurse asks questions, and Felix nods and shakes his head. When they've determined he's physically okay, they check out Layla. Since she's further along, they can do an abdominal ultrasound.

"And that's the baby's heartbeat," the tech says softly.

"That's the baby?" Felix asks, finally speaking. He's lying next to his mom, against her side, but he sits up to check out the monitor.

"It is," the tech says, explaining all the parts.

"How does the baby get in there?" Felix asks, curious as ever, making Layla smile.

"It's science," the tech says.

Once the ultrasound is done, the tech leaves us alone.

I'm about to ask Layla how she's doing when there's a knock on the door.

"Yeah?"

Simon steps inside the doorway. "Layla." He nods. "You both okay?"

"We are," she says, tears filling her eyes. "Thank you."

He nods then looks at me. "I need to talk to you for a second."

"I'll be right back," I tell Layla, leaning over and kissing her forehead, then kissing Felix's. "If you guys need anything, I'll be right outside the door."

"He's alive," Simon says once we're in the hallway and the door is closed. "At least for now. He's in surgery. I hit him in the chest, and they saved his fucking life."

"They were doing their jobs."

Simon glares. "A little more to the left and I would've hit his heart."

"You don't want that blood on your hands," I tell him, as much as I would've loved for him to have killed David. He sure as fuck deserves it. "If he survives, he'll be going to jail. Kidnapping a minor, attempt to commit murder. We heard the shit he said."

Simon nods, but I can tell the only way he'll be satisfied is if David's heart were to stop beating. And that's why I trust him with my family's lives.

After suggesting they both speak to someone about what they went through, the doctor discharges Layla and Felix, and we head to a hotel since our house is a crime scene.

Felix, like the four-year-old he is, snaps out of it the second he sees our room has a private one-lane bowling alley. After our parents visit, giving Layla and Felix love and affection, we spend the afternoon bowling, going swimming, and playing in the arcade while Layla stays close, watching but not participating.

When it's time for bed, Felix asks to sleep with Layla, and she of course tells him he can. I kiss them both good night, prepared to sleep in another room, when Felix says, "You can sleep with us. The bed is big enough for ten people."

I glance at Layla, making sure it's okay, and she nods once. I keep my clothes on and climb into bed behind her, pulling her into my front, so I can feel her warm body against mine. Felix lays his head down on the pillow, and within minutes, he's passed out. I assume Layla is asleep as well, but then she carefully turns over to face me.

"Hey," I say softly, tucking a few loose strands behind her ear.

"Hey," she says back.

We lie in silence for several minutes, and then, like a dam at capacity, her lids fill with tears, and they spill over. Not wanting to wake Felix, I pull her face to my chest and hold her tightly. "It's okay," I whisper, kissing the top of her head while she quietly cries into my shirt. "Everything is okay."

292

Epilogue

Layla

TWO MONTHS LATER

"WOW, THIS PLACE IS BEAUTIFUL." I GLANCE AROUND AS CAMDEN PULLS MY CHAIR OUT FOR me, and I have a seat. Life can get busy, especially with his line of work, so he insisted on weekly date nights. I wasn't about to argue since it meant my amazing, handsome husband was taking me out and spoiling me at least once a week. I mean, what woman would say no to that?

But tonight is a special occasion because, after two months of wondering what would happen to David—since the bullet didn't kill him—it's all over. He was charged with several crimes, including kidnapping and endangering a minor and attempted murder on two counts—since his plan was to kill Felix and me and end his own life—and found guilty of all of them. He lost all his parental rights to Felix, and today, he was sentenced to life in prison. It's been hard on Felix since he's young and doesn't understand everything, only knowing his daddy was mean to him, so we're seeing a therapist every week, which I think is helping.

"You look stunning," Camden says, sitting next to me and rubbing my small bump. The guy can't keep his hands off me, and it's only gotten worse since I started showing. His mom warned me the Blackwood men loved pregnant women, but I didn't fully get it until I experienced it.

"I was thinking, before you go on tour, we can do a weekend getaway since Felix is still in school," I suggest as we look at the menu.

"That sounds perfect," he says, taking my hand and kissing the top of it. "Where were you thinking?"

"I don't know. Somewhere we can relax since I can't really do much being pregnant."

"We'll figure it out." He lets go of my hand and moves his hand down my belly to my thigh, massaging the flesh. Since I'm wearing a dress that's on the short side, he's able to glide his fingers easily under the material and tease me.

"Not here," I hiss, glancing around. You never know who's watching or taking a picture.

He chuckles softly. "C'mon, I'll make it quick. You know I can get you off in like five seconds."

I glare at him. "I don't want to get off in five seconds. I want to fully enjoy it."

He backs off slightly, but the entire time we're eating and talking, he makes it a point to still touch me… everywhere but there, and by the time we get home—Felix is spending the night with my mom—I'd be completely okay with him making me come in five seconds. But of course, that's not what he's going to do.

He lays me out on the bed, undresses me so I'm completely naked, and then starts working me over slowly, sucking on my neck, tweaking my nipples, massaging my thighs. Not once, though, does he touch my clit, and I know it's because he's going to draw it out and make sure I can't say he got me off in five seconds.

When his fingers dip into my warmth, I wiggle my ass, silently telling him I want some ass play. He grins and grabs the lube, squirting some onto his finger. His tongue licks my center—everywhere but my clit—and his fingers push into my ass, deliciously filling me.

"More, please," I beg when he uses his other hand to finger my pussy.

"I'm not sure if you're ready for more," he murmurs, kissing my belly, just under my belly button.

"I am," I breathe. "Please."

"Hmm… I don't know. I need to make sure you're *fully* enjoying this."

He dips his face between my legs and laps straight up my seam, brushing softly against my clit. It vibrates in need, and I squeeze my legs together, making Camden chuckle.

"Please," I whine. "I need to come."

He laughs against my pussy, but does as I say, taking the swollen nub between his lips and sucking on it. Sparks go off behind my lids, but then he stops.

"Camden, please," I moan, riding his fingers that are still in my ass.

His tongue glides back and forth along my clit, taking me higher and higher until I'm dangling off the edge. Then like the perfect lover he is, he takes me right over it, sending me flying as I experience a mind-blowing orgasm.

Once I've come down, he removes his shirt, using it to wipe his fingers and face, and undoes his pants, exposing his long, thick cock. I take it in my hand and stroke it a few times before I guide it into me. The moment we become one, we both sigh in contentment. He makes love to me, switching between soft and sweet and hard and rough. It'll never get old, being with Camden. I'll never have enough of him. I'll always want and need more, and he'll always give it to me.

When we've both come, we take a shower together and then climb back into bed. I love the moments after sex when it's just the two of us. We talk and laugh and just *be*. Camden is so great about simply being in the moment with me. Life can be crazy and chaotic, but when we're together, it's as if all the chaos is under control, even for just a moment.

"I'm going to miss you while you're on tour," I tell him. They take off in a couple of weeks and will be gone for two months. He made sure they'll be back long before my due date, not wanting to chance me having the baby and them having to cancel any shows.

"You and Felix should just come with us,"he says for the millionth time, even though he knows it's not happening. I'm planning to visit him—with and without Felix—but being on tour full time with a rock band is not a place for a child or a pregnant woman.

"We'll visit…"

"I don't want to go more than a week without seeing you," he says, pulling me into his arms, his face resting on the top of my head that's laying on his chest.

"We'll video chat, and I'll visit. It's only a couple of months. It will fly by."

"I already miss you, and I haven't even left yet."

I smile at his sweet words. "We'll make it work. We were apart for five years, and we found our way back together."

Camden takes my chin and lifts it slightly, so I look at him. "I'll always find my way back to you." He presses his lips to mine, and I sigh into the kiss, getting lost in him.

When the kiss ends, I lean forward and press my lips to his tattoo, located right over his heart. He always said he wouldn't get one until he had something worth putting permanently on his body.

So I was shocked when he told me he wanted to get a tattoo one day. I went with him to Forbidden Ink, the tattoo place where the guys always go when they're in New York to get their work done.

He wouldn't tell me what he was getting, but I was in tears once it was done and he showed me. It's the same tattoo I got: a camera. Only his isn't shattered like mine is. Instead, it's perfectly intact, and where I had written "Shattered," the title of his song he sang about me all those months back, he has "Pieced Back Together," the title of the new song he once again wrote about me—only this time, it's about our love putting all the shattered pieces back together. It might not be perfect, but it's ours, and I wouldn't have it any other way.

CAMDEN AND I ARE CUDDLING IN BED, BETWEEN ASLEEP AND AWAKE, WHEN MY PHONE buzzes with Kaylee's name on the screen.

"Hey, Kaylee. How are you?" There's sniffling over the phone, and my hackles rise. "Kaylee…"

"I need you, Layla."

"Where are you?"

"At home… in New York."

"I'll be right there." I'm already jumping out of bed and getting my clothes on. "Kaylee needs me."

"I'll drive you," Camden says.

"Thank you."

When I get to Kaylee's apartment, the one she shares with her mom and stepdad, Camden kisses me and tells me to text him once I'm inside and to let him know when I'm ready to come home.

I haven't even knocked when the door swings open and Kaylee's standing there, her face splotchy from crying. "What happened?" I ask as she throws her arms around me and buries her face into my neck, sobbing heavily.

"I was fired from Evolution." Evolution is the PR company that hired her.

"What? Why?"

"Sam fucking York accused me of trying to sexually assault him. It's so ridiculous, but they, of course, took his word over mine and fired me on the spot. Four years of college all down the drain," she cries.

"You don't know that," I tell her.

"Yes, I do. Once it gets out what he's accused me of, no PR company will hire me. I'll be blacklisted everywhere."

"We'll figure it out," I tell her as I hug her tightly, trying to rack my brain with ways to help her. "There has to be something we can do."

The Love & Lyrics Series isn't over!

Did you know Braxton, Declan, and Gage have books?
Check out the whole *Love & Lyrics Series*.

Did you know Camden's parents have their own book?
Check out *A Chance Encounter*.

About the Author

Reading is like breathing in, writing is like breathing out. – Pam Allyn

Nikki Ash resides in South Florida where she is an English teacher by day and a writer by night. When she's not writing, you can find her with a book in her hand. From the Boxcar Children, to Wuthering Heights, to the latest single parent romance, she has lived and breathed every type of book. While reading and writing are her passions, her two children are her entire world. You can probably find them at a Disney park before you would find them at home on the weekends!

www.ingramcontent.com/pod-product-compliance
Lightning Source LLC
Chambersburg PA
CBHW060617310726
48982CB00003B/589